THE BOYS NEXT DOOR

DAN GREENBERGER

HANNOVER
20km

"Men have knowledge of the present.
As for the future, the gods know it,
alone and fully enlightened."
—CONSTANTINE CAVAFY

"Everybody's got something to hide
except for me and my monkey."
—JOHN LENNON

Appian Way Press

Photograph by Astrid Kirchherr, courtesy of Ginzburg Fine Arts
Cover Design by Andjela Vujic

dangee@msn.com

ISBN: 9798655706583
Printed in the U.S.

For Genevieve

PROLOGUE

September 20, 1960

If this horrible, head-splitting racket doesn't stop soon I swear to God I'm going to hang myself.

It's 4 o'clock in the morning. I'm tired of banging on the wall, tired of stuffing toilet paper in my ears, tired of burying my head in pillows and dirty clothes.

This is not music. This is weaponized sound. Someone has figured out a way to beat a person senseless using a thing that could be described, generously, as a "song." Maybe it's the work of the Devil. Maybe this is how he's chosen to appear, and how he plans to drag me, ears bleeding, into the depths of hell.

I think about confronting my neighbors. I think of calm and rational things to say. "Guys, I need to sleep." "Fellas, have some consideration." I go over these sentences in my head, or I whisper them aloud, like I'm rehearsing a play. My goal is to sound respectful but firm, urgent but not desperate. Surely I can reason with them.

Other times I fantasize violence. I imagine that I erupt and do something horrific, some very specific act of brutality that makes me question, on a deep level, what kind of deranged monster I am.

These thoughts do not relax me, either.

So I count the hours till dawn, calculating how much sleep I'll get if I start now, or in five minutes, or in an hour, and how tired that will make me tomorrow at school. I eventually conclude that getting out of bed and taking any action at all will only awaken me further and delay my getting back to sleep, and so I lay here, repeating the cycle for another night, outraged, frustrated, and exhausted.

During the War, the Germans piped music into the concentration camps. It wasn't loud and aggressive like what my neighbors are playing now, but it was similarly high-spirited: waltzes and other popular music of the day. ("The Beer Barrel Polka" a.k.a. "Rosamunde" was a favorite.) While the music helped to drown out the screams of the victims, it functioned more importantly as a form of psychological torture. The contrast between the upbeat songs and the unspeakable violence taking place in their midst was intended to break the will of the prisoners, to make them meek and docile, and march willingly into the ovens.

I would welcome death at this point. At least it'll be quiet. And I won't have to listen to "the Beatles."

PART ONE

September 5, 1960 (two weeks earlier)
per Luftpost

Dear Mom and Dad,

Hallo aus Deutschland!

I have arrived, and I love this place! What an adventure, and what an opportunity! I love that I'm so *anonymous* here. Like a secret agent, dropped behind enemy lines and instructed to "blend in." (Isn't this what American life has always been about? The freedom to reinvent oneself, to start over and write your own second act? Even if it's only for one semester.)

The city is beautiful. I took a long walk by the river this morning—past the harbor, bustling with ships; past the old warehouses and the fish market and the smoke-stained buildings—and then the only thing you notice is the trees, framing the river just so, their leaves starting to erupt with fall color. Everyone tells me how gorgeous this city gets when it all turns brown and the air grows thick with the smell of burning leaves. (If there's one thing that Germans have a talent for, it's throwing things on a big pile—books, Jews—and setting them on fire.)

I shouldn't joke. I know you would have preferred that I do a semester in England instead. But I think it's important for Americans to be here, and especially American Jews. We can't stay enemies forever. I have to believe that the Germans are fundamentally decent people, because, in the words of Anne Frank, "In spite of everything, I still believe that people are good at heart." We have to move on.

Because war doesn't matter! Wars come and go. Only art lasts forever. The plays of Shakespeare, the symphonies of

Beethoven . . . and the poems of Rilke (sigh). Yes, he remains my favorite poet and his is the life and career on which I will model my own. I'm a little peeved that the school doesn't offer a course in Rilke, but I've signed up for German Literature and, needless to say, he's the towering colossus in that group. Plus, everybody here has read *Letters to a Young Poet*, which is awfully nice for a change.

Even though I'm registered at the University of Hamburg (go Hamburgers!), I'm taking my classes at the College of Fine Arts, the *Hochschule für bildende Künste*, or HFBK for short. It's a swell place, just one big building right on the river, and the kids seem interesting, if somewhat aloof.

The only problem I've had so far has been finding a place to live. (Not a small problem.)

When I got here on Thursday, I was informed by the housing office that I was not on their list, so they didn't have a room for me. Not a dorm, not a broom closet—nothing! Never mind that I was enrolled at their university, never mind that I had traveled four thousand miles from America: *I was not on their list!* I dragged myself, protesting indignantly, from one office to another, each tended by a bored-looking administrator whose entire universe consisted, apparently, of The List, and the fact that I wasn't on it.

I finally got in to see the registrar, who somehow managed to be the least interested of them all. "We do have a bulletin board," he offered, with a yawn. "Perhaps you can find something there."

I wanted to hit him.

The bulletin board, of course, was all in German. Phone numbers (I don't have a phone), addresses (I don't have a car), all the while dragging around my steamer-trunk suitcase and my typewriter. I hadn't slept or bathed for God-knows-how-long, so yes, I probably got a little emotional. A little flustered. I don't think I was actually crying, but I was making some unattractive, high-pitched sounds while jumping up and down with frustration—probably like I did as a child when you told me I couldn't have ice cream for breakfast.

"Are you okay?"

I turned to the voice.

It was a girl. Very pretty: thin and elegant, high cheekbones, blond hair cut short like Audrey Hepburn. Her name is Astrid. I don't know why such a beautiful thing would ever stop to have pity on a whimpering, hysterical specimen like myself. But she did.

In my halting German, I explained my situation. Her English wasn't so great either, but she soon got the picture. She laughed (not in a nasty way) at the expression on my face, and I can't say I blame her. Tired/dirty/frustrated/hysterical is not a winning look for me.

She told me she knew a guy who had recently rented out a room to some friends of hers, and he might have another one available.

I piled my stuff in her car (a Volkswagen Beetle, every bit as sleek and uncluttered as she was) and she drove me to the guy's place, about twenty minutes away. It was my first real look at the city, but I couldn't take my eyes off Astrid. She's not at all like the girls at Columbia—she's exotic and sophisticated. And, in a strange way, a little boyish, which is both unsettling and highly attractive.

"This place I am taking you," she said, turning toward me, "it is . . . I don't know how to say it . . . *wild,* you know?" (She pronounced it "*vild.*") "Like the Wild West?"

I tried to picture what she meant. Gunslingers? Tumbleweeds?

She pulled the car over to explain. "Alan," she said, her steely blue eyes hitting me full-force. "Are you willing to try something that is a little . . . *exciting*?"

I swallowed hard.

"Understand," she said. "This part of Hamburg is *full of life*—yes? It is *with energy,* you know? It is . . ."

"Vild?" I croaked.

"Yes," she said. "If you are willing."

I was able to summon a smirk. "I think I can handle a little *vild*."

I'm not sure she understood what I meant (it's an idiomatic expression, and I must be careful with those), but it didn't matter. She understood the attitude.

When we got to the destination, I looked around and quickly realized what she meant. The Grosse Freiheit is what you'd call the red-light district of Hamburg: bars, clubs, tattoo parlors, kebab stands. It's where the sailors come when they want to get drunk and blow off some steam. An odd place for a rooming house, I thought. But she beckoned me in.

"Hamburg is so dead!" she shouted, over the din of two motorcycles that swerved to avoid her. "So much of it gray and sleepy. People with—how do you say it?—eyes closed, no joy, no excitement. Here is where they come to *live*!"

I followed close behind her, dodging traffic, and into the building. It wasn't a rooming house at all, but a small movie theater, the Bambi Kino, which appeared to be showing an American cowboy movie in German. The tiny auditorium was on the ground floor, and then two stories—apartments, I assumed—just above it. She led me past the lobby and into a small office in back. The man behind the desk looked up.

"Bruno, *das ist* Alan. Alan, this is Bruno."

I shook hands with Bruno. Not what I would call the

warm and welcoming type. Actually about as nasty-looking a man as I've ever seen. Short, barrel-chested, with hands that looked permanently swollen from punching people in the face. He and Astrid spoke rapidly in German—I didn't understand much, but I picked up the words "student," "homeless," and "rich American." It was that last part that seemed to make an impression.

He stood up and gave me the once-over, limping around me like an injured dog who smells meat. "Fifteen marks a week," he said, spitting out the words like broken teeth.

"Can I see the room first?" I asked.

He raised his eyebrows, like I'd insulted his mother, and barked something in German at Astrid. She barked back, and a heated exchange followed. Finally he scowled at me, dripping with contempt, and told me to follow him upstairs.

As we trudged up the narrow passage, I realized his left foot was deformed. It twisted awkwardly away from his leg, like a wobbly wheel on a shopping cart, and dragged behind him. On it he wore a thick-soled shoe that seemed to be made mostly of wood. *Not a wooden leg,* I thought. *A clubfoot. An angry German with a clubfoot is going to be my landlord.* And up the stairs he dragged it: *klump, klump, klump.* (He tells people that he lost his foot in the war, but Astrid says he actually got his start performing in the circus, as part of a freak show.)

When I saw the room, I thought I might actually be sick. It was really just a storage room: it smelled of mold and cigarettes, and was stacked to the ceiling with hot dog buns and rancid cooking oil. There was one small window in the corner and a rusted sink that looked like blood might flow from the faucet.

Astrid must have seen my reaction. "Don't worry," she said. "It is a good place. Safe. My friends here are happy. And they *sprechen Englisch.*"

I looked around at the godforsaken property, barely the size of a bathroom, in a horrible building, a horrible part of town, owned by a horrible, club-footed Nazi . . . and then I looked at Astrid. She seemed so happy, so hopeful. No question I'd be seeing a lot of her if this were my home. I imagined the late nights together, the two of us talking, studying, learning each other's language. We'd laugh about Bruno, walk downstairs to catch the end of a movie, get a cup of coffee . . .

Of course I said yes.

I realize this is a problem men often have. Logic, good reason, wise decision-making—these sometimes evaporate when a good-looking woman enters the scene, and I may have fallen victim to just such a trap. Maybe "trap" isn't the right word, maybe it's more like a form of hypnosis; and they say you won't do anything under hypnosis that you wouldn't do in real life. You simply become more suggestible, and that's how you end up clucking like a chicken, or agreeing to live in a squalid rat-hole with a circus freak as your landlord.

I've cleaned up the place, and honestly it's beginning to feel like the right decision. I've come to appreciate the gritty realism of it all. I live in a movie theater! How cool is that? Or maybe I'll just call it a garret. I live in a garret! (Which do you think sounds better?) It's here that I will write my poems, and here that my adventure will unfold.

When Astrid left, she gave me her phone number (she has a *business card,* and it's the coolest thing I've ever seen). I don't know if I'll actually have the nerve to call her, but I'm sure we will see each other again. She comes by often, she says, to see her mysterious friends. (Evidently they're musicians from England.)

The expedition begins. Mysteries abound.
Germany is great.

Love,
Alan

September 6

I had just finished writing my letter and climbed into bed when I heard the noises.

It sounded like twenty or thirty people charging up the stairs. (Yes, I'll confess: my first thoughts were "Gestapo" and "Anne Frank.")

Then I realized it was only a handful of people on the stairs, but very loud and very drunk. I heard voices and laughing and, I thought, some words in English. They were Astrid's friends.

They all shuffled into the room next door and closed the door behind them. I expected that things would quiet down, but the laughing and drunk-talking continued. I was tired and annoyed, but also curious. I lay in the dark for ages, it seemed, listening to the sounds coming through the wall. They were definitely speaking English, but I had trouble understanding the words. It was some strange accent (Scottish?) and they seemed to be talking about a girl, but it wasn't so much a conversation . . . it was funny voices, and shouting, and teasing, and laughing. So much laughing. They must have been drunk out of their minds. I heard singing at one point, but just a phrase here and there, nothing that I recognized.

Maybe they're throwing a party, I thought, but I heard no one come or go. Astrid hadn't told me how many of her friends lived here—I figured it was two or three. But this sounded like the whole ensemble.

I lay there with my ear to the wall, weirdly fascinated. I felt like an anthropologist, observing a previously unknown tribe of monkeys. I pictured an orchestra made up of primates, blowing into their tubas and French horns, wearing fake noses and silly hats. Sleep lapped at my brain. Eventually things quieted down, and I listened as, one by one, the monkeys went to the bathroom down the hall for a final piss—I counted four, possibly five—and then settled in for the night. When it became quiet again, I was finally able to sleep, and did so like a dead person.

I saw nothing of my neighbors the following day. When I left in the morning, I tiptoed past their room and listened. Nothing. Snoring. By the time I got to school, I'd put them out of my mind completely. And when I returned to my room at night, they were gone. Maybe I'd imagined the whole thing.

Later that night, however, it became clear that I hadn't.

I'd gotten into bed early, anxious to catch up on my sleep, and sleep I did, until I heard the noises. I looked at my watch. It was 3 a.m., exactly the same time as their appearance the night before. And it couldn't have sounded more familiar. The clomping up the stairs, the laughing, the jeering, the comic voices. The door closing behind them. The same funny accents, the same stupid jokes, the same laughing, laughing, laughing.

All my curiosity from the night before had vanished. I had no desire to "study" my next-door neighbors: I simply wanted them to shut up. I wanted to sleep. I put my pillow over my head and lay down, but it wasn't going to work. After fifteen minutes of quiet fuming, of feeling that I shouldn't escalate the situation, that I should be the bigger man here—I could finally take it no more.

I banged my fist into the wall. "Hey! Could you please keep it down?"

It felt good to get that off my chest. They simply weren't thinking about anyone else, and they needed a reminder. I know what it's like to be drunk, I'm not some party-pooping wet blanket killjoy –

"Fuck off!"

I stared at the wall, my mouth dangling open, frankly a little shocked. Weren't English people supposed to be polite? *So sorry, old chap, we'll put a sock in it.*

"Look, guys," I said, trying to sound reasonable. "It's three in the morning. Some of us are trying to sleep."

"Why don't you go fuck yourself to sleep?" A huge cackle.

I was so angry, I was shaking. It's a horrible, helpless feeling, being kept awake at night. Like being tortured in your own home: the slow drip-drip of sound onto your skull, splintering through to your brain.

I wanted to march in there and—what? Kick their heads in? Smash them with a baseball bat?

Who was I kidding? This is Germany, there *are* no baseball bats. And there were five of them—at least. The chorus of laughter erupted again and again.

"Shut up!" I yelled, pounding on the wall.

"Shut up!" came the reply, in a high-pitched, womanly voice. More screams of laughter. "Shut up!"

I clutched my pillow to my chest. I took deep breaths. I concentrated on bringing my heartbeat down. Peals and peals of laughter.

I took out my copy of *Letters to a Young Poet* and tried to read. Letter Four, where Rilke defends the solitude of the artist's life, often has a calming effect on me. I read the words: "But your solitude will be a support and a home for you, even in the midst of very unfamiliar circumstances, and from it you will find all your paths."

From next door, somebody howling like a coyote.

I'm not sure how long this went on—me trying desperately to find some peace in the great man's words, and more drunken raving from next door. Finally, there was a brief lull, and a knock came at my door.

It was one of them.

My heart pounded. Had they come with clubs? With knives? Who were these people? "Friends" of some girl who had given me a ride? They could be psychopaths, for all I knew. I pretended to be asleep.

The knock came again. And I realized—I had to face this. Whatever *this* was, I had to stand up for myself. I didn't start this fight, but I'd be damned if I walked away from it. I took a deep breath and opened the door.

It was just one of them. And not at all what I expected. He was a teenager with a baby face, at least a few years younger than me.

"Hello," he said, "I'm Paul."

I'd never seen a man wearing leather pants before.

"I guess we're makin' a bit of noise, aren't we? Sorry about that. We get back late, you know, we've been working, we're all poomped up."

I had no idea what he was talking about. "You're musicians?" I said.

"Yeah that's right," he said, with a jaunty smile. "We play at the Indra. You know it?"

I shook my head.

"You should come out some time, it's good fun. We bash out a few tunes, have some laughs—and a lot of good-looking girls, you know. Anyway, we'll try to be quiet. Good fences, good neighbors, right?" Another jaunty smile, with a wink.

I nodded, still at a loss. He was so positive and upbeat, and looked like such a child, and yet he and his gang had been hurling obscenities at me only minutes before.

"So we're all right?" he asked.

"Yes," I said, "I suppose we are."

"Well give us a oog, then."

"I'm sorry, a what?"

"A hug. Come on, give us a hug."

And he put his arms around me and hugged me. I can't remember ever being hugged by a stranger. Maybe this is an English thing I'm not aware of. I know Italians like to hug.

"What's your name?" he said.

"Alan."

"Night then, Alan. Sweet noddies!" And off he went.

Dear God, I thought. *Maybe they're homosexuals.*

September 7

I often find myself, in the course of these endless, sleepless nights, thinking about Astrid.

Which is strange, since falling in love is absolutely the last thing I want to be doing right now. I had pretty much given up on the idea completely, and assumed that it would never happen again—or, at the very least, that it would take months, if not years, for me to feel the tiniest sliver of attraction toward another human being. I thought that part of me was broken.

To say that Suzy broke my heart is giving her more credit than she deserves. There were a lot of factors that went into my heartbreak; it's just that Suzy happened to have control over all of them.

The timing she used was particularly hurtful. Six hours before I left. *Oh by the way, I think we should end things*... And the absolute certainty of the decision. No, she didn't want to "take a break." No, it wasn't *because* I was going away for a semester. She said she'd been unhappy with our relationship for some time, and now she wanted to finish, once and for all. Better that we do it now, she said, rip it off like a Band-Aid, so I could be "free to explore."

Living abroad is a scary thought, especially if you've never lived more than a couple of hours away from your home and family. It would have been nice to have a girlfriend back home to send me letters and tell me she missed me and fill me in on everything that's happening back at school. (That was my idea for a writing project while I was here: I would write my own *Letters to a Young Poet*. But since Suzy is pretty much the only young poet I know, who am I going to write my poems to now? Dear God, please not my parents.)

I asked if we could still write to each other, and she was dead set against that as well. It had to be a clean break so she could move on with her life, so *she* could feel free to explore, even if it wasn't something as dramatic as moving to Germany. (Is she angry that I'm going abroad and she isn't? She never expressed any interest in doing so. And, frankly, she never loved the idea of a Jew living in Germany—she never understood the statement I was trying to make.) "I wish I could just erase you," she said. Not *forget* me, you understand, but *erase* me, remove all traces, scrub herself clean.

I asked her if we could have sex one last time. She didn't like that idea either.

I honestly thought Suzy and I would get married someday. Not until after college, of course, but I always thought we would be one of those classic couples: high school sweethearts who keep coming back to each other, one of those relationships that starts early and lasts forever. And I thought she was on board with the idea, feeling what I was feeling, right up until that last night.

I was numb for the whole plane ride, which was too bad, since I'd never been on a plane before, and I think I might have enjoyed it if I hadn't been sick with my thoughts of Suzy. Sick because now the plane wasn't speeding me toward an adventure; it was hurtling me into a sense of loneliness more profound than I've ever known. How quickly plans can change. How quickly excitement turns into dread. And every minute, the flight was taking me miles and miles farther from home.

This is my pledge. I will not run away from this pain: I will embrace it. I will let the sorrow inform my art, and turn my loneliness into poetry. I will become a celibate monk, devoting all my spirit and love inward, into my soul and onto the page. I will study hard and work hard. And by the time my semester is over, I will have written the greatest poetry of my life, and be ready to share it with the world. That is what Rilke would do.

I'll just have to forget about Astrid.

September 9

per Luftpost

Dear Artie,

Hallo aus Deutchland! How's it hanging, old chap? I thought I'd take a break from all the *sturm und drang* in my life and drop a line to see how things are going back at dear old Columbia.

Hamburg is amazing. There's an energy to this place that's unmistakable—and actually quite exhausting. I wonder if, someday, "Hamburg in the '60s" will evoke the same magic as "Paris in the '20s," and inspire the same legacy of great art. There are so many artists here! And so many of them are living on the dole! The Fatherland has a very generous attitude toward its young creative types, so nobody is forced to get a crap job working for idiots during the day, just so they can go home at night and create—they just create! It's very appealing, but also a little Communist. I wonder how Senator Kennedy would feel about it.

Is anyone there still interested in the election? Honestly, I couldn't care less. Nixon and Kennedy are both bureaucrats, and both servants of the moneyed class. The only difference is, one of them looks like a movie star and the other like a professional bowler.

Do you see much of Suzy these days? You've probably heard by now that she and I have split. Sad sad sad . . . but it was a mutual breakup. With me so far away, I thought it was only fair that she should be free to explore. I hope it was the right decision. Sometimes I wish I'd never gone away at all.

I've wanted so many times in the past few days to write

her a long letter and get everything off my chest, but I don't know what good it would do. I'm 4,000 miles away and committed to stay here until at least the end of the year, maybe even longer. How could I expect someone to stay committed to me?

I never even considered what this trip would do to my relationship with her—I just assumed that she'd wait for me and I'd wait for her. I imagined myself having some fun in Hamburg and never telling her about it, but, in truth, I also imagined that she would have some fun in New York and never tell me about it. And I thought that would work. Never take anything for granted, I suppose, especially a woman.

I have no desire to go shopping for a new *fräulein* (even in a city crawling with eligible *fräuleins*), so I'm doing a lot of writing instead. I've started a poem cycle on deformity, death, and decay. I know it sounds depressing, but you see so much of it here—the whole city is wounded, the whole country. My landlord has a clubfoot (he's going to be a character in the poem), and you see all sorts of people on the street with missing limbs and eye patches, the *mutilés de guerre*.

Sounds like a lot of fun, right?

Anyway, must go and read some Goethe for tomorrow's class. Please report back on Suzy or anyone else who misses me terribly.

Your Pal,
Alan (The Wandering Jew)

P.S. My neighbors are driving me crazy. They never shut up!

September 10

I keep hoping I'll bump into Astrid at the college, but there hasn't been even a glimpse. I did some asking around, but nobody seems to know her. I even tried to find out if she was registered for classes this semester, but she's not on the list. (Which doesn't surprise me, since *I* wasn't on the list either.)

I also haven't seen her at the Kino, visiting her friends. Maybe she's been there while I'm asleep. The boys next door have an upside-down schedule, and seem to do nothing in their rooms except catch up on their sleep and ruin mine.

I know I could call her. That would be the brave, bold move. But not necessarily the right move. I'd have to do it from a pay phone, for one thing, and I hate pay phones. Especially German pay phones, which are ridiculously complicated. The telephone is not a good instrument for the two of us, anyway. We need an in-person encounter. We need a bumping-into. We had a great physicality with each other, I thought, that day in the car, and I need to find out if that meant anything, or if I had just imagined it.

So I made a bold move. It was Monday, the day all the clubs are closed, and I figured the musician-boys were having a day off. Maybe if I introduced myself to them in person—as good neighbors do—then not only could they lead me to Astrid, but perhaps they'd also have a little more consideration for my eardrums at 3 in the morning.

I knocked on their door around noon. I figured that was probably when they got out of bed. The door opened. There was only one of them in there, but this wasn't Huggy Paul. He looked roughly the same age, though, bleary-eyed and hung over.

"Hi," I said. "I'm your neighbor. Alan."

He didn't seem terribly interested. "Pete Best," he said, without offering his hand.

I looked past him into the room. Another storage room like mine, but bigger and even more horrible, with a smaller room just off it. I counted five mattresses on the floor, along with beer bottles, ashtrays, cigarettes, food wrappers, cereal boxes, guitar cases, amplifiers, suitcases, dirty clothes, a blanket that looked like a British flag, tattered newspapers, dirty tissues, and a small puddle that may or may not have been vomit. It was difficult to believe that human beings could survive in such squalor. Maybe this is how musicians live.

"So there's five of you?" I said.

"Yeah." He rubbed his eyes, half-asleep. A long pause followed.

"So listen," I said. "There's this German girl, Astrid. Do you know her?"

"Yeah," he said. Another lazy pause.

"I've been trying to get in touch with her," I said.

"Right," he said. Another pause. It's not even like he's being rude. Just boring, or socially inept, or both.

"Any idea how I could find her?"

He ran a weary hand over his face. "Lives in the suburbs, I think." And then he stopped talking again, and just stood there, staring at the floor. Bored with me? Bored with his own life? At least this one's not a homosexual.

"So you're a musician?" I asked.

"I'm a droomer."

"A what?"

"Drummer. Drums." He stifled a yawn.

"Good. Good. See you around," I said. Pete the drummer. What a magnetic personality.

"Oh," he said, just as I was walking away. "I think Astrid's coming to take our picture on Wednesday."

"Really?" I said, "Wednesday? This Wednesday?"

"Mmm."

"What time?"

"Don't know."

He closed the door, and that was the end of our visit.

By coincidence, I ran into Pete again about an hour later. We were both buying coffee and strudel at Café Moller down the road. So I guess you could say we had breakfast together, even though his communications were rarely more than a grunt. But I was able to extract a few pieces of information. The five of them were from Liverpool, in the north of England. They'd only been here for a few weeks. They played mostly American music. And Pete was the newest member of the band, having joined only recently. I got the sense that Pete didn't get along very well with the others, so while they were off "mucking about," Pete hung out by himself, going for long walks and sitting in cafés. A little bit like me.

He seemed lonely, but not the least bit bothered about it. British reserve, I suppose. If I were a better person, maybe I would reach out to him and initiate a friendship. Strangers in a strange land, united by a common language, all that...

But God, he's just so boring. Extracting a sentence from him is like pumping water from a dry well. I had nearly given up the effort completely when he surprised me by remembering a vital fact.

The photographs with Astrid were scheduled for 2 o'clock on Wednesday.

"She's pickin' us up," he intoned. "Takin' us somewhere."

Boring, perhaps, but useful.

September 12

I'm blowing off my Shakespeare class today. I was supposed to memorize a monologue and perform it in front of the others—which is too bad, since I already know Hamlet's "too, too solid flesh" bit from my acting class last year, and that would have been impressive. But I really want to see Astrid, and I knew she'd be coming by to take photos.

I stayed in my room all morning. I don't have a view out to the street, so at about 1:30 I went up to the roof, where I'd be able to see her coming. Sure enough, just after 2, I saw her get out of her car and walk into the building.

I bolted back inside and down the staircase and quickly assumed a casual demeanor just in time to say—

"Astrid!"

"Alan!" She gave me a hug. Not casual or half-hearted, but strong, almost masculine in its force.

"What are you doing here?" I asked. (This is why it's good to take acting classes.)

"I am seeing my friends. Taking pictures! Have you met them?"

"A couple of them," I said. "Very colorful characters. How are you?"

"*Gut, gut,*" she said, and added, with a dramatic wave, "I am throwing myself into my art!"

Just like me.

"The room is working out great," I said. "Such a great location, so full of life—"

"Hey," she said with an excited smile. "You want to come watch?"

It took me a second. "Oh! Watch you take their pictures!"

"Yes, yes. Come. We have fun."

"Actually, I was hoping . . ." I looked at her. She still looked like a boy, but God, so beautiful. (Am I attracted to boys all of a sudden?) She had a camera case on one shoulder and a big bag draped over the other. Of course she wasn't going to drop everything just to run off and have coffee with me. Or come visit me in my room. Or have savage, Olympic-quality sex with me until sundown.

"I'd love to," I said.

She instructed me to wait outside and say hi to her friend Jurgen, who was driving the van. I didn't realize there would be a van. "Great!" I said.

It occurred to me, as I walked downstairs, that this probably wasn't the best bump-into-Astrid-type situation I could have engineered. Yes, I'd be spending time with her, but also with five—no, make that six—other guys, all of whom probably had designs on her. (If there's one thing I know about musicians, it's that they tend to be oversexed.)

I don't like competing with other guys. It's why I hate picking up women in bars. There's something so animalistic about a bunch of males competing with each other for the attention of a female, strutting about, showing off their plumage. It's vulgar.

I almost bailed out on the whole thing right then and there, but then I thought, *Can I really afford to miss this opportunity*? I knew almost nothing about Astrid, and I'd been failing miserably in my attempts to track her down. It's not perfect, but it's an opening.

I saw the van parked right in front, and I introduced myself to Jurgen, who spoke perfect English. He seemed to be roughly my age and had the same chiseled, artsy look as Astrid. I casually asked if she was his girlfriend, and he said no.

Former girlfriend. Good.

In a few minutes, Astrid came down the stairs, followed by the five musicians. I'd never seen them all together before, or in the light of day, and they looked even younger than I'd thought. They all wore scruffy jeans and boots, and a variety of grubby unpressed jackets, mostly leather. They looked like a motorcycle gang. I found it a little strange that they wouldn't *dress up* a little to have their photo taken—or even comb their hair—but maybe this was some Northern English fashion statement. To me, they just looked ratty and filthy.

They loaded their instruments (banjos?) into the rear of the van, which also held Astrid's photo equipment. I sat in the front seat with Jurgen and they all piled into the back. I watched through the rearview mirror.

"Who's he?" one of them asked, indicating me, making a face one usually reserves for food that's gone bad.

"He's your neighbor, John," said Astrid.

"The American," said another.

I turned around and gave them a friendly wave. "Alan," I said. "How do you do?"

John glanced at me and turned to the others. "Why's he coming with?"

"Be nice, John," said Astrid. "He's a nice boy."

John gave me a nasty, aggressive look that felt like a glob of saliva hitting my face.

"Maybe," said one of the others, "he's taken a fancy to our Astrid. Do you suppose that's it?"

I turned away from him and looked out the window, mortified. They are every bit as rude and loathsome as I'd imagined.

"I don't see Astrid falling for a pimply git like that," said

John, in a low, drawly voice. "I think he's living in a fool's paradise."

"Don't listen to John," said Paul, in the seat right behind me, and patted my back (there's that physical contact again). "You flirt with Astrid all you want."

I could only hope that Astrid's English wasn't good enough to register what they had just said, but I think she understood. She shot me a coy look, as if to say, *Don't worry about them, they're just being idiots.* I struggled to say something charming and funny in return, but nothing came out. Finally I turned my back on all of them and looked forward at the road. I heard a few giggles behind me.

We drove about fifteen minutes, through neighborhoods I'd never seen. I kept up a steady conversation with Jurgen, who was interesting, but I was only speaking for Astrid's benefit. She'd see that I was thoughtful and well-spoken, and, most important, a good listener. (Women like that.)

From behind me, I heard more laughter. Little sniggering whispers. I don't imagine they were all about me, but I resented them just the same. I felt bad for Astrid, and a little protective of the poor girl, surrounded by a pack of ill-mannered greaseballs. But she didn't appear to be suffering, and laughed at every one of their stupid jokes.

We finally reached our destination: a fairground at the edge of town, recently outfitted for a carnival, but now empty of people. A big banner at the entrance proclaimed, *Hamburger Dom Funfair.* A hazardous-looking roller-coaster stood at the center of the field, surrounded by booths and snack bars and a whole contingent of trucks waiting to haul it all away. It struck me as an oddly cheerful place for these hooligans to pose, but I have faith that Astrid knows what she's doing.

While the boys unpacked their gear, I had a moment alone with her.

"I love it here," I said. "So . . . *evocative*."

I could see that she didn't understand the word. I tried again.

"Where do you plan to shoot them?" I asked.

"*Die vagons*," she said. "The trucks."

"Ah!" I said. "Or . . ."

She looked at me, eyebrow raised. I let it sit there for a moment.

"Or," I continued, "maybe you use the *snack bars*. You know, something funny. Like one of them ordering a pretzel. Or spilling their ice cream." I did a funny pantomime of somebody dropping a scoop of ice cream.

She looked at me quizzically.

"They seem like they're funny guys," I said. "I think something funny would be dynamite." (Dammit, another idiom.)

She smiled and patted my cheek. "You are so sweet," she said. (She's very touch-y, very hands-on. I like that.) "But no. You will see."

She led the boys to an open-sided truck parked at the base of the roller-coaster. The lettering on its side read "HUGO HAAS—HANNOVER." Four of them held guitars (electric guitars, but not plugged in), while Pete dragged around a single drum. She stood them against the side of the truck, trying different poses, different positions. I saw what she was going for—some interesting lines from the coaster tracks, the girders, and the open-bedded truck. But then I see those silly boys, those pale, scrawny teenage Marlon Brandos, and that ruins the whole effect. Trying so hard to look like bad boys, but I don't think they're fooling anyone. Except maybe Astrid.

I kept my distance and stayed out of her way. She seemed

fully engaged with the project, energized by it. And so very beautiful. She must be an artist, I thought—how could she not be? A true artist—especially a visual artist—knows that the first piece of creation is the Self. If you can make yourself look that gorgeous, you can probably make a photograph look pretty good, too.

I leaned against our van, a good distance off, with Jurgen, watching Astrid move the boys around, like she was playing with dolls. I paid close attention to their interactions, trying to gauge whether Astrid had any interest in them romantically, or they with her. It was hard to tell. There was some joking around, but on the whole it was a businesslike session. At one point she touched one of them on the shoulder, directing him to move slightly to his left, but it wasn't a lingering touch. She seemed much more interested in the photo she was trying to take.

"They are very good," said Jurgen, noting my interest. "Very talented. They play rock and roll. You know?"

"Like Elvis Presley?"

"Yes, exactly."

I had to confess that I don't particularly like rock and roll. It's so completely derivative of Negro music, of rhythm and blues. I think it's fine if it's actually *done* by Negro artists. That, to me, is genuine. But when white boys start doing it, it's almost like a parody. And especially white boys like Elvis Presley, who is, after all, such a hillbilly. I suppose these boys from the north of England are a little like England's version of hillbillies.

"What's their band called?" I asked.

"The Beatles," he said.

"Like the car?"

He laughed. "No."

"Like the insect?"

He laughed again. "Like the beat of a drum. The Beat Poets. Beatniks."

"Oh," I said, "I get it." I didn't have the nerve to tell Jurgen (who seemed like a fan) that if you have to ask twice what a title means, it's probably not a very good title.

Once they finished the group shot, Astrid broke them off into smaller groups and took some more photos against the other trucks. Moving from one location to the next, I noticed, she spent most of her time talking to one "Beatle" in particular, the thinnest and palest of them all. The guy who never took off his sunglasses, even in the van. Jurgen noticed me watching.

"That's Stuart," he said. "The bass player. I think Astrid fancies him."

"Really?" I tried to sound casual. But I could feel my back arch as I stepped forward to get a better look. "Talented bass player, is he?"

"No." Jurgen laughed.

Of course he isn't.

"But he's a very good artist. Quite remarkable. And very smart. Astrid thinks he's a genius."

"A genius?" I said. "Him?"

"He paints these wonderful canvases. He won all sorts of prizes at school. They think he'll be a famous artist someday."

At first I thought he was joking, because I couldn't imagine *anyone* seeing talent in any of these young thugs. But Jurgen seemed quite convinced of it; and as I watched Stuart pose with his sunglasses and his bass guitar, I felt a pang of jealousy—not of his alleged talent (and yes, it was only an allegation), but because Jurgen believed it and so, evidently, did Astrid.

But then I had a revelation. The way Jurgen had described Stuart, the things he'd said about him—this is precisely how people might well describe *me*. I'm not being immodest here: my poetry did, in fact, win a prize at school last year, a very prestigious prize, and I think I'm well respected as a result. And, of course, my school is Columbia University. God only knows what passes for a school in the north of England.

So if this is the type of man Astrid is attracted to, someone who is very smart and considered very talented, then good for me.

"Why is he playing in a rock and roll band?" I asked.

"I don't know," said Jurgen. "It's good fun, I suppose."

I took a closer look at Stuart. The sunglasses were a pretentious touch, no question, but I could see what he was going for: the aloof bohemian-artist type, hiding his sensitivity from an adoring public. His pale, finely chiseled features reminded me of someone, and then it hit me: *he looks like Astrid.* They could be brother and sister. Maybe that was the attraction: the sibling they never had—or even just a case of misplaced narcissism.

But for heaven's sake, he's so thin and pale. He looks sickly, like someone who hasn't been exposed to sunlight for a year. I read somewhere that young people in America tend to be better nourished than our European counterparts, owing to the wartime shortages they suffered, which is a terrible tragedy, of course. But I also think we Americans have a higher respect for healthy living. We're robust and energetic, with clear skin and tan faces—that has to be more attractive to a woman, hasn't it?

I walked over to where they sat, chatting, on the running board of an old ice cream truck. They were all smiles and giggles. I felt a wave of nausea. I don't want these two to fall in love. I don't want them to be happy. I want them to fail, just as I did. If anyone gets to fall in love with Astrid, it's me.

"How's it going?" I asked, with a casual wave.

"*Gut, gut,*" she said. "Alan, do you know Stuart?"

"No," he said, "we haven't met."

I shook his hand.

"I understand you're an artist," I said.

"I used to be," he said with a modest smile.

Astrid squeezed his arm. "He is a wonderful artist. But he likes being rock and roll star even more."

Stuart shrugged, as if to say, *I'm just so good at everything, it's hard to choose.*

"I took a class at Columbia with Helen Frankenthaler," I said. "Do you know her?"

"No," he said, disinterested.

"Abstract expressionist, you know, New York School. Fascinating woman. I can't say I *love* her work, but I guess I'm more of a representational kind of guy. Give me Cézanne and a bowl of apples, right? That guy could *paint.* Not that I believe representation is the only valid visual aesthetic, I simply think one needs to paint realistically, and master that, before moving on to abstraction—"

I realized that I was blathering and they were no longer paying attention, but I couldn't make myself stop. I was able, at least, to change the subject.

"So what kind of stuff do you paint?" I asked.

"Oh, this and that." He shrugged.

"He is, how do you say it, *eklektisch,*" offered Astrid.

Stuart smiled. "Eclect-ish? Is that really a word?"

"Yes," said Astrid, teasingly defiant. "*Eklektisch.* Like, many different styles."

"German is such a ridiculous language," said Stuart.

"No it isn't," she said, bumping him with her shoulder.

"Yes it is!"

It was all so flirty it made me sick.

Stu turned to me. "Alan, do you know what they call meatloaf? It's called *Leberkäse*. Which means 'liver cheese.' Doesn't that sound bloody marvelous?"

"Stop it, you two," said Astrid, smacking him on the shoulder with her gloves. Then she smacked me on the shoulder for good measure. This snapped me out of my funk. Maybe she's flirting with both of us.

"Come, we go back to work now," she said, pulling Stuart to his feet. "Maybe I can make you smile this time." She tickled him. It got the desired effect.

"Bloody woman," he said, which made Astrid laugh, too, as they walked off together to plan the next shot.

She didn't stop to tickle me.

September 15

Is it possible that I'm attracted to Astrid precisely because she looks like a boy? I've been dwelling on this thought for a couple of hours now, and it's disturbing on a number of different levels.

First of all, I'm pretty sure that I'm not a homosexual. Astrid is very much a girl, even if her face and haircut vaguely resemble those of a boy. "Boyish" could simply be a descriptive adjective and nothing more, like calling her "thin" or "blonde."

Second, I've never been attracted to a boy. At least, not that I know of. But do we ever know these things for sure? Do these distinctions exist deep within our psyches and emerge only at some unexpected point in our lives? Maybe we're all composed of parts that are heterosexual and parts that are homosexual and we all just live at different points on the spectrum.

I must stop with these crazy thoughts.

Or maybe my attraction to someone who's "boyish" is simply a reaction to Suzy. The word that's most often used to describe Suzy, by myself and others, is "curvy." She is a curvy girl. And there's no question that I was attracted to that curvy-ness in ways that are even now getting me sexually excited despite the fact that I am dead to her.

So maybe, as part of my grieving process for the loss of Suzy, I am attracted to someone who is quite the opposite of curvy, at least in terms of the relative size of her sexual organs and her female attributes (including Suzy's long, luscious hair). Maybe I'm not really attracted to Astrid at all; I'm just so unattracted to the memory of Suzy that I've become attracted to the polar opposite of her.

Or maybe I'm a homosexual.

September 16
per Luftpost

Dear Mom and Dad,

I received your care package today—thank you so much! I've gone through the bag of pistachios already, as well as the dried fruit. I'm saving the peanut brittle for later. Peanuts usually make my face break out, and I think it's important to make a good first impression here in Germany.

My classes continue to be good. My Shakespeare teacher is a very interesting guy named Karl Wensinger. I may have mentioned him to you—he's a well-known poet in Germany (well, he's been published, anyway), and he's one of the reasons I chose this program. He's not teaching a class in poetry-writing this semester, which is too bad, but I think I can work with him on an informal basis. I can't even imagine what a German poet would think of my work (I've always imagined that my sensibility would be very popular in Europe), but I'm sure his take on me will be fascinating. Maybe he can introduce me to some of the literary types in this country. Maybe even a publisher?

I went to speak with him after class the other day, to introduce myself and explain that I was a poet as well. He was nice enough and seemed interested, but when I asked if he would read one of my poems, he apologized and said he couldn't do that. If he read my "outside projects," he'd have to read everybody's, etc., etc. Such an annoying response. What's the point of doing anything well if you're always lumped in with everyone else? ("I'm sorry, Mr. Shakespeare, if I read *your* play then I'll have to read *everybody's*.") I suppose I'll just have to work on him a little. Eventually he'll see that I'm a kindred soul.

I took a long walk through the city today, and it was very stimulating. The city is dominated by water, with a large port, lakes, canals, and the River Elbe. (Did you know that Hamburg has more canals in it than Amsterdam and Venice combined?) Each of the neighborhoods has its own character and I'm fascinated by them all. So much life and energy! Thousands of different people going about their business in thousands of different ways. Sometimes I look in the windows of these densely packed apartment buildings, and I think about how different their lives are from my own. I hope that during my stay here I can get to know a great many of them, and see the world through their eyes.

There is beauty everywhere I look, and so much here for me to learn.

Love,
Alan

September 16

per Luftpost

Dear Artie,

Hamburg is one fucked-up city.

I took a long walk today, and by the end of it I felt physically ill; not from the rigors of the walk, but from the level of depravity you see from one end of this city to the other.

The neighborhood I live in (St. Pauli) is the most overtly sexual place I've ever seen, and not in a cheerful way. It's what I imagine Times Square would be like if the Nazis had won the war. There are sex shops on every corner. (And I must confess, I always wondered exactly what the term "sex shop" meant. And now I know: it's a wide-ranging description that encompasses a great variety of goods and services. It can be a retail shop that sells sexual toys and sexy garments and even furniture made specifically for sex. There is a store down the street where I can buy dildos, latex masks, and a wide selection of cock rings. It can be a bookstore, like the one on Feldstrasse, whose shelves groan with pornography of every shade and stripe: books, magazines, newspapers, posters, journals—the scope and variety of which rivals that of the New York Public Library.)

In Hamburg, sex shops are simply no big deal. They're everywhere, and nobody cares. It's not unusual for the locals here to use sex shops as points of references when giving instructions. "You are looking for the bakery? It's right across from the store that sells battery-operated vibrators; you can't miss it."

Around the corner from my apartment is Herbertstrasse,

an entire street that's been designated "for adults only." There are big metal barricades at either end of it, informing visitors that anyone under 18 years of age—and all women—are forbidden. The street was originally cordoned off by the Nazis, as they were unable to stop the practice of prostitution in the area; they decided to simply hide it behind walls where it couldn't be seen by the casual citizen.

At first, I wasn't sure why—twice I was asked to "show my papers"—but then I saw all the storefronts that have live women sitting behind glass, looking out onto the street. (As Dorothy Parker said, "You can lead a horticulture . . .") If you're interested, you tap on the window, she chats you up, then invites you inside to discuss a price. (I know all this from my landlord, who seems well-acquainted with the custom.) The women are scantily dressed, with sad expressions and too much makeup, and are remarkably unattractive. Evidently they do a thriving business, though, as a new shipload of hungry sailors arrives on the dock almost every week. Let me know if you're interested, Artie; I can get you some phone numbers.

A little further inland is the delightfully named Schmuckstrasse (*schmuck* meaning "jewelry," among other things). It also has an air of depravity to it, but is a little more dark and mysterious. Even my landlord told me to stay away.

"You will catch a horrible disease," he said. "It will make your cock hurt for months."

Naturally I had to go and look.

I discovered that sex is bought and sold on this street as well, but the purveyors of said erotica are not ladies: they are men *dressed up as ladies*. The scientific term, I believe, is *transvestites*. Much like unicorns and jackelopes, it is a species I'd heard rumors of, but never actually seen in the flesh.

My education continues.

I can't help but think that seeing all these sights, and experiencing the outliers of humanity, will make me a better artist. Witnessing the full blossom of man's depravity will not only broaden my view, but encourage me to lift my sights ever higher, and better appreciate what is good and beautiful in life. As Rilke said, "No great art has ever been made without the artist having known danger."

Maybe he was talking about venereal disease.

Your pal,
Alan (The Sexual Pioneer)

September 16

I decided I need to buy condoms. It's not like I'm planning to have sex anytime soon, but you never know when those things might happen, and Hamburg has got to be crawling with dangerous pathogens. I see the sailors from all over the world and I think of all the germs and the dirty sex they're having with cheap prostitutes and low-class German girls . . .

I must confess, I've never used a condom before. The two times that Suzy and I did it, we used a combination of diaphragm and the new "birth control pill," which Suzy insisted on (I think the idea of a pill that prevents pregnancy is absurd: it's unhygienic, unreliable, and will never catch on). Condoms I think of as being for seafarers and roustabouts, so it would make sense that they would be easy to come by in Hamburg.

I went to an *Apotheke* near the college and the man behind the counter was not surprised when, in a whispered voice, I asked for *die Kondome*. (A nearby university with an energetic male population must surely make it a well-stocked item.) He handed me a small box—*Willie Boy Kondome* read the label, aimed, perhaps, at the American sailor market—discreetly wrapped in a plain paper bag. He was handing me my change when I heard the rap of knuckles on the pharmacy window.

It was Astrid.

Oh dear God, I thought, and thrust the bag deep into my pocket.

"*Hallo* Alan!" she said, entering the shop. "How are you?"

"Good! Good!"

She must have seen the panicked look on my face. "Are you all right?" she said, looking concerned.

"Yes! I just . . ." I gestured toward the pharmacist and tapped the package in my pocket, struggling to find words. "I got some Alka-Seltzer." I have no idea why I said that.

"What is Alka-Seltzer?" she asked, looking even more concerned.

"Well, you call it something different here, I forget. Just for headache, stomachache . . ."

"Oh no, you are sick?" She took off her glove and touched my face, feeling for a fever. (Is it just my imagination, or does she go out of her way to touch me?) Her hand was warm and smelled vaguely of peppermint. The combination of condoms burning a hole in my pocket and Astrid's soft touch on my forehead was enough to make me burst. "Can I bring you some soup? My mother makes a wonderful *Eintopf* with chicken and carrots and dumplings."

I groaned just a little bit. She must have thought I was reacting to the food. "Really, not necessary," I said. "I'm already feeling better."

She didn't believe me completely but made a brave face and nodded. "Maybe you are a little homesick, too, yes?" And she looked at me with such kindness.

This is what fascinates me about Astrid. She's so cool and elegant, and yet filled with warmth and compassion. She's a woman of opposites, shifting imperceptibly from one to another. Sexy but motherly. Boyish but also girlish. (And Suzy, by the way, never once in our relationship expressed sympathy for me when I was sick. It was some strange neurosis on her part: she couldn't see a sick person without making some comment about "faking it" or chiding them to "get over it." She saw illness as a personal failure, and sympathy for it a weakness.)

"Yes, maybe a little homesick," I said. It felt easy to be

honest with her. Vulnerable, even.

She nodded twice, three times, staring deeply into my eyes. "It's natural to be homesick," she said. "You miss your family, and they miss you. But you have me, and you have my friends next door. You will do well here. This is the right place for you. You are living your adventure. Yes?"

I nodded, even as I got a little lump in my throat. I didn't even realize I was homesick, and yet here I was, suddenly overcome with a wave of it.

"Good," she said, now in a stern voice. "Now go home and get some rest. Sleep. I promise you. You will feel much better. And I . . . must get back to work."

I asked her where, and she said at a photographer's studio. I didn't ask which one—and I'm kicking myself now that I didn't—but it must be right in the neighborhood because I watched her stride down the street, with no sign of a car or public transportation.

Just before she left, though, she said something significant. She had just given me a firm pat on the shoulder ("I must not hug you if you are sick") and then stopped to give me a long, quizzical stare. "You have very interesting eyes," she said.

I smiled skeptically. "Really?"

"Yes," she said. "Very interesting."

No one's ever told me that before.

September 17

It is now 4 a.m. and I am living in hell.

The musicians came home at 3, as is their custom. They stomped up the stairs with the requisite joking and funny voices, but were a little quieter tonight. Maybe they were tired after their long show, maybe just feeling down—who knows? Who cares? I turned over in bed to face the other wall, and felt myself drifting back into sleep. I could hear a quiet conversation, but I couldn't make out the words. Then I heard the first guitar.

I didn't recognize it as a guitar at first. In my semi-conscious state, my first thought was, *Somebody's plucking a rubber band.* Gradually I came to realize that I was hearing an electric guitar that wasn't plugged in, hence the lack of reverberation or anything else that sounded remotely like music. I thought I could probably sleep through it (I've gotten considerably better at sleeping through their late-night giggle sessions), but then another guitar joined in, and then another. And then the singing.

Oh dear God, I thought, *they're playing music.* They've just played all night in a club, and now they come home and play even more? They must be on drugs. (My uncle Ernie played briefly in a swing band, and he told me that his bandmates smoked marijuana almost nonstop.)

And let's be honest. When I say they were playing "music," I'm being generous. I didn't recognize the song, but it sounded vaguely familiar, possibly some Negro boogie-woogie number:

The best things in life are free

But you can keep 'em for the birds and bees
Now give me money
That's what I want

I wrapped the pillow around my ears and buried my face on the mattress. This was a nightmare. If they'd been playing, say, a Bach minuet, or a gentle French *chanson*, my goodness, it would be like a lullaby. This was the opposite: hard, aggressive, angry. (I sense a certain amount of anger in all Negro music—and why shouldn't it be? It's their music of protest, after all. But to hear it coming from a white, English motorcycle gang is both laughable and insulting.) And those horrible, vulgar lyrics . . .

Money don't give everything, it's true
But what it don't give, I can't use
Now give me money, that's what I want
A lot of money, that's what I want

Negro music is an expressive genre, no question, but I think we can all agree that its power comes from the primal rhythms and raw, long-suffering sense of emotion. Certainly not from the words.

I am a poet. Words matter to me. Each syllable of a Rilke poem, or a Shakespeare sonnet, runs riot with meaning, with sound, with association. Each word is an opportunity to build a new world and construct a new meaning.

Yeah gimme money, that's what I want
A lot of money, that's what I want
That's what I want, that's what I want
So gimme money, that's what I want

That's what I want, yeah,
That's what I want

It's absolutely revolting. If the sheer inanity of the lyric wasn't enough to send me hurtling into a dark night of despair, I also had to endure a discussion of how to play this monstrous tune, a continuing argument between members of the band. Possibly Paul and John.

"Let's try it slower."

"I'm not trying it slower."

"Can't we just try it slower?"

"We're not turning it into a fucking show tune. We've got enough of your fucking soft numbers for the fucking grannies—"

"What if we slow down the bridge?"

"WE'RE NOT SLOWING DOWN THE FUCKING BRIDGE!"

This went on for ten minutes.

Finally I could take it no longer. I jumped out of bed and pounded on the wall. "Guys! Please, could you keep it down? Thank you!"

I threw myself back into bed and curled myself into a ball, waiting for the mockery and taunting to begin. There was silence, for a moment, but then . . .

"Good evening, Alan," came a voice, low and comical, like a cheesy American lounge singer. I think it was John. His voice was deeper than the others. "How ya doin', Al baby? You havin' a good time?"

"I'm tired," I said. "I want to sleep!"

"Al baby, tonight is your lucky night," he said, still doing the lounge singer voice. "Me and the boys got a sensational new number. Would ya like to hear it?"

"It's the first time we've played it," chimed in another.

"A world premiere."

"Look, guys," I said to the wall, in my most reasonable voice. "Why don't you go out to a bar? Have a good time with other people . . . like you. You can sing as much as you want."

"But we want you to hear it, Al baby, we think you'll dig it."

"Well I don't dig it—I don't dig it at all!"

There was a pause. "You hear that, fellas? Al baby doesn't dig it at all."

"Does he say why?"

"I'll tell you why," I shouted. "It's loud, it's vulgar, it's completely atonal!"

"Atonal, you say?"

"Yes! It's discordant! It's not soothing or satisfying in the least!"

There was a long pause. I could hear them talking quietly among themselves. I thought that would be the end of it, or that perhaps they were plotting some terrible revenge. But at long last John came back to the wall.

"Are you still there, Al baby?"

"Yes," I said, pillow over my head again.

"How 'bout I sing you a lullaby instead?"

I took a deep breath. "Look," I said, "Just—"

And he started to sing.

Little cowboy, say goodnight
Nighty night, sleep tight
Dreamy sweet dreamy
And blow out the light
Nighty night, sleep tight
Close up your clamballs

And count up your sheep
Sleep tight little cowboy
Slippy slippy slippy slippy slippy sleep

What any of this meant, I didn't have a clue. A private joke at my expense? Some hidden meaning in the seemingly random words? I was too tired to care. I waited for another verse, but it never came.

"Alan?" It was John again. "Are you still awake?"

"Yes," I said.

"Sorry, mate. You'll just have to listen to the fuckin' song."

Someone counted off—"One two three four"—and the music kicked back in.

Your lovin' give me a thrill
But your lovin' don't pay my bills
Now give me mo-oney . . .

Just another night for a Jew in Germany.

September 21

Yes, it would be easy enough for me to move, at this point. I know enough people in Hamburg now that I could probably find another accommodation, maybe through one of the kids at school, or maybe even through Astrid.

But no, I will not. It's a matter of principle. I am a good, quiet tenant who minds his own business. My neighbors are loud, detestable vulgarians whose antics are surely a nuisance to everyone in the neighborhood, all of whom need their sleep, too. I must stay, and they must go—it's as simple as that.

I made an appointment to see Bruno. He is well known in this part of town. In addition to the Bambi Kino, he owns a couple of nightclubs just down the road, the Indra and the Kaiserkeller, both of which feature live music and rowdy, boisterous crowds. I've never patronized either one of them, and I doubt I ever will. They are both acknowledged as breeding grounds for degenerates and thugs. I do sometimes see the Kaiserkeller during the day, when it's closed for business: that's where Bruno keeps his office, and where I go to pay my rent and pick up my mail.

He was sitting at his desk, opening letters with what looked like a Nazi war-issue switchblade, when I came in.

"What do you want?" he asked, and didn't wait for my answer. "I have letters for you." He pulled a short stack of mail from his drawer and dumped it on the desk, not even looking up.

"Herr Bruno," I said. "I must ask you to do something about the musicians. The English boys."

He curled an eyebrow.

I told him about the problems I'd been having with them, how they were keeping me awake with their late-night hootenannies, and how necessary it is for me to get a deep and restful sleep every night to keep my mind clear so I can be fully present for my studies and for my art.

He looked at me like I was from Mars. "Levy," he said. "Let me ask you something."

"What?"

"Are you a cocksucker? You like sex with boys?"

"What? No!" I said. And felt a quick panic that maybe this is why he had rented me the room in the first place—that maybe cocksucking is part of the rent.

"Good. I am glad. You are good tenant. I like you."

"Well . . . thank you . . ." I said, and buttoned the top button of my shirt.

"But the English boys, they are good tenants, too."

"They most certainly are not!" I said. "They are horrible people! They're loud, they're disrespectful, they're dirty . . ."

"I know what kind of people they are," he said. "They play in my club every night. But you see, they make me money. You are nice American boy, but you do not make me money. If I have to choose between them and you, I choose them."

I leaned forward. "What if I told you they were breaking the law?" I said.

"Are they?"

"Well I'm sure they must be," I said, twisting my mouth in disgust. "They have very loose morals, and poor hygiene. I think they may be Communists."

Bruno smiled. "In my country," he said, "we do not put people in jail for these things. We have perhaps more freedom than the USA."

I was a little offended that a German who opened his

letters with a Nazi switchblade would lecture me, an American, about social justice, but I chose to ignore it.

"What if I found you some proof?" I said. "That they had committed a crime?"

Bruno considered it for a moment, then gave a condescending smile. I could tell he thought I was out of my depth, an American schoolboy playing junior detective. Perhaps he was right.

"Levy," he said. "You are a Jew, yes?"

I told him that I was.

"Come with me."

He led me out of his office and down the stairs. The nightclub is actually in the basement, and though it was empty, it emitted an overpowering smell of sweat, tobacco, and bleach. I followed him—his leg dragging like a short, knotted rope—past the stage area, through another door and into a small boiler room. The furnace, black and ancient, burned with a noxious rumble and made the room uncomfortably hot.

"You see this?" He indicated some small pellets in the corner. "Rats," he said. "Filthy, disgusting rats. They eat garbage in the alley and now they come inside."

"That's horrible," I said, though it didn't surprise me that Bruno and a rat colony had managed to find each other.

He shook his head, looking grim. "I must kill them."

"Well," I said, "you could call an exterminator."

"No! I must kill them myself! I will not allow them to destroy my club!"

I tried to look sympathetic. His passion on the subject felt a little overblown, and was making me uncomfortable.

"How do you think I should do it, Levy? Poison?" He leaned in close. "Gas?"

I cleared my throat. "Well . . . I suppose either one."

"Or is such a thing *unthinkable*?" He gazed even harder at me, searching my face, so close that I could smell his breath, which reeked of sausage. "You think for me to leave poison and kill them, kill them all, indiscriminately, this is *acceptable*?"

I took a step back. Perhaps he was just interested in hearing a Jew's opinion on the subject, but he seemed unusually excited at the prospect of indiscriminate killing. I replied calmly, in a reasonable tone of voice, "Well, I mean, rats do spread disease."

"Yes!" shouted Bruno. "Yes, they spread *disease*! They are horrible, filthy creatures!"

"I should probably leave," I said.

"Yes! Thank you, Levy. Thank you. You are right. It must be done. I will kill them all."

And with that, he led me out of the boiler room, dragging his foot back up to the office. Neither of us spoke. I was happy to emerge from the dark pit, a perfect murder scene if ever there was one.

"Wait," he said. "Your mail."

Outside, I leafed through three letters: one from the university, one from Artie, and a small pastel envelope with the handwritten return address, *A. Kirchherr*.

Astrid.

I tore open the envelope and stood in the shadow of the nightclub, while the riffraff of the Grosse Freiheit passed me by unnoticed, and I read these words:

Dear Alan,

May I take your photograph, too?

xxx,

Astrid

And just like that, I was transported. Away from Bruno

and rats and boorish neighbors and an ex-girlfriend who lives in New York City. I was no longer alone. Now, at least in my own mind, I was with Astrid.

Maybe it's time to admit that I'm falling in love.

September 26

The photo session had to be engineered carefully. It was the perfect opportunity for some serious one-on-one time, and, more important, an artistic collaboration. We can see if our visions are compatible. And I like the fact that, as the photographer, she'll be looking at me the whole time.

First, I had to respond to Astrid's letter, and I decided to do so in a forceful and aggressive manner: I went to see her in person. Through a series of inquiries, I learned that she worked for a well-established photographer in town named Reinhart Wolf. As I'd guessed, his studio was quite near the college, and, after two unsuccessful sorties (it appears that she only works there in the afternoon), I found her there, seated at a desk in the outer office, all alone.

By showing up unannounced, I'd be able to see her reaction in real time, spontaneous and unrehearsed.

I couldn't have asked for a better response. When she saw me walk in, she burst into a big smile, warm and genuine.

"Alan!" She rose from her seat and gave me a big, deep, affectionate hug. She was dressed a little more formally today: an aqua cashmere sweater, a single row of pearls, and a tight skirt. She looked like a French fashion model, and more beautiful than ever.

I don't think there's any way in the world I could be a homosexual.

She showed me around the studio and introduced me to Herr Wolf, but all I could think about was how gorgeous she looked, and how effortlessly she fit into the world of high-class photography. To be honest, I've never known a professional artist; i.e., anyone who makes a living in the arts. There are my professors at school, I guess, but they're academics. Herr Wolf is a working artist, and Astrid is clearly being groomed as another, like the apprentices who worked for Michelangelo and eventually became great masters themselves. There's a world of difference between someone like me who aspires to be an artist, and someone who actually is one. And it fits Astrid perfectly. Everything about her—the way she dresses, the way she moves, the way she speaks—feels like a work of art.

And I love the way she mangles the English language. We got to talking about art school (she had graduated the previous year) and she said that she found so many of her fellow students there to be "extremely woolly."

A pause, as I considered this. "In what way?"

"You know," she said, "woolly. Like, how do you say it . . ."

"Covered in wool?"

"No," she said, and smacked me on the shoulder, which felt like a tickle. "You know, they have seen a lot, they have traveled."

"You mean *worldly*?"

"Yes!" she said. "Woolly."

Adorable.

She lay one of Herr Wolf's photographs on a table in front of us. A ship in the harbor, or something. I found myself looking instead at Astrid's shoulder, the curve of it, and how it framed the back of her head. Standing so close to me. It would be so easy to touch her shoulder, but of course I couldn't.

"It's nice," I said, idiotically.

She smiled but kept her attention fixed on the image. "I love the light," she said, resting a hand on her hip while her eyes darted around the page. "You must learn to see only the light. Not the ship, not the harbor. Just the light. The pattern. You know?"

"Yes," I said. "It's almost an abstraction." My mind raced. I don't know very much about photography. "It reminds me a little of... you know, the French guy... the photographer..."

"And think about this," she said, her eyes lighting up with something that resembled mischief. "This light... this exact light..." She indicated the whole scene. "It existed once, but it does not exist now. You know? It is gone. If you saw this place now, it would not look the same."

She was trying hard to find the words in English. Trying to explain her complicated theory using words that were far too simple. I could only watch her and enjoy the performance.

"It existed for a moment," she continued. "Yes? It touched the camera, it touched the film, and now, many months later, it touches us. Yes? Even though it is gone. You understand?"

I nodded.

"So. This is like when you look at a star, you know? In the sky. You are seeing light from ten thousand years ago, but it just reaches you now. The star may be gone, it may be dead, but you are seeing it now, you are seeing the *photograph*."

I tried to follow what she was saying, but I was distracted by her eyes, the way they rose and fell with each syllable, animating her words and lighting up the room. She must have seen me smile. She stopped talking and ran a quick, self-conscious hand through her hair. She turned back to the photo, a little more businesslike, and said, "I like this part," pointing at the bottom of the ship. "How do you say it?" She made a V with her hands.

"The hull?"

"Hull?" she said, and turned toward me. "How do you spell that?"

When two people don't speak the same language, I think, they rely less on words to communicate, and more on things that speak even louder—smiles, gestures, body language. They all become exaggerated, and fraught with meaning. I wanted so desperately to touch her, not for the purposes of sex (well, not entirely) but simply as a form of expression. It's like when you're dancing and the music's too loud; words are unnecessary. You exist purely in the realm of the senses.

Yes, that was it: I wanted to dance with this woman. I wanted to hold her, to feel her warmth, her motion, her breath on my neck. I wanted to sway with her, while we drank in the music, with no words to get in the way.

The boyishness, I realize, is simply an illusion. She is a woman, all right, and her sexuality is there for all to see, but it wears a disguise. It masquerades, in small, subtle ways, as something that belongs to a boy. It doesn't actually convince you, but it confuses you. It makes you question what you see, and look even harder.

"By the way," I said. "The answer is yes."

She gave me a puzzled look.

"I'd like it very much if you took my photo."

"Yes! Right!" she said, as if it had slipped her mind, even though I'm sure it hadn't.

"Maybe we could shoot it down by the harbor," I said, indicating Herr Wolf's photo.

"No," she said, with a little scowl. "No ships. Just you. Your face. No hulls."

"Or," I said, a little mysteriously (and this I had planned, but only if the mood seemed right), "we could go out of town. Maybe for the weekend. We could drive out in the country, stay at a bed and breakfast..."

"Mm," she said, narrowing her eyes. I could tell immediately that I had gone too far. I was pushing too hard, and I never should have used the word *bed*. Stupid stupid stupid.

"How about this," she said, choosing, gracefully, to ignore my transgression. "The Kino. Where you live. I love the posters. And the big, you know, the sign?"

"The marquee?"

"Yes," she said. "The marquee. That is where we do it. All right?"

Having nearly blown the whole thing, I agreed to it immediately. We would meet on Tuesday, at noon, at the Kino.

I thought it best to make my exit then and there, with a win under my belt, but she stopped me. "Do you want to see the photos I took of the English boys?"

Of course I did.

She dug a small envelope out of her desk and laid a dozen or so photographs down on the table, all of them black and white.

They were stunning.

Never mind that the five boys were thoroughly uninteresting characters; it was the images themselves that were remarkable. The light. With the color drained away, the Hamburger Dom Funfair—as happy and carefree a setting as you'll ever find—was grim and industrial, bleak and menacing. It looked like Hamburg: bombed-out by the war and living in shadows. Exactly the feeling that I'm trying to evoke in my poem cycle. (I'm more positive than ever that Astrid and I share an artistic sensibility.)

And I had to admit, she even managed to make the boys look more dangerous and less idiotic than they are in real life. They stared, unsmiling, directly into the lens or just off to the side, statuesque and vaguely defiant.

I noticed that many of the photos featured Stuart, with his silly sunglasses and cut-rate James Dean look. "Does he always wear the glasses?" I ventured.

Astrid looked at the photo and smiled. "That is Stuart," she said softly. "That is Stuart."

There are a million ways I could have interpreted her gaze at his photo, or the way she tilted her head as she spoke his name, but I chose not to. I had no desire to bring Stuart into the conversation, and I let the matter drop.

September 29

I had two days to prepare.

My first project, of course, was to clean my room. At the very least, she would see it; at best, she'd be spending some time here.

A man can live like an animal for long stretches of time, burrowing deeper into his own filth, absorbing more of his own foul smells. Women, however, have no tolerance for such things: they prefer a neat and orderly living environment. (My biology teacher, Mr. Mumbrue, attributed this to the female nesting instinct—a theory Suzy took great exception to, that led to one of our worst fights ever, one in which she threw a plate of chicken paprikash in my face. At Barnard, this is known as "feminism.")

I attacked the various surfaces of my apartment with a sponge and a bucket of warm water and bleach. Each layer of cleaning revealed another layer of dirt, graduating from dust to soil to soot, to something resembling black tar. After many hours and much physical strain, the room felt clean. Or at least not poisonous.

Second, I resolved to buy myself a great outfit. One of the German kids at school told me about a boutique on Moenckerberg Strasse that sells bohemian French-style clothing. French seems to be the fashion among the artsy types at school, as well as for Astrid and her circle of friends. And I suppose that makes sense, considering that German fashion, as far as I can tell, consists either of lederhosen or an S.S. uniform.

I decided to go with a black turtleneck sweater. I remember seeing that look in a French movie (possibly *every* French movie)—simple, classic, artistic. I also bought myself a black beret, but I don't know if I'll have the chutzpah to pull that one off. I looked at myself in the mirror. I felt like Jean-Paul Sartre.

Lastly, I considered the amount of time I'd be spending with Astrid during the shoot. When I watched her photograph the English boys, she was quiet for the most part, even while they talked and joked among themselves. I wanted the sheer power of my physicality to do my speaking for me, but at the same time I had to keep her engaged. There mustn't be any lulls in the conversation. And that's when I came up with my plan.

I would memorize a Rilke poem. *In German.*

And what better poem to recite than the beautiful "Autumn Day"—*Herbsttag*—the poet's masterful meditation on the inexorable march of time? After all, the photo shoot would take place on an actual autumn day, and I could pretend to think of it off the top of my head when we discussed the weather, which we were bound to do. Besides, if you're going to photograph musicians with their instruments, why not photograph me with my Rilke? I can't think of anything that would come closer to my essence. And the words are so beautiful...

Herr: es ist Zeit.
Der Sommer war sehr gross.
Leg deinen Schatten auf die Sonnenuhren,
und auf den Fluren lass die Winde los.

I spent a full hour rehearsing it in front of a mirror. I'm a pretty good actor when I put my mind to it, and this felt like the role of a lifetime, for the prize of a lifetime. If I absolutely nail it, I think I can make her cry.

> *Befiehl den letzten Fruchten voll zu sein;*
> *gieb ihnen noch zwei sudlichere Tage.*

What a spell I will cast!

When Wednesday arrived, I waited for Astrid like before, listening for the telltale footsteps coming up the stairs. I'd bought myself a small hand-mirror at a beauty shop (I told the clerk it was for my wife) and I checked my reflection frequently. I paced back and forth, over and over, rehearsing my lines, until finally I had to stop. I was starting to sweat and I didn't want to stain my shirt.

At noon exactly, I heard her approach. And then the knock on my door.

We hugged. Oh, those hugs of ours. How absolutely *right* she feels in my arms.

She remarked that my room was much cleaner than the boys' next door, which she likened to a *Schweinestall* (which I eventually translated into "pig pen"). I told her I had never actually been inside.

"Why do you not make friends with them?" she asked. "They speak your language, they are nice boys."

I told her that our schedules were just so different, our lives so completely different.

It was best, I thought, not to mention how much I despised them all, with their noise, and their music, and their silly *Englishness,* night after night. Or how much it galled me that Stuart, my anemic, pasty-faced rival, slept in a bed not thirty feet away from my head, every night, surrounded by his fellow *Schweine.*

"Tell you what," I said. "If it would make you happy, I'll

try harder to be friends with them."

"*Gut*," she said. "That does make me happy." She patted me on the cheek.

Women are so easy to manipulate.

"Come." She took my hand. "Let us take photos."

She led down to the front of the Kino, and sat me on the top step that led to the lobby. Over my shoulder was a poster for an Italian melodrama called *La Dolce Vita*. (Astrid said it was wonderful.) I tried a number of different looks and different expressions while Astrid clicked away. She moved my legs a little, from one side to the other, but didn't "direct" all that much, apart from telling me more than once to stop smiling.

In my own mind, I was trying number of different characters. (This was a cinema, after all.) Stoic cowboy, dashing spy, mysterious drifter, man with no name, man with a dark secret . . . And, of course, my specialty: Sensitive Poet.

"Beautiful day, isn't it?" I asked.

"Yes," said Astrid. Click click click.

"A beautiful *autumn* day," I said. "Have you ever—"

"Alan?" she interrupted. "Can I move you over here?" She motioned to the wall that faced the street.

I stood, hands in my pockets, trying my best to project unsmiling artistic anguish.

"*Gut, gut*," she said.

I took a deep breath. "An Autumn Day," I sighed.

Herr: es ist Zeit.
Der Sommer war sehr gross.
Leg deinen Schatten auf die Sonnenuhren,
und auf den Fluren lass die Winde los.

Still clicking away, Astrid grinned. "What is this?" she

asked. "A poem?"

"Yes," I said. "By Rainer Rilke, you know him?"

"Oh yes," she said. "I love Rilke."

Of course she loves him. We were made for each other. Stuart had probably never heard of Rilke.

I continued my performance, and I could tell it was working. She took more photos than ever—the slow click of her lens now shooting rapid-fire. I wasn't just saying the words—I was inhabiting them. Feeling them. Living them.

And Astrid felt it, too, I could tell. Her movement became more fluid, and I could see the beautiful words wash over her, bringing her pleasure, like a warm summer breeze. She was moved—not only by the melancholy words of the great poet, but also by the commanding presence of a young man deeply and helplessly in love.

Befiehl den letzten Fruchten voll zu sein;
gieb ihnen noch zwei sudlichere Tage.
Wer jetzt kein Haus hat, baut sich keines—

"*Hallo,* Astrid."

I stopped.

It was one of the English boys. The little twerpy one who rarely spoke.

"*Hallo,* George!" said Astrid, and hugged him. Her hugs are highly affectionate, it would seem, to just about everyone.

"Who's the monkey?" He nodded toward me.

"Your neighbor Alan," said Astrid, a little scolding. "He came with us to the Funfair. Remember?"

"Hello, neighbor," said George.

"Hello," I said, and shot him a nasty look, as if to say, *keep walking.*

"Have you seen the photos?" Astrid asked.

"No," he said. "John tells me they're fantastic."

"Well, John likes any photo of himself, doesn't he?"

"Yes, he's the man of his dreams."

Astrid laughed, like that's the funniest thing she's ever heard.

"Ahem," I cleared my throat and shot the weaselly little George another dirty look. He was starting to feel like something stuck to the bottom of my shoe.

"Sorry to interrupt," he said. "Do you mind if I sit and watch?"

Oh for heaven's sake, no.

"Of course," said Astrid. "Sit, here."

George sat on the top step, the one I'd just vacated. Astrid watched him settle in, wrinkled her brow a little, and then started taking pictures—*of him*! It was just too horrible. Not thirty seconds before, I was holding this woman enthralled, writhing in poetic bliss, helpless in my grasp—and now look at her. Fawning over this greasy little delinquent.

"Shall I leave the two of you alone?" I asked.

"No, no, of course not," said Astrid. "I am sorry. George has had his session already."

George shot me a knowing smile. The little bastard.

Astrid got back to shooting me, but the moment had passed. I didn't dare break out the Rilke again; it would be pointless. I tried to regain some of my haughty, artistic grandeur, but somehow, with an audience watching, it felt a little silly.

Astrid suggested I put on the beret. I did, and immediately felt even sillier.

George leaned over to her and whispered. "He has a raw sensuality, hasn't he?"

"Shush!" Astrid kicked him in the shin.

"A moody magnificence."

Now she was giggling.

I felt myself beginning to sweat. It was like being onstage when you forget your line, and then your pants drop to the floor. I took a deep breath and tried to compose myself. As an actor, when these things happen, you don't run offstage and go home—you simply ignore the distraction, concentrate, and move on.

I did some sense-memory exercises to bring me back into the moment. I thought of my dead grandfather. I thought of my friend Ronnie from junior high who tried to outrun a Metro North train, only to get hit by it and dragged to his death. I thought of my childhood cat, run over by the neighbor's car. *Death death death,* I thought, and tried to make that come out of my eyes.

George kept making wisecracks under his breath. At one point I made out the words "Captain America." Astrid kept shushing him and stifling her own giggles. This was beginning to feel like torture.

"Alan?" she said, lowering her camera. "Do you smoke?"

I looked her in the eye, mean and moody. "Sometimes," I said.

"Let me try some with you smoking. Do you have a cigarette?"

I didn't. The truth is, tobacco makes me dizzy and nauseated, so while I'd considered it, I thought it was too risky.

"I've got a ciggy," said George. "Here you go."

He handed me the cigarette and lit it for me. I blew the smoke ever-so-slightly in his face and he retreated. I took a small puff, careful not to inhale too much. I used it more as a prop, holding it like Humphrey Bogart, gesturing with it like

Dean Martin. It turned out to be very useful. I relaxed a little, and I was starting to move again. I leaned against the wall and kicked one foot up, my shoe against the wall, the way I'd seen James Dean do it in a movie. And I could tell Astrid was back into it as well. The clicks of her shutter came more frequently, and she weaved around me, getting different angles.

"Please," she said, "do the poem again."

I looked at the English boy and I thought, *Okay. You want poetry, I'll give you poetry. Let's see if you can handle it.*

"Autumn Day," I said, with a cold, direct simplicity. "*Herbsttag.*"

Dramatically, I lifted the cigarette to my lips and took a big drag, which I sucked down into my chest.

And that's when the bomb went off in my lungs.

Evidently, German tobacco is quite a bit stronger than American, and it felt like a fireball in my thorax. I coughed like a drowning man, straining to expel the poison from my body: a wracking, knee-shaking rasp from the depths of my soul. I hacked, I wheezed, my eyes watered, my nose ran like a fountain—and the worst sound of all was the click of Astrid's camera. She was getting this on film.

George finally fetched a glass of water from upstairs, and within ten minutes I was able to breathe freely again. They were no longer making fun of me—I think they were genuinely scared I was about to die. We all agreed the shoot was over; there was no use delving any deeper into my swollen, snot-stained face. I looked like the loser of a particularly one-sided heavyweight fight.

Astrid tried her best to cheer me up, saying she had gotten some great shots. I tried to believe her. I can't imagine anyone looking more pathetic or less manly than I did.

But maybe she's right. If the photos turn out great—and

there was no reason to think they wouldn't—she'd forget about all this and remember only the photos. No one remembers the process. They only remember the art.

George excused himself. "Are you coming tonight, luv?" he asked Astrid.

"Not tonight," she said. "It's my mum's birthday. But tomorrow."

George shook my hand. "You should come, too, Alan. You can sit and make fun of us. We're very silly."

And off he went.

Astrid had to rush to get home. I was sad to see the session end so poorly and so soon, but she planted a kiss on my cheek and made me promise not to smoke any more cigarettes. "We are making good photos together," she said, and drove away.

October 2

I've been thinking a lot lately about sex.

Not necessarily sex involving myself and another person (though I've been thinking of that, too) or even sex involving just me (there's been some of that, as well), but sex in general, sex as a concept. I've been taking long walks by myself around Hamburg, exploring the different neighborhoods, taking in the *gestalt* and feeling the *zeitgeist*. I'm beginning to think that sex is really what Hamburg is all about.

The city was bombed extensively during the war, and much of that rubble still remains. You can't walk more than three or four blocks without coming upon a building in partial ruin, or a heap of bricks, blown apart by some explosion and never carted away. But even the other parts of the city, the ones not damaged physically by the war, feel like they've been broken spiritually and emotionally. There's a gloom that hangs in the air, smelling faintly of death. I was struck by this almost immediately when I got here, and that's when I decided to write my poem cycle about death and deformity.

But then my walks take me to the Reeperbahn, and closer to home in St. Pauli, and what you see there is not death and destruction, but the loud, primal wail of SEX. The strip clubs, the prostitutes, the whorehouses, the free flow of alcohol and cheap hotels that rent rooms by the hour. Here in Hamburg, there is a blossoming of sex, well beyond anything I've ever seen in the United States. (In New York, Times Square has a small number of strip clubs, and Las Vegas, I've heard, has even more, but those are mere whispers compared to the full-throated howl one hears in Hamburg.) It's loud, it's vulgar, it's neon-lit—and sometimes I'm completely disgusted by it: the half-naked women who sell their bodies, the drunken sailors and roustabouts who spend every *pfennig* of their hard-earned money on the momentary pleasure of a grunt, a spasm.

Is it not the life force, bursting through? Isn't this the tiny seedling that appears suddenly atop the mound of ashes and dirt, signifying the return of spring, despite man's best efforts to destroy it?

My own experience with sex has been limited, I admit. I think of it as low in frequency, but high in athleticism and spiritual discovery. (Yes, Suzy has been my one and only.) In America, we're talking about sex more than we used to. You see it in novels and movies. But in Hamburg, people are actually *doing* it—more than anyone, maybe, *ever*. It's not inaccurate to say that the people of this city are *completely obsessed with sex*. And maybe that's not a bad thing. I believe that, once this particular seed starts to sprout, it will continue to grow, and will do so exponentially. The life force will build and build, throughout Germany and throughout the world, and I believe that someday we will see a flowering of sex that all races, all religions, all people of the world will share, in an overflowing, cosmic embrace.

Jesus, I'm horny.

We are making good photos together.

What exactly did she mean? What was she trying to tell me? I think over and over again about the shoot and how it played out, but I keep coming back to that one line.

We are making good photos together.

A photo exists as a memory, certainly. So, we're making good memories together? Yes. The more things we do together, the more experiences we share, the more "photos" we add to the catalog of our memories. Or maybe we make a "good photo together" in the sense that our identities are becoming linked, that "me" and "you" are becoming "us," the way that my friends Kenny and April refused to take individual photos for the Columbia yearbook, but insisted on posing together, squeezed into a single frame, reduced (elevated?) to the identity of "Kenny and April"?

Or maybe "making a photo together" evokes something like procreation—a man and woman *creating* something together that represents a synthesis of their DNA, something that is born, is cherished, and eventually outlives them both.

We are making good photos together.

During my walk last night, I passed the Kaiserkeller, further down the Grosse Freiheit, and I heard music. I was a little shocked at how loud it was, even from the street. (I couldn't bear to venture inside.) Loud, blaring electric music, amplified to such a degree that it lost all semblance of melody and sounded like industrial noise. I couldn't imagine how anyone would want to sit there and listen to it. How could you talk? How could you even think? How could you not go deaf?

According to the poster on the door, there were two groups on the program. One was called Rory Storm and the Hurricanes, and the other was my next-door neighbors. *Strange*, I thought, because Paul told me they were playing at Bruno's other club, the Indra. Maybe they played both. That would certainly account for their late evenings.

Not that I particularly cared, but I discovered the terms of their employment the next day.

I was sitting by myself in the Café Moller, enjoying a beer and a rollmop (pickled herring wrapped around raw onion, which has quickly become a favorite of mine), when I saw Pete, the drummer, walk in.

He was bleary-eyed, barely awake. He had a cup of coffee

and a plate of strudel balanced precariously on a tray (even at 2 p.m., this was his breakfast) while he scanned the café for an empty seat. As it happened, the only one available was directly across from me. I could see him try to avoid it, but eventually he approached.

"Mind if I?" he mumbled.

"Please," I said, "be my guest."

He tore into his strudel, chewing audibly while he stared at the floor. Not the slightest attempt at a conversation. What a strange, antisocial man.

I couldn't bear the silence. "Pete, right?"

"Yeah." He went back to his strudel.

"I, uh, I think I heard you fellows last night. At the Kaiserkeller."

"Yeah?"

"Yeah. I mean, I was walking past. But I thought you played at the Indra."

"They closed it down," he said. "Some old biddy complained about the noise. They turned it back into a strip club."

"Ha!" I said. "Another strip club! Just what this city needs."

"Yeah." Pete took a long sip of coffee and stared at his shoes.

It was almost impossible to reconcile this dour, silent misfit with the never-ending noise-cloud that I've come to associate with him and his friends. Maybe there was more to Pete than I realized. Or maybe there was less.

"How do you like being in a band?" I ventured.

"It's all right," he said.

"You fellas get along?"

"Yeah, I suppose."

He stared into his coffee cup.

This wouldn't be easy.

After what seemed like a minute, he continued his thought. "Sometimes, though . . ."

I leaned forward, hoping to encourage him.

"Sometimes I get a bit sick of them all." He looked me straight in the eye, like he was making a confession. "They're loud, you know."

"Yes!" I said. "Extremely loud. Believe me, I've noticed."

"Sometimes I just . . ." his voice trailed off. I waited. Twenty seconds? Thirty seconds? At last he continued, "I just want to tell them to shut the fuck up."

I laughed. "Yeah, you and me both," I said.

He looked at me again. The eye contact was a little jarring.

"In fact," I said, "if you *could* get them to shut up—at night, I mean—I'd be awfully grateful. It's hard for me to sleep."

"Yeah," he said, and nodded his head sympathetically. "I get it." He took a last sip of his coffee and pushed his chair back. I put up a hand to stop him.

"By the way, you know your friend Stuart?"

He nodded.

"Do you think he and Astrid are . . . you know . . . in love?"

He stared down at the bottom of his coffee cup and squinted. Deep in thought? Conflicted? Hung over? At last he answered. "Yeah. I don't know."

I leaned forward in my chair, desperately wanting him to finish the sentence. "*Yeah* as in yes?" I said. "Or *you don't know*?"

Pete nodded, reassuringly. "Right," he said (not answering the question). And then added, "I'll keep me eyes open, mate."

I now have a dim-witted spy who reports directly to me.

October 6

per Luftpost

Dear Mom and Dad,

Sorry it's been a while since my last letter. I've been very busy with my classes and spending long hours in the school library, which has become a haven. As cool as it is to live upstairs from a movie theater, it's also a giant pain. It's like having fifty people come over to visit—*every single night*. Twice or three times a night, in fact—and all of them sharing my bathroom.

Technically, I suppose it's no worse than living in a dormitory, like John Jay Hall, where we all shared a bathroom and I saw some horrible things; but there's something unnerving about sharing a toilet with strangers, who have no ongoing interest in the place or any pride of ownership. It's a little disturbing what people can do in a bathroom that isn't their own, but I'll spare you the details.

So yes, I've been spending a lot of time at the school library (not a big, imposing one like Columbia, but small and vaguely industrial). The silence is absolutely wonderful. The other day I was sitting at one of the carrels, reading Shakespeare, and someone next to me was chewing gum. You know how annoying it is when someone is chewing gum, and you hear the squish of their saliva and the snappy, cracky sound of the gum in their mouth, and their jaw wrenching up and down? This *wasn't annoying at all*! It was blissful. There was something so quaint about it—a noise so small and insignificant, like rain tapping on a windowsill. I found myself tuning into it, listening to the rhythm and the variations, like a piece of avant-garde music. I've come to appreciate the tiny sounds of this world, because they're such a welcome change from the big, unruly sounds that dominate my life.

And by that, of course, I mean my next-door neighbors, the musicians. Their late-night tomfoolery continues to assault me and deprive me of my sleep. I try to be sympathetic. I understand that they haven't had all the advantages that I have. They are simple creatures, uneducated, perhaps the product of poverty, disadvantage (domestic violence?). But people have to understand that their actions have consequences—that when you shout at night and sing bawdy songs about someone called "Long Tall Sally," you are disturbing the lives of everyone around you.

I've spoken to my landlord about them on several occasions. He's sympathetic to my plight but, like every other businessman in the world, all he cares about is the money. I tried approaching the police about the noise, but that fell upon deaf ears as well. The club owners and the *polizei* are all in bed together here, all on each other's payrolls, all bowing down to the power of the almighty Deutschmark. (Good thing we beat them in the war so now they understand the difference between right and wrong.)

I don't mind. I'm keeping an eye on my beastly neighbors. It's only a matter of time before they slip up and piss someone off and get dragged off to jail, or worse. That will be very satisfying.

School is also a bit maddening, to tell you the truth. I had another run-in with my Shakespeare professor, Herr Wensinger. He's a talented poet—I read a few of his works in translation, and they're good, even if he's no Rilke. As a teacher, though, I find him a little arrogant. We've been reading *A Midsummer Night's Dream* and Wensinger assigned us a two-page paper, which I found a little ridiculous. What can you possibly say about Shakespeare's comic masterpiece in two pages? So I decided to write a poem. I called it "Puck Thyself." Maybe not the cleverest thing I've ever written, but it was well-crafted and heartfelt, and I thought it did a good job of evoking the playful spirit of Shakespeare's comedy. And perhaps it would make Herr Professor understand that I'm not just another student, but a poet, like he is.

Wensinger went ballistic. He gave me an "F" and scrawled *"SEHEN SIE MICH"* at the top. (I had to ask: "SEE ME.") When I went to his office hours, he was downright belligerent.

"Do you think this is some kind of a joke, Herr Levy?"

No, I told him, I didn't. I consider myself a poet, and I chose to respond to Shakespeare's poetry with a poem of my own. As a mark of respect.

"Ah. So you think you are just like Herr Shakespeare?"

No, I said, I'm not as *good* as Herr Shakespeare, but I have the right to express myself, the right to *try*.

"Herr Levy," he said, and took a long draw on his pipe (which smells, for some reason, like hard boiled eggs). "I don't care if you are a poet or not. As your teacher, I care that you respect me. When I tell you to write an essay, you will write an essay. Do you understand me?"

Yes, Herr Wensinger.

"Good. Maybe you will learn some manners while you are in my classroom. And some humility while you are in my country." He tossed my paper back down on his desk with a resounding thwack, like garbage on a bonfire.

I picked it up. Maybe he expected me to get angry, or burst into tears, but I didn't. I looked at him and I said, "I've read some of your poetry, sir."

That took him by surprise. "Yes?" he said.

I told him I thought it was very good.

He gave a condescending smile. "I am flattered," he said, though he clearly wasn't. His face is tense and reptilian, with small, pointy features and slicked-back hair.

I made a little joke. "Not as good as Herr Shakespeare, of course," I said. "But you should definitely keep at it."

I've been told that Germans don't have a great sense of humor. It's just not a part of their culture; maybe it's a sense of irony or perspective that's missing, I don't know. But in retrospect, I probably shouldn't have made a joke.

Wensinger shot me an icy look. "Good day, Herr Levy." he said. "And close the door, please."

I understand that artists can be difficult. They can be horrible human beings and still be great artists. Yes, Wagner was a raging anti-Semite. Hemingway is, by all accounts, a ratfink to his wives and children. But they are artists, and I'm willing to forgive their moral turpitude in exchange for the greatness of their work. I will just have to deal with Herr Wensinger's shortcomings, and he will have to deal with mine.

Yes, even I have a few.

Love,
Alan

October 8

Dammit, I still haven't heard from Astrid. It doesn't take a week and a half to develop photos. (Does it?) I fear they *are* developed, but the results are so unspeakably ugly that she can't even bear to acknowledge them. There's nothing more toxic than a bad photograph—it becomes the official history of the moment, no matter how distorted it may be. (Me coughing my lungs out, leaking from the nose.) I think this is why I'm more of a "word guy" than an "image guy."

I'll give her two more days to get in touch with me, and then I'm taking matters into my own hands.

October 10

Still nothing. I'll give her two more days.

October 12

I was ready to give her another two days, but I realize I must change my behavior. This is the new me: I can't be so passive. Fortune favors the bold.

Once again, I decided to forgo the telephone and force an in-person encounter. I showed up unannounced at Reinhart Wolf's photo studio, but Astrid wasn't there. Herr Wolf explained that she was on vacation for two weeks. This surprised me, as I didn't remember her mentioning anything about a vacation. I asked Herr Wolf if he knew where she had gone; he said he had no idea. I thanked him and left.

A vacation? It seemed so strange. People always talk about their vacations (that's why they go on vacations, so they can talk about them). We spent a whole afternoon together and the subject had never come up. Plus we were *making good photos together*—and even if that wasn't code for *falling in love*, it was at the very least a collaboration, a creative partnership, and I couldn't believe she would just leave town without telling me how our photos had come out.

Maybe it was a family issue, maybe some kind of emergency? I considered the possibilities as I walked home. It could be a million different things, I realized, and there was no possible way I could guess. I simply didn't know that much about Astrid (or she about me). As I continued to walk, however, I felt a change coming over me. I began to sense an opportunity. I could turn this negative into a positive.

I would write Astrid a letter.

Of course. And not just a letter, but the greatest letter I had ever written. A beautiful, poetic, heartfelt, lyrical, funny, wise, and insightful letter. A Rilke letter. I could give the letter to Herr Wolf who could pass it on to Astrid's family, and they could get it to her, wherever she was. It would be in her hands within a matter of days.

I walked past my apartment and continued on to the Planten un Blomen, the beautiful public park with an even more beautiful Japanese Garden. I was in the mood to walk. I began to compose the letter in my head. The October air was crisp with ideas.

First of all, I'd have to ask her about the photos. That was, after all, the *raison d'être* for the correspondence. I'd ask casually, then quickly move on to other subjects. I'd be funny but passionate: it wouldn't be a love letter per se—more like a rumination on love—though I'd make it very clear (in an artful way) how I felt about her. Probably two to three pages, written in longhand.

I would open myself up to her. I would let Astrid see me for the first time, not in the realm of photography, which was her world; but in the realm of words, which was mine.

I continued to walk, forming sentences in my head. These are my favorite times as a writer, when the poem is churning inside your gut, ready to burst forth into the world.

After more than an hour, I headed back home. I would make myself a pot of tea, flop on my bed, and write. I could feel the pen and paper in my hand already.

That's when I saw them. Outside my building, buying tickets for the Kino, for the early showing of *La Dolce Vita*.

It was Astrid and Stu.

I turned my back and pretended to look into a store window. I was stunned. I'd spent the past hour thinking in great detail what I wanted to say to this woman. I couldn't bear the thought of making small talk with her instead—or the nausea of seeing her arm in arm with Stuart. I thought I might actually get sick.

I started to walk away, but then I saw another opportunity. (Maybe this is the new me: the person able to recognize the potential for moving forward, in pursuit of one's goals.) So I lingered until Astrid and Stu went inside. And then I bought a ticket for myself.

I went to my room for about ten minutes, until I was sure that the film had started, then I crept into the darkened theater. I took a seat near the door and waited for my eyes to adjust, and . . . there they were. About five rows in front of me, a little to the left. I could swear I smelled her perfume.

I couldn't take my eyes off them—trying to read their relationship, their chemistry, their comfort with each other. My great fear was that they'd spend the whole movie making out (like Suzy and I did during *The Diary of Anne Frank*), but that didn't seem to be the case. They watched the screen with great interest. Every now and then, Astrid would whisper something in Stuart's ear; he would either smile or whisper something back. Maybe she was translating the German subtitles for him. Even if that's all it was, I could still imagine how wonderful her hot breath must feel in his ear.

They didn't appear to be holding hands, nor did he have his arm around her shoulder, in the classic movie-theater-grope maneuver. These were all good signs. Maybe they were here together purely as artists, admiring the art of the filmmaker. (What little I actually saw of the film, I thought was pretty good. Very moody, very stylish, very Italian.)

All I know is, if it was me sitting in a dark theater with Astrid, I would be making physical contact. It's just too good an opportunity—and even the old me wouldn't let one like that go by.

About an hour into the film, Astrid said something to

Stuart, laughed, and ran her fingers through his hair. Affectionate, yes; sexual, not necessarily.

When the movie finished, I darted out the back before they turned around. I went outside and across the street, pretending to shop in the same store window. If they didn't come out of the theater, it would mean they'd gone upstairs to Stuart's room, and that would be a disaster. Fortunately, they emerged a moment later. They seemed deep in conversation. They took off down the street, and I followed.

I lingered about a block behind them, as they walked down the Grosse Freiheit in the direction of the river. Perhaps that's where they were heading. But after following them for a couple of blocks, I started to feel a little . . . creepy? Intrusive? Vaguely pathetic?

I decided I couldn't spy on them anymore. No good could come from it. I'd be horribly disappointed or partially reassured, but in either case I'd feel like a weirdo, lurking in the shadows with his hand down his pants. Astrid deserves better than that, and so do I. I stopped and turned back home. I glanced one last time to see the couple disappearing into the distance, and that's when I noticed they were holding hands.

October 12

Dear Astrid,

I dreamed of you last night. It was a curious dream, and if there exists a meaning to it, I am unable to say. I was lying on a sandy beach, squinting up at the sun, and I saw a beautiful girl flying a kite. And the kite looked so free and alive as it danced in the wind. And I realized that the kite was me. And the girl was you.

I hope you are well. I came to see you at Herr Wolf's, and he told me you were on vacation. I hope you are somewhere wonderful, though for me personally, sometimes the very best vacations are the ones we spend at home.

Did you ever finish those photos we made together? I had the most wonderful time, creating them with you. I loved the way you took control of the project, reimagining everything—the light, the shadows, the emotion—exactly according to your design. You have the touch of a master (or is it mistress?), and I can't wait to see the results. And wasn't it funny when I tried to smoke the cigarette? I've been laughing about that for days.

But if the photos are not ready to be seen, don't rush them. Art should never be rushed. As Rilke said:

> *Let your judgments have their own quiet, undisturbed development, which must, like all progress, come from deep within, and cannot in any way be pressed or hurried. To allow every impression and every germ of a feeling to grow to completion wholly in yourself, in the darkness, in the unutterable, unconscious; inaccessible to your own understanding, and to await with deep*

humility and patience the hour of birth of a new clarity: that is alone what living as an artist means: in understanding as in creation.

Oh Astrid, my days are so full, my nights so empty! I am far from home, living in a place that is deliberately unfamiliar and lacking in the comforts of my past. I wonder sometimes why I was so eager to live like this. I think what I crave, what I've always craved, on some level, is solitude. Not loneliness, you understand, but solitude. The ability to live within oneself, to find peace in one's thoughts and feelings, and turn them, with time, into art. What a gift it is, what an opportunity! How lucky we are to welcome the silence, knowing what fruits it will ultimately bear!

And when we have created our art, how much freer we become to seek out companionship, and how much easier it becomes to receive it. A productive solitude is like a good night's sleep: it leaves us refreshed and energized to face the pleasures of daylight, with renewed vigor and appreciation. The person who thrives in silence is also the person who thrives in love. For art and love are but two sides of the same coin, and we pass our time on this earth circling from one to the other, between solitude and embrace.

Yes, dear Astrid, we are making good photos together. What else can we make?

Your humble servant,
Alan

October 14

I must have slept extremely well last night. I didn't hear anyone outside my room, or footsteps on the stairs. I didn't hear the envelope slide under the door.

But when I woke in the morning, there it was. A single manila envelope with my name on it. I checked the hallway—no one there, no noise coming from my neighbors' room.

Inside was a small note that read: "xxx, A."

And an 8-by-10 photo. Of me.

At first I didn't recognize myself. I suppose, in part, it was the size of it. I'm not accustomed to seeing myself quite so . . . *enlarged.* And in black and white. It's the kind of photo, frankly, I'd expect to see in a movie magazine, with a signature at the bottom along with a roundly insincere greeting.

But it was me. I was sitting in front of the Kino, on the stairs, in front of the film poster. Only a small section of the poster was visible: the rest of the frame belonged to me. It must have been early in our shoot, because there was no beret and (thankfully) no cigarette. Just me, looking deeply and attentively into the lens. Maybe it was during my recitation of the poem.

I'm still trying to be objective about it but honestly, frankly, sincerely . . . I look magnificent. I look like a movie star.

Not any star in particular, just an extraordinarily good-looking, confident, celebrated person. Part of the effect, to be sure, was the lighting, which was impeccable: dark and shadowy, to match the serious look on my face, but dappled with enough sunlight to give my brow and cheekbones depth and dimension. The background—a little textured brick, the edge of a film poster, a glimpse of stairs—merely served to throw focus onto my face.

Only a handful of times in my life have I seen a good photo of myself. My face tends to look fat, and I have a knack for blinking or flinching just when the shot is taken. There's a good photo of me in my high school yearbook (a candid one near my locker) and a couple of good ones from my family's vacation to the Grand Canyon, but that's pretty much the end of the list.

It wasn't that my hair looked good (though it did), or that I looked thin (which I did). It was my expression. It was a personality coming through, and not even one that I recognized as my own: it was someone thoughtful and sensitive and wise and generous. Someone who looked out at life with a bemused curiosity. Someone who challenged the world but also took in its beauty. I didn't know I was capable of such a look.

But Astrid did. She found a soul in me. One that I never knew I had.

How could she see into me so thoroughly? And this person in the photo, this person who looks vaguely like me, is it something she found, or something she created? She had managed, somehow, to invent *me*, but it was her version of me. She must think I'm absolutely beautiful. Or decided that I should be.

It was an act of great *intimacy*. She had seen me naked, and managed to convey that nakedness to the world. And how easily I had *made* myself naked, without even realizing it. That was her genius, too: she got me to drop all my barriers, all my walls and hiding mechanisms, and open myself up—in ways I never have before.

Nakedness.

The more I stared at the photo, the more I thought of Astrid. I wanted to see the person who could make me look like this, make me feel like this. I wanted to see into her soul and capture it, the way she had captured mine. I wanted to see her naked. I wanted us to be naked together.

I was getting sexually aroused. I couldn't help it. I was getting tremendously stimulated, physically, and . . . well, it was early in the morning, when I often get erections and think about sex.

I continued to stare at the photo, and reached one hand past my loosely strung waistband and down into my pajama bottoms. I was hard as a rock.

I was thinking of Astrid, saying her name over and over again, looking at the photo of me—and God I can't believe how good I look—and then I close my eyes and think of her: picturing her legs, her skin, her softness, her breasts, her ass—and I see her, and then I see me, and then I see her one last time and I climax, erupting like a volcano, all over the black-and-white image of my face.

October 15

As I read over my previous entry, I find it a little disturbing. It's a very odd thing, to masturbate to a picture of yourself. I hope I made it very clear that I was thinking of Astrid the entire time. She is a woman, after all.

Anyway. After cleaning myself up and blotting the photo dry, I began to think about the note she left along with the photo. "xxx, A." Yes, it was affectionate (x = kiss, evidently, even in German). But awfully brief. *Unusually* brief. No additional information, no invitation, no reaching out. Not even a "so, what do you think?" How could she deliver such a shimmering work of beauty without the slightest explanation?

Maybe she was embarrassed. She'd rendered me so beautifully and so nakedly—maybe that made her uncomfortable. Maybe her overwhelming attraction to me came as a surprise to her, and now she was pulling back a little, being coy and modest. Or perhaps a little frightened, even, by the magnitude of her feelings.

Or maybe not.

I tried to put Astrid out of my mind. I had German Lit at 11. I stuck the photo in my notebook. I couldn't bear to leave it at home. I wanted it near me.

I showed it to a couple of kids in my class, Dieter and Greta (a bunch of us went out for lunch afterward), and they had the same reaction.

"Das ist you?"

With a modest smile, I assured them it was. Greta studied the photo, and then stared at me, almost in disbelief. Like she'd never seen me before. Like a light had switched on in her mind: *What an attractive man. Why have I never noticed?* We chatted for the remainder of our lunch. Greta's a good-looking girl. Not quite Astrid's level on the sexy-genius scale, but she has a wholesome vitality that is quite attractive.

As I walked home from our lunch, I thought what a remarkable tool this photograph was. The control it seemed to exert over people's feelings. Here was a better, more attractive version of me, and I was free to use it at my will. It would certainly have to go on my first book of poetry. Maybe I should hand it out along with my poems, so my readers could judge the beauty of the words against the beauty of the person who had produced them. Such were the almost painful levels of narcissism I was feeling when—

"Alan?"

It was one of the English boys. Paul, the baby-faced one. He hugged me. (I don't know what it is with Paul and his hugs. I don't get a sexual vibe from them, but I don't know what they mean.) "Are we bein' better about the noise?" he asked, with apparent sincerity. "We're makin' the effort, you know."

"I suppose it's been a little better," I said. "But it's still kind of loud."

"Right, right." He scowled, disappointed. "Well, I'll have a talk with the lads. A man needs his sleep, doesn't he? 'Early to bed and early to rise, makes a man healthy, wealthy, and wise.' Do you know that one?"

"Yes," I told him. "Benjamin Franklin." I had to explain who Benjamin Franklin was.

"No kiddin'?" said Paul. "Me dad used to say that. I figured it was an old song. Fancy me dad quotin' Benjamin Franklin. You heading back to the Kino?"

We agreed to head back together.

Paul is quite a bit more chatty than Pete, and, as we walked, he kept up a lively conversation on a variety of topics—the weather, the architecture, German men, German girls (he found them very attractive, particularly the ones with the "*grosse booben*")—for ten blocks at least, and then finally he asked, "Are you seeing much of our Astrid?"

I felt, for whatever reason, that I could confide in him. "Well, no, frankly," I said. "I think maybe she's avoiding me."

"Why would she do that?"

"I don't know," I said. "Maybe she's confused. Maybe there's too much going on in her life." I reached into my notebook and handed Paul the photo. As if that would explain everything.

"Bloody hell," he said. "Did she do that?"

"Yes," I said.

"Bloody brilliant, that girl. Look at that. It's fantastic." He held the photo next to my face. "Who's the movie star you look like? You know the one I mean?"

"Sometimes, people tell me . . ." I shrugged, ". . . Gregory Peck."

"Yes!" he answered. "Gregory Peck! That's exactly right. Absolutely the spittin' image. Caw, what I wouldn't give to look like him."

"But honestly," I said, beating back my vanity. "How could someone take a picture like that, and then just disappear? How could you collaborate with someone and create something as good as that and not want to discuss it? "

"I don't know," said Paul, "but I'll tell you this." He looked down at the photo again, studying it carefully, considering what it all meant. "You are one handsome son of a bitch."

It made me laugh.

"The girls haven't got a chance with you, mate."

I have to admit, Paul has a certain charm.

"Well, listen," he said, "if you want to see Astrid, you

should come to one of our shows. She's there every night."

"Really?" I said. "Every night?"

"Nearly. I mean, we play the whole night long, but she usually drops by for an hour or two. She brings those artsy-fartsy friends of hers. Jurgen and thingy."

She was there *every night*. And presumably, they served alcohol. Why am I always the last to see the obvious, even when it's right in front of my eyes?

"And you know, Alan, you might just like us. Do you fancy music?"

I told him, somewhat grudgingly, that I liked jazz. When he pressed me about pop music, I could only admit that I like Paul Anka and Andy Williams.

"Okay," he said. "I wouldn't mention that to John. But yeah, I think Paul Anka's all right. "Diana" and that. Do you know he made his first record when he was fourteen? Fourteen years old and it went to number one! In England *and* in the States! And I think he wrote the bloody song, too."

Paul seems to know quite a bit about music.

"I hate hearing stories like that," I said.

"Right?" said Paul. "Makes you feel like a failure, doesn't it? Like what have I been doin' my whole life?"

I shrugged. "Still plenty of time for us late bloomers."

"Anyway," he said, "you should come see us. We do some pretty songs, too, you might like 'em. Now if you excuse me, I have to buy some ciggies—they're so bloody cheap here!"

I put up a hand to stop him. "Listen," I said. "Do you think there's anything going on between Astrid and your friend Stuart?"

Paul squinted into the distance. "Mmmmm," he said. "I'd say I've noticed a bit of it . . . you know . . . a bit of *soomthin'* goin' on."

"I see." I couldn't tell if he was being honest or just trying to spare my feelings.

"But I'll tell you something about Stu," he said. "Just between you and I."

I ignored the faulty grammar (something I have a hard time doing, but I wasn't about to interrupt).

Paul leaned into me. "Stu is a rotten musician. He's bloody awful. He's a pain in the arse. And . . ." He tapped on the photo in my hand. "He doesn't look like Gregory Peck, now does he?"

He gave me a wink and a thumbs-up, and trotted off.

I think I like Paul.

October 17
per Luftpost

Dear Artie,

I think I'm finally starting to get over Suzy. I feel silly that I've spent so much time—nearly six weeks!—moping about how she broke my heart, and feeling that I would never fall in love again. I remember you saying once that you never really get over a girl until you get involved with the next girl. Well, it's happening.

Her name is Astrid. She's German, and a photographer. Very beautiful, very sophisticated, very European. She and her circle of friends call themselves "exi's," as in "existentialists." So just imagine Jean-Paul Sartre, with the body of Brigitte Bardot, and an accent like Marlene Dietrich. I hope you'll get to meet her someday. I would so love to come back from Germany with Astrid by my side and parade her in front of all my Jewish relatives. ("My son! Dating a Nazi!")

And speaking of which, I had my first anti-Semitic experience last night!

I was having a beer with some of the kids from school, and they were asking me about America. What's it like there? How's the food? Do I know any Negroes? And this one stuck-up girl, Helga, says, real innocently, "I hear you have a lot of Jews in America." I was a little taken aback, but I smiled and said, "Well, you know *I'm* one, right?" The table went stone silent. You could hear a pin drop. "Oh?" she said. The painfully awkward moment didn't last long, someone made a joke, and it passed. But I felt like something had changed. I'm sure they'll be nothing but nice to me, but I almost wish they didn't know, and I wish I hadn't said anything. In this country, at this moment, I'd rather operate as an Undercover Jew.

Anyway, I've got to run to my cinema class. Another laff riot from Ingmar Bergman! My sides hurt already!

Your pal the Nazi sympathizer,
Alan

P.S. Did I mention that I'm living in the garret of a radical cinema house? *Tres bohème, n'est-ce pas?*

October 18

I've been in an odd mood the last few days. On Thursday, the day after I ran into baby-faced Paul, I took the day off school. I'm not really sure why. I convinced myself in the morning that I was sick, that a horrible cold or influenza was coming on, but within an hour or so I realized that wasn't true at all. Maybe I was tired, maybe I was depressed, maybe I just needed a day off. I stayed in bed for most of the day, reading Rilke, sleeping, reading a little *King Lear* but quickly getting tired of it and sleeping again. I looked at Astrid's photo of me, pleasured myself, and slept some more.

I didn't have any dreams while I slept, but I had quite a few while I lay awake. I dreamed that a knock would come on my door, and it would be Astrid, bringing me another photo from the shoot, one that looked even better than the first, and we'd sit and look at it together while she explained to me her creative process—and I'd have trouble paying attention because I'd be so hypnotized by her eyes and her perfect cheekbones. Then she'd look at me, the same way she looked at the photo, as if I was a work of art, created by her. Then she'd run her hand through my hair, to remind herself that I *wasn't* a work of art, but a three-dimensional, living, breathing, hot-blooded animal. And then we'd kiss. And then . . .

I had to put the photo away, so I'd stop.

As the day wore on, I came to realize that I was kidding myself. Astrid wasn't coming to my door, not today, anyway, and probably not tomorrow. If she'd wanted to see me here, she would have knocked when she dropped off the photo. It's possible that she just doesn't want to see me at all. And if I'm honest with myself, that's probably why I've spent most of the day in bed.

But I remember something my father once told me, probably the single best piece of advice I ever got from him. He said that when people fall out of touch, when they don't return your calls or your letters, it usually has nothing to do with you: it's because of something going on in *their* life, something you know nothing about. So don't take it personally.

This gave me some comfort, and kept my general funk from escalating into a full-blown depression.

By the time it got dark outside, I realized one thing very clearly: if I wanted this woman, I would have to go out and get her. And I would have to get her from a seedy bar in the red-light district of Hamburg, the last place in the world I would feel comfortable. (I've never enjoyed bars. I dislike the noise and I seem utterly incapable of ever getting the bartender's attention to order a drink.) But I would have to do it.

On Friday I went back to school. I flirted briefly with the idea of finding someone to go with me to the Kaiserkeller on Saturday night. (I figured that was the most likely night to find Astrid there.) But I had to be careful. I didn't want to bring another girl (that would be stupid), but I also didn't want to bring some good-looking guy whom Astrid might be attracted to. I needed someone ugly.

Fortunately, there's an ugly kid in my Shakespeare class named Dieter. He's barely over five feet tall with thick glasses and a strange speech impediment (which I suppose is really just a lisp with a German accent). I asked him if he had any interest in seeing a band play at the Kaiserkeller.

"Die Kaiserkeller?" he said, surprised. "You mean that place on the Grosse Freiheit?"

Yes, I said.

He shook his head gravely. "Oh, you do not want to go to

the Kaiserkeller. That is a very rough place. These are not good people."

"Well, you see, there's this girl—"

"Alan," he said. "People get their throats cut at the Kaiserkeller. People get smashed in the head with beer bottles! I think this is a very bad idea." He looked at me with an expression of deep concern and walked away, as if even talking to me was too dangerous.

PART TWO

October 20

I walked into the Kaiserkeller at exactly 9 p.m. on Saturday, and it was exactly ten seconds before the first beer bottle flew past my head. It was thrown by a drunken American sailor in the direction of a drunken British sailor, who ducked just in time. The bottle smashed against a brick wall decorated, appropriately enough, with pictures of ships and nautical paraphernalia (and now beer and broken glass, too). The sailors' dispute seemed to be over a young German lady who, if she was not a prostitute, might as well be wearing a Halloween costume labeled PROSTITUTE.

The sailors tore into each other with their bare fists and quickly scrummed themselves to the floor. At that point I heard a whistle, which I realized had been blown by one of the waiters, a thug in a waiter's jacket, and within seconds, three more thug-waiters appeared and proceeded to beat the shit out of *both* the sailors before picking them up and throwing them a measurable distance out the door through which I'd just come.

What a friendly place!

I navigated my way through a fog of tobacco smoke, vaguely in the direction of the bar. The room was packed, elbow to elbow, and Dieter was quite right about the clientele: a rogue's gallery of rough-and-tumble types, dressed in leather and cheap jewelry, all scarred faces and missing teeth. The presence of ladies did nothing to soften the mood. Most of them appeared to be sex professionals, yet I couldn't imagine any of them costing more than a sandwich and a cup of coffee. Nor did the presence of so many members of the armed forces do anything to make me feel safer. The servicemen (most, but not all, sailors) were just as mean and despicable as the German thugs; they merely operated on an accelerated timeline. They had *x* number of hours in which to get drunk, pick a fight, get laid, and get out of town, and woe to any man who stood in their way. (I made it a point to steer clear.)

The room—it was the basement of a brick slab on the corner of Schmuckstrasse—was annoyingly loud, even though there was no music playing when I walked in. At the far end of the room I could see a stage with a drum kit and some microphones. I assumed the musicians were on a break. I pushed my way toward the stage, hoping to God I would see a familiar face. Before long, I did.

"Astrid!" I shouted, thrilled to see her—or anyone who could help get me out of here alive.

She didn't hear me. I yelled again and waved my arm. She still didn't hear me. I saw that she was sitting next to Jurgen, whom I recognized from the photo shoot, and also with another young man I didn't recognize. They looked so completely out of place: three chiseled, artsy, beautiful faces in a sea of pock-marked degenerates.

I tried to push my way toward them, but it wasn't easy. I apparently got too much elbow into a sailor on my left. "Hey!" he said. "Are you American?"

"Yes!" I said, brightly.

"Well fuck you," he said. His breath smelled of burning tires. I kept inching forward. After what seemed like an eternity, I got to the table where Astrid and her group were sitting. "Astrid," I said.

Her face lit up when she saw me.

"Alan!" she shrieked. "Alan Alan Alan!" She jumped up and gave me a warm hug and a big excited kiss on the cheek. After all the time I'd spent thinking about her and longing for her touch, it almost didn't seem real. "We finally got you to come here!" she shouted over the noise. "Good for you! I am so excited!"

Jurgen gave me a smile and a hearty handshake as well, genuinely pleased to see me.

"Come, we get you a chair. Alan, this is Klaus, he is with us too."

"Please join us," said Klaus, pulling up a chair from another table. "You are from America, yes?"

"Yes!" I said. "New York City."

"Ah! New York City!"

I squeezed in between Klaus and Astrid. She grabbed hold of my arm and held on tight as they grilled me with questions. What was New York like? How tall are the buildings? Is it dangerous to walk around at night? I felt like a celebrity: all eyes on me while I held court, a beautiful girl hanging on my arm. It wasn't exactly the Algonquin, but it was close enough, and I couldn't help but grin.

"New York is the greatest city on the world," I declared, brash New Yorker that I am.

"Have you ever been to Paris?" asked Astrid.

I had to admit I hadn't.

"For me, Paris is the greatest city in the world. But then, I have never been to New York. So I guess we will never know." She sounded a little tipsy.

"Well then," I said. "I will have to show you New York, and you will have to show me Paris."

She held out her hand. "Deal," she said, and we shook on it.

Even a handshake with this girl is an international adventure.

"So Alan," said Klaus. "You like rock and roll?"

"Of course," I said. "I mean, it hasn't been the same since Elvis went into the army." (Thank you for that one, *New York Times.*)

"You are in for a treat," said Astrid. "The English boys are very good, you will see. Have you gotten to know them?" She made a little pout, expecting me to answer in the negative.

"Yes," I said. I had a lovely visit the other day with Paul."

"Oh! That makes me happy."

"Well, you asked me to, darling, and so I did." She didn't flinch when I said "darling." To me, it's a word one uses only with a girlfriend or a wife, so I threw it out there as a test signal, but it's possible she's not familiar with the term.

"Paul is very sweet," she said.

"Yes," I said, "a lovely young man."

"He's a bit of a show-off—"

"*Ja,* a bit of a show-off!" echoed Klaus.

"But a very nice boy."

Jurgen asked me what I wanted to drink. I said beer (it's the local currency) and handed him some money, but he insisted on paying. He and Klaus began the long and perilous journey to the bar, which left me alone for the moment with Astrid.

I leaned closer, so I wouldn't have to shout. "So," I said. "The photo."

Astrid giggled, with what appeared to be embarrassment. "Did you like it?"

"Sweetheart, I love it!" (She's got to at least know *that* word.)

"But it's so . . . stupid!" She let out a big laugh. (Still embarrassed, I'm sure.) "I'm sorry, I don't mean stupid, you are a very handsome man—"

"Well, it was your vision of me, your artistry—"

She laughed again, even harder. "You look so serious in it! So Hollywood! You know?"

"You mean my Hollywood Asshole look?" I said, striking the pose.

This only made her laugh harder. "Yes, that guy! Him! You do it a little too well, I think!" She was laughing helplessly.

It wasn't the reaction I'd expected. Was the whole thing a joke to her? No, no, I think it was a combination of her being embarrassed and her being tipsy. It was actually quite endearing and I couldn't help but laugh, too. I loved this silly side of her, and it felt good, it felt intimate, to laugh so hard with her.

She wiped her eyes. "Well," she said, her voice cracking. "I'm glad you liked it." Another burst of giggles. "Maybe I can try another one sometime."

"I'd like that very much," I said.

I wanted so much to lean over and kiss her right there, but at that moment I noticed a familiar face making its way onto the stage. It was Bruno. He scowled at the audience.

"Damen und herren," he said into the microphone. The crowd paid no attention. He scowled some more. *"Damen und herren. Von Liverpool . . . Die Beatles!"*

There was a smattering of applause. And out came the boys.

First in line was Stuart, wearing the sunglasses—even at night, even in a dimly lit basement. (How could Astrid not see through his pretensions?) Next came Pete, trudging businesslike to his drum kit, not smiling, not acknowledging the crowd, dynamic as always.

Then George, with a coy wave to the crowd, followed by Paul, all boyish smiles (and a wave to our table), and finally, John. They were in the exact same outfits they had worn in the photo shoot: leather jackets, jeans and t-shirts, all scruffy and unkempt. The crowd applauded each one of them individually, which surprised me. I had never imagined that people actually *liked* this group. Although Astrid certainly did.

Paul stepped up to his microphone. "*Guten abend*, everybody. Thanks for coomin' out. *Wie gehts? Ja? Wie gehts?*"

John approached his microphone. "Good evening, you fucking Nazis."

What did he just say?

"Can I get a *Sieg Heil*?" He marched a quick goose-step to the left, and then another back to the right.

A few people in the audience laughed, a few yelled back at the stage. I turned to Astrid, not quite understanding.

"They think that's funny?" I asked.

She smiled. "I guess they do."

"One two three FOUR!"

And suddenly, an explosion of music. I hesitate to call it music: it was so loud that at first I actually believed a bomb had gone off. The whole room shook. I could feel my body, even the internal organs, trembling with the vibration: like a physical assault with sound waves. I can't imagine why such volume was needed in such a small room. I began to fear for the structural integrity of the building.

They're really rocking in Boston,
Philadelphia, P.A. . . .
Deep in the heart of Texas
And round the Frisco Bay

I instinctively put my fingers in my ears, but when I saw how much Astrid was enjoying the noise, I took them out. Her eyes were glued to the stage. She bobbed her head to the beat, and positively beamed with pleasure. I couldn't help but notice that her eyes drifted frequently to Stuart, even though he was facing the other direction. Occasionally I caught him turning to face our table: he'd see Astrid, smile briefly, and then turn away.

Sensing those little moments between the two of them was disappointing, to be sure. I had hoped that their—what? Their attraction? Their relationship?—might have cooled by now, or perhaps ended completely. But I saw the way she looked at him, and clearly there was something still there. Why else would she be here? It certainly wasn't because of the music.

Or maybe it *was* because of the music. That's why Klaus and Jurgen were here; surely they didn't have a crush on the boys, too.

Or maybe they did. (I find the whole subject of sexuality a little bit confusing these days.)

I snuck my fingers back into my ears. Three electric guitars were creating most of the disturbance. I'd always thought the electric guitar to be a thin, twangy sound, but that was clearly not the intention. There was no subtlety or shading to their tone, just flat-out volume, each note louder than the next. Stuart played bass guitar, but I could see that *his* excessive volume was lagging just a bit behind the others'. He kept his back mostly to the audience.

Pete did a good job of keeping the beat, but even halfway through the first song, he looked bored.

And then there was John, the singer. An interesting voice, I suppose. A little pinched and nasal, but powerful: he maintained a volume that nearly matched the guitars, which is no mean feat, and I could imagine him going through box after box of throat lozenges. It sounded more like shouting than singing.

Sweet little sixteen
She's just got to have
About a half a million
Famed autographs
Her wallet's filled with Negroes
She gets them one by one . . .

(*What* did he just say?)

In addition to their thundering guitars, the boys made things even louder by stomping their feet in time to the music on the flimsy wooden stage. (They wore matching cowboy boots, presumably for just such a purpose.) That made the room shake even more, and contributed to the very palpable sense that the whole building was about to collapse and bury us beneath the rubble. Maybe this is why the Germans love this music—it makes them nostalgic for the days of Allied bombs raining down on their cities.

The crowd seemed to enjoy it. Quite a few of them were dancing, though many more merely continued with their conversations—I can't imagine *how*, but they did.

And no one enjoyed the music more than Klaus and Jurgen at my table. They were standing and clapping along, yelling at the stage every so often, either "Yeah!" or "*Ja!*" (same difference), and stomping on the floor, adding more noise and vibration to an already deafening environment.

Paul sang the next song, which I recognized as Ray Charles' "What'd I Say." George sang the song after that, some silly number about the Sheik of Araby, still at the same ridiculously high volume, still pounding the beat with the heel of his cowboy boot.

I was getting a headache. I attempted to converse with Astrid, but it was absolutely pointless while the music played. I didn't do much better during the break between songs: the boys onstage kept a running commentary going, a weird comedy routine consisting of "Sieg Heils" and insults, and pretending to be cripples and hunchbacks. (Were they making fun of Bruno? I couldn't tell by Bruno's reaction: he was busy patrolling the bar and breaking up fights.) It wasn't what I would call sidesplitting material, but it seemed to engage the audience, many of whom yelled back at the performers before being drowned out completely by another eruption of music.

Pretty much all I could get out of Astrid was an "Aren't they wonderful?" and "Pretty great, *ja*?" which I nodded along with, a giant fake smile on my face.

There was no way I could put up with another hour of this. My head was throbbing with pain. I tapped her on the shoulder.

"Do you want to go somewhere?" I shouted.

"What?" She shouted back.

"We could go somewhere quiet!"

She looked confused. "Aren't you having a good time?"

"Of course I am, I just . . ." I didn't have anything to finish the sentence with, and she turned her head back to the music. Suddenly I felt a little foolish, expecting her to leave with me, just like that. She was here with her friends, having a good time on a Saturday night. She loves the music and she loves her friends: I couldn't blame her for that. And as for Stuart . . . well, maybe this wasn't the time to make her choose between the two of us.

I tapped her shoulder again. "I'm sorry," I shouted. "I have a test in the morning! I have to go study!" I mimed reading a book.

I'm not sure if Astrid understood me or not—she looked puzzled—but I had to get out. I blew her a kiss (she blew one back), waved goodbye to Klaus and Jurgen, and sprinted up the stairs to the outside.

The cold air felt wonderful. I took deep breaths to flush out the nicotine that had gathered in my lungs. My ears rang for the full duration of my walk home, and for another half-hour after that. It was nearly an hour of not being able to hear anything, or anyone—an hour without a sense of hearing, deaf and helpless in the world.

Why would anyone subject themselves to that?

October 22

per Luftpost

Dear Mom and Dad,

I got your letter—and thanks for the box of peanut brittle, as well. I don't want to discourage you from sending such things my way (the candy here is terrible!), but unfortunately a piece managed to dislodge one of my fillings. I had to scramble to find a dentist here, which is an experience I wouldn't care to repeat. A German dentist is just as grim and sadistic as you would expect him to be, but this one, Herr Gottlieb, was somewhat philosophical about his cruelty. During the painful parts of the procedure, he would repeat, in a low voice, "We must suffer . . . we must suffer . . ."

School continues to be okay. I wish I could say I've made a lot of friends, or that I find the other students to be interesting and engaging, but I don't. They are a little cold, to tell you the truth, and not terribly sophisticated. They don't seem the least bit interested in art or literature, even though it's what they've chosen to study. I think a lot of them consider the arts to be an easy major, and they're just coasting through without much serious, critical thought. All the guys ever talk about is sports and girls, and all the girls ever talk about is boys and shopping.

We go out for lunch occasionally, or a beer in the afternoon, but I always find myself feeling like such an outsider. Jokes go past me and aren't explained, little knowing glances shot back and forth. Perhaps I was naïve to think that an American would be welcomed here; maybe there is some residual bad feeling from the war. Or maybe it's just the nature of German society: a German in our country, I think, would be made to feel far more welcome than this. Americans are warm and inclusive; it's who we are.

Honestly, the only people I've met here who interest me at all is the group of German artists, "the exis," who I met through Astrid (the photographer). I think they come from wealthy families, so they've seen a bit of the world—they're all madly in love with Paris and dying to see New York. I'd love it if I could take Astrid there some day. Mom, how do you think your son's German girlfriend would go over at the B'nai B'rith? Would they be shocked? Secretly impressed? Kick you out of the bridge league?

Anyway, sorry again that my letters home tend to be so whiny and complain-y. It's not that I'm so unhappy—just letting off some schteam.

Though it would make me feel better if you sent more money.

Love,
Alan

October 23

It appears that winter has come early. It's been chilly for the past few days, but last night it was positively frigid. According to the newspapers, it got to about minus six degrees. (When I first got here, I thought reporting the temperature in Celsius rather than Fahrenheit was charming and exotic. Now it's just annoying.)

My room is unheated. I get a little warmth from the movie theater below, but as soon as that's locked up for the night, the heat disappears and the temperature plunges. I slept last night wearing socks, a sweater, and a scarf, my thin blanket wrapped tightly around me, and it still wasn't enough. When I woke up, my breath billowed and my teeth were chattering like a wind-up toy. I quickly discovered why: the bottom half of my bed was soaking wet. My first thought was *how odd that it's not frozen solid,* but that last tiny bit of optimism quickly vanished when I saw what the problem was. A pipe on the ceiling had broken and was dripping cold, filthy water all over my bed things.

I don't know if you, future reader, have ever experienced the joy of waking up cold and wet. I have once before, on a canoe trip to Lake Namekagon when I was in summer camp. It rained all night long and our tent leaked and my sleeping bag, when I woke up, had the texture of cold, soggy bread. It was about as miserable as I ever remember being in my childhood, and if it toughened me up at all, it still wasn't worth it.

It would have been lovely to jump in a hot bath and soak for the better part of an hour, but oh, that's right, I don't have a bathtub in this festering stink-hole I call home. There's one single shower, which I share with the English boys, and it usually gives me about ninety seconds of hot water before it turns ice cold. This morning, for whatever reason, it gave me five seconds of lukewarm piss-water before turning into shards of ice, which sliced into me like a thousand knife blades. My body shivered uncontrollably. I wrapped myself in a towel and ran back to my room, where I struggled to put layers of clothing over my trembling and unresponsive limbs. After ten minutes doing jumping jacks, the shaking finally stopped. I ran to the Café Moller, where it took two giant pots of tea to get any feeling back in my extremities.

This is no way to live.

I bundled myself up and trudged the three blocks to the Kaiserkeller, still shivering, clapping my hands together and bouncing from toe to toe, willing my bloodstream into heat and action.

Bruno looked up from his desk. His slightly horrified face made me realize what a pathetic sight I must be: wild-eyed and messy-haired, like a man who had just emerged from a glacier.

"*I* . . . am freezing!" I announced, with a sense of drama that bordered on the operatic.

"*Ja,*" he said, looking puzzled. "Why?"

"I'll tell you why!" I bounced up and down, now animated with anger as well as frostbite. "Because that *room,* that *pit,* that *torture chamber* that I live in, is freezing!"

"It's been chilly—"

"One of *your* pipes is leaking water all over my bed!"

That seemed at last to register, although his concern probably had more to do with water damage than me freezing to death. After a short amount of grunting and fussing, he gathered up his toolbox, and we trudged off together to fix the leak. We walked in silence for a couple of blocks before he turned conversational.

"Tell me," he began. "How are you getting along with the English boys?"

"Still bothering me," I said. "Still keeping me awake at night."

"Do you know what those bastards did to me? They played at another club."

"Is that bad?"

"Is that bad? Do you know what a written contract is, Levy?" He was practically shouting.

Bruno explained that the boys' contract required them to play exclusively at the Kaiserkeller, but they had been secretly playing dates at the Top Ten Club, a rival establishment owned by some other miserable bastard. To Bruno, this was a betrayal, an attack on his livelihood, and "a filthy English knife in the back."

He shot me a serious look. "Maybe you are right, Levy. Maybe it is time to get rid of them."

I flashed back to our conversation about the rats in his basement. "Well," I offered, "it depends what you mean by *get rid of.*"

He gave me a knowing smile. "There are many ways to get rid of people," he said, and let this sink in. Then, matter-of-factly, "Isn't that what you want?"

I considered the question. If he was to "get rid of" the English boys, not only would my sleep improve, but Stuart would disappear, now, wouldn't he? That could be a very good thing, vis-à-vis the Astrid situation. But then I looked at Bruno. There was more than a little crazy in his eyes, even on an average day. I'd like to believe that he wasn't talking about murdering five young men, but how on earth could I be sure?

How could a Jew, in any good conscience, advise a German to "get rid of" a roomful of marginalized human beings?

"It's up to you," I said. "Do what you want."

Maybe it wasn't my most heroic moment ever. Perhaps I could have been a little more dissuasive about the whole homicide option. But if they did somehow go away, my life would be much improved. And maybe Astrid would be mine.

"Herr Bruno," I said. "What's the age limit for the Kaiserkeller? Children aren't allowed in, right?"

"You must be eighteen years old," he said. "The police make sure of it."

I took note.

When we got to my apartment, Bruno balanced himself on a chair and started banging away on the broken pipe. It must have echoed through the rest of the building. After a few moments there was a knock at the open door, and Pete stuck his head in.

"Oh," he said. "Hey."

Bruno looked down on him in full fury. "Well, well! One of my little traitors! One of my English rats!"

Pete either didn't understand or didn't care. He gestured to me instead: would I mind stepping outside? I did.

"So," he said. "I've got some information, you see, about Stuart and Astrid."

"Go on," I said. Just the mention of her name made my heart speed up.

He looked down at his shoes, and took another one of his endless pauses. "Well, you've got to understand, he's my bandmate, right? I mean, we're not tight, you see, I'm not his best mate or nothin', but still, I mean, it's something, right? He'd be plenty cheesed if he found out. I'm right up with me mates, and I wouldn't give something up like that unless . . ."

"Pete," I said. "Do you want me to pay you for the information?"

"Yeah?" he said, scrunching up his face. "Yeah?"

I sighed and reached into my wallet. The smallest bill I had was a five-mark note, which seemed to be plenty for Pete.

"Right," he said, and melodramatically looked both ways. "I think they like each other. Sometimes they meet up for a drink. At the Gretel and Alfons. I don't think they're actually *doing it,* yet, but you know . . ."

It hung there for a long moment.

"No," I finally said, "I don't know. What?"

"Well, a girl and a bloke go out for a drink, I mean, that's it, innit?"

"Well, I don't know if that's it," I said. "I've been out drinking with girls, and it doesn't always lead to sex."

"Really?" Pete was genuinely surprised. "So you have a *drink,* with a *girl,* just the two of you, and you don't end up doin' it?"

"Well, *usually* I do," I said, not at all convincingly.

Pete shrugged. "Well, to each his own, I suppose."

Suddenly I found myself hating Pete intensely. Pete, I realized—Pete, the dimwitted but good-looking drummer for a bad-boy rock and roll band—probably gets more sex in a week than I've had in my entire life. Duller than dishwater, and yet I just knew, I could just tell, he was absolutely swimming in sex. I could practically smell it on his clothes.

"All right, then," he said, and slapped the money into his pocket. "I've got ya covered." He gave me a conspiratorial wink, and walked off down the hallway, trailing a dull, musky scent.

October 24

Bruno fixed the pipe, but my blanket and sheets were still soaking wet, and naturally he refused to pay for new ones. He offered to loan me some of his own bed linens, but I declined. I have no doubt they would be stained and crusty and smell like food. (I can imagine Bruno sitting in bed at night, reading pornography while snacking on liverwurst and wiping his hands on the sheet.)

I have a little money saved up, and while it pains me to spend it on something so dull as bedding, there are some times when you just have to throw money at a problem. I paid a visit to Horten's, a big department store on Moenckeberg Strasse, and bought the cheapest sheets I could find. (Though I splurged a little on the blanket: being warm at night is an essential luxury, and worth every *pfennig*.)

As I walked back to my sad little apartment along the Grosse Freiheit, I found myself in front of the Gretel and Alfons. It looked warm and lively inside. And, according to my highly paid informant, it was the last known location of a certain Astrid Kirchherr. It was unlikely that she'd be inside—and if she was, she might be there with Stu—but maybe fate had brought me here for a reason. I went in, my two oversize shopping bags in tow.

The bar was full but not crowded. It was a Monday night and pretty mellow, by Hamburg standards. I quickly scanned the room and didn't see Astrid. But I did see a roaring fireplace at one end of the room and that was good enough. I was considering what very stiff drink I should order when I noticed, at a table near the bar, John, Paul, and George.

Ugh. I turned away from their table, but it was too late.

"Alan!" Paul waved from his chair. I pretended not to notice. "Alan!" he called again. I waved back. "Come join us!" he shouted.

Oh God. I was in no mood for their tomfoolery after the day I'd had, but Paul looked genuinely happy to see me, and his charm is hard to resist.

I felt a little foolish, lugging my giant department store bags—they brushed against people and clunked into chairs—but Paul extended his hand and slapped me warmly on the back. (No hug this time: perhaps he was playing it cool in front of his friends.)

"Hey guys," I said.

"Hello Alan," said George.

"Howdy," said John. It occurred to me that I'd never really spoken with John. Of all of them, he seemed the least friendly, and more than a little intimidating. He always looked like he was sizing you up, a tough guy looking for a fight. He was clearly the leader of this street gang, and he let everybody know it. He stared at me dead-cold and said, in his peculiar nasal drawl, "Whatcha got in the bag?"

It took me a moment to realize it was a question. "Sheets and blankets." I told them about the broken pipe and the soggy bed and how Bruno was too cheap to make the place fit for human habitation. They snorted in agreement.

"Bruno! Caw he's the worst!" said Paul.

"And quite the looker, isn't he?" said George. "He looks like he fell out of an Ugly Tree."

"And hit every branch on the way down," Paul added.

"And by the way," said John, "What do you reckon a fella like Bruno did during the war? Do you think he was one of the ones who did the killing, or one of the ones who looked the other way?"

"Oh I think he was a killer," said George.

"Yeah that's what I think, too," said John. "I think they brought him in for the juicy bits. I think his specialty was torture-then-murder." He turned to me. "What do you think, American?"

I cleared my throat. "Well, I don't think *every* person in Germany is necessarily a murderer. I think you have to give people the benefit of the doubt."

John looked at me quizzically. "You're a Jew, aren't you?"

"Yes," I said. I couldn't tell if he was trying to pick a fight or not. It's not the first time in my life someone has asked me that question, and I've learned that you can never be sure of what's coming next.

But John retreated, leaning back in his chair. "I'm just sayin', maybe you more than anyone would be curious about a thing like that."

I shrugged. "If there's evidence, yes. Otherwise it's just speculation."

John lifted an eyebrow and took a sip on his beer. Bemused, perhaps, and not in the mood to fight. Paul gave me a friendly tap on the shoulder. "You fancy a drink, Alan?" he said. "Come on, join us."

I supposed one drink wouldn't hurt, and I ordered a schnapps.

"So where's the rest of the band?" I asked, innocently. By "the rest of the band," of course, I meant Stuart, but I didn't want to arouse their suspicion.

Paul shrugged. "Pete's off doing his own thing, doing his Pete business. As for Stuart, well . . ." His voice trailed off.

"I'm afraid he's with your little friend," said George.

My stomach clenched. It made me angry to hear George say it. I could tell he took a certain pleasure in delivering the news.

"Do you still fancy her?" said John.

"I think she's wonderful."

John took another swig of beer. I could feel him judging me, that I wasn't worthy of a girl like Astrid, but I don't care what he thinks.

"Well, I wouldn't give up on her," said Paul. "If you're that keen on the girl, you should keep trying."

"Now why would you tell him that, Paul?" said John. "Why would you build up his tiny little hopes?"

"Well, you never know, do you? Things happen. People break up. She and Stu are pretty tight now, but who really knows the secrets of a young girl's heart?" (Paul has a tendency to sound like he's talking in song lyrics.)

There was a pause, and we all looked at John. "Stuart," he said at long last, "is a very *serious yoong chap*." (John has a habit of talking in funny voices, and said that last bit in a Scottish brogue.) "He's not all about the easy fuck. You know? He's deep. He throws himself into things. I've never seen him so stuck on someone as this. I think he's head over heels."

"Oh, don't listen to him," said Paul, nudging me in the ribs. "I think it's one of those things. You've found her, now go and get her."

My schnapps arrived. I drank it in one gulp and ordered another, which seemed to amuse my companions. It tasted so nice and hot, and it seemed to settle my head, now spinning with all manner of thoughts about Astrid. It was all so confusing.

"Tell us about America," said John.

I was happy to. They asked if I knew any cowboys (no) or Negroes (yes), and whether I owned any guns (no). They wanted to know what New York was like and if the girls put out and if everybody had a car. But mostly they wanted to know about American music. They peppered me with names I'd never heard of—rock and roll singers, I would imagine—and record labels I'd never heard of either. I told them I was more interested in jazz.

"Jazz?" snorted John. "You like bloody *jazz*?"

"Oh, now you've done it," said George. "You've set the boy off."

"Nobody *likes* jazz!" John went on. "Rich toffs like you *appreciate* jazz. With your turtleneck sweaters and your pipes and your snappy little fingers."

"You don't think Charlie Parker is a great musician?" I asked.

"Oh he's all right," sniffed John. "But the music, it doesn't speak to me, you know? It's not vital. It doesn't grab hold of you the way rock and roll does. Rock and roll is something you *feel*. It gets through to you. It's *real*. Rock and roll is the only fucking real thing in the world, as far as I'm concerned."

"I don't know about that," I sniffed right back.

"All right, then," said John. "What does it for you? What makes your throbber stand up?"

"Poetry," I said. "Art. Love. Those are pretty real to me."

I could see a flash in John's eye, the urge to attack me, but once again he let it go. He made a noncommittal "hmm" instead, and went back to his drink.

"The thing is," said Paul, "jazz is just so *old*. Me dad likes it. His generation. But it doesn't tell me what's happening *right now. This minute*. Music is constantly changing. Do you want to live in the present or in the past?"

"And I'll tell you something else," said John. "Your friend Astrid? She and her artsy friends? They all grew up on jazz, they thought it was oh so posh. Then they heard rock and roll, and that was it."

"If you want to make it with Astrid," said Paul, "it might be helpful if you liked the same music."

I must admit, the thought had occurred to me. The fact that she enjoyed this ear-splitting assault they called music, and could sit through one of their shows every night of the week, was bound to be an impediment at some point. I've known couples who broke up over music. If she and I shared an artistic sensibility—and I sincerely believe we do—how could we be so completely different in our musical taste?

"Oh, he's never going to like rock and roll," said John. "He walked out on us the other night, didn't he?"

"Yes," said Paul, mock offended. "That was a bit of cheek."

I explained that I hadn't walked out, I just had to study for a test, and I meant no offense. I don't think they took any. They were just joking. Before long, we were all joking—laughing about the pompous Germans, the hard-working Hamburg prostitutes, and, of course, our landlord, the "Hunchback Hitler." I'll say one thing about my neighbors: they do enjoy "taking the piss." I almost forgot about Astrid.

I stayed for one more schnapps, and got to feeling seriously schnozzled, which I enjoyed thoroughly (and will pay for tomorrow with a giant hangover). At 9, they left to go play their first set of the evening, and I left for a warm, dry bed.

October 25

per Luftpost

Dear Mom and Dad,

I'll have to make this brief, as I have a lot of studying to do for my midterms tomorrow. I seem to have caught a bit of a cold. I have a raging headache and a sore throat coming on, and no energy whatsoever. A pipe in my room burst and soaked my bed with water—on the coldest night of the year—and I had to buy all new sheets and blankets.

Any chance you've sent me that money I asked for in my last letter? I could probably use a little extra at this point, as well. I'm trying hard to keep to my budget, but things are expensive here. And wet.

If I can buy a couple more blankets, I think I have a pretty good chance of not catching pneumonia.

Love,
Alan

October 26

I took my only midterm exam today, in Shakespeare. Both my cinema class and German Lit class required term papers instead (two pages each! It's like being in grade school again), but leave it to Herr Wensinger to design a fill-in-the-blank quiz on the world's greatest poet. (Romeo falls in love with _____. Claudius kills Hamlet's father by pouring poison in his ______.) I honestly don't understand why he puts so little thought or energy into his classes. From what I understand, he's published only two thin collections of poems, and even though they were well received, that's hardly a huge career.

But again, I must try to understand. The man is an artist.

But so was Hitler.

I finished the exam in half the allotted time and tossed it, rather flamboyantly, onto Herr Professor's desk. He looked up at me with a scowl and his eyes followed me to the door. I think he's one of those teachers who's happy only when his classes cause pain and anxiety for the students.

I was hoping to go out for a drink with someone afterward to celebrate, maybe Greta and Dieter. But they seemed genuinely stumped by the test—suffering through it like the good little soldiers they are—and I waited for them to finish. But after twenty minutes I got bored and walked home instead. I haven't done very much writing lately, I thought, and I should really get back to my poem cycle.

As I trudged up the stairs, I heard footsteps coming down. It was Pete.

"Hey, Alan," he said. "I was just knockin' on your . . . you know . . ."

"My door."

"Right. So listen." He looked both ways down the hallway, and lowered his voice. "I've got some more, you know, *information* on you-know-who and you-know-who."

I sighed. "I'm a little short on cash right now."

Pete gave an it's-your-funeral kind of shrug. Shit. He probably knew absolutely nothing, and even if he did know something, he was too inarticulate to actually explain it. But could I really be sure?

I sighed again. "What if I buy you a coffee?"

Pete stared down at his feet, shod in the same cowboy boots they all wore onstage. "Strudel as well?"

"Fine," I said.

As we walked toward the café I asked, "So, what have you got?"

"Let's get the strudel first," said Pete.

After his first bite of the first pastry—I bought him two—he addressed me with the solemn look of a doctor delivering a cancer diagnosis. "I saw them kissing."

"What kind of kissing?" I felt a tightening under my collarbone.

"You know. Toongs and that."

"Mmm," I said. It made my flesh crawl to think of pasty little Stu sticking his tongue into Astrid's mouth.

"Both of them, really goin' at it. A right old snog." He demonstrated, on his hand.

I held up my hand to stop him. "Got it."

Pete went back to his strudel. There was a beat of silence.

"Do you think they've . . . ?" I let the question hang there.

Pete had a long chew, narrowed his eyes, and finally looked up. "Think they've what?"

"Had sex!"

"Oh. Hm. Don't know." He went back to chewing.

"Look, I really can't pay you for every piece of information..."

"No," he said. "Truthfully, I don't know. Sometimes the lads'll have a toss with somebody, with me right there in the room. I can't tell you how many times I've had to wait out one of their bloody fuck sessions, but not Stuart. I think he's too posh to do it with someone else in the room."

I watched him tear into the second strudel, a glassy look in his eye. It didn't sound right to me. "He's your bandmate, right? You live with the guy. Doesn't he talk about it?"

"Very strange duck, our Stuart," said Pete. "Doesn't say much about girls. First time I met the bloke, I thought he was queer."

"Do you think maybe he is?"

Pete gave me a wary, why-are-you-asking look.

"I just mean it would be good for me if he was," I said.

He looked even more distressed.

"Because then he wouldn't be interested in Astrid!" Jesus, it was like explaining to a child.

He seemed eager to drop the subject, but I thought I'd keep digging.

"I have friends in New York who are homosexuals," I said. Pete sneered in disgust. "They can be perfectly nice," I said. "And sometimes—"

"Look," said Pete, getting annoyed with the line of questioning. "Stu is John's mate, right? There's no way John is hanging out with a bloody poofter. And he wouldn't be sharing a room with a bloody poofter, that's for bloody sure."

"So Paul's not a 'bloody poofter' either, huh?"

"Good God, no," said Pete. "He and John do just fine with the girls. They get almost as much as me. Yeah they don't admit it, but sometimes it's like a thing with us, a competition, and guess who usually wins?"

"You?"

"Me." said Pete, and took an aggressive bite from his strudel.

Jesus, the whole band is a sex machine.

"I'll tell you one thing, though," said Pete. "Paul hates Stu. And Stu hates Paul. Caw, they go at each other like bloody cats and dogs."

"Why do they hate each other?"

"I don't know," said Pete. "See, Stu is John's mate, but Paul is John's mate, too. It's like they're jealous of each other."

"Well, that doesn't sound the least bit homosexual to me," I said.

"Hey! Just pipe down with that, all right?" Pete practically shouted. I had to smile. I'd never seen him looking fully awake, let alone excited or angry.

"Sorry," I said. "I didn't mean to imply."

Pete settled back. "It's just fuckin' unpleasant, is all," he said. "Either fightin' all the time or makin' jokes—and the jokes always turn nasty. I don't see this group staying together, to tell you the truth. " He frowned, and stared out the window. "I got a lot of mates back home, a lot of blokes I could be playing with. And I got me Mum. Don't know why I came here in the bloody first place."

It was an odd, endearing little moment. The bad-boy drummer, positively drowning in sex, homesick and missing his Mum.

"Pete," I said. He lifted his head like a hurt puppy. "I think you're the most talented guy in the whole band. Whatever happens with these guys, you'll do just fine."

Pete seemed genuinely touched. "Yeah," he said. "Right? They don't call me Best for nothin'."

October 28

I walked into town yesterday to buy myself a pair of earplugs. They were not easy to find, or to ask for. I went into a couple of different stores asking for *ohr steckers,* but no one seemed to understand. I stuck my fingertips in my ears to demonstrate, but this only got me strange looks. Finally, at a third store, an elderly woman got it, after I made the sound of loud music and fingers in my ears. "Ach!" she said. "*Ohrstöpsel!*" Of course, silly me. *Ohrstöpsel.*

I got to the Kaiserkeller at 11:15. I was hoping things would be winding down by that point, but it was a Friday, and there was no sign of anything, or anyone, winding down. From across the street I could already hear my next-door neighbors at work, and I braced myself for the onslaught. I inserted my *Ohrstöpsel,* and proceeded down the stairs and into the club.

The scene within was even more unruly than my last visit. All the same drunks, degenerates, louts, thieves, gangsters, and whores—but now with more energy to burn, and more alcohol in their bloodstream.

At the far end of the room, the boys were blasting away. I couldn't tell what song. (Did it really matter?) Even with my eardrums firmly blockaded, I could feel the volume shaking the walls, and my stomach, and the floor beneath my feet. The earplugs were definitely a good idea. The volume was overbearing, but at least it wasn't painful.

I spied Astrid at her usual table—in the same seat, even—and flanked, as before, by Klaus and Jurgen. I didn't wave this time, but got up right behind her and gently touched her neck. She turned and burst into another big smile. "Alan!" she appeared to say, and jumped up to hug me. (How can she be so affectionate with me if she's in love with someone else?)

Klaus and Jurgen gave a friendly wave but soon got back to bouncing to the music. Astrid shouted something in my ear, but I have no idea what she was saying. I nodded and replied, matter-of-factly, "Rock and roll."

That seemed to be the right answer. She patted me on the shoulder, comrade-like, and I squeezed into a seat right next to her. She shouted something else into my ear, which seemed to reference either the song, or something that was happening onstage, or maybe the sound system. It didn't matter. I was happy to be next to her, and feel the blast of her breath in my ear.

With the sound muffled, and my ears protected from the volume, it was actually quite relaxing to sit there and take in the show. Without the constant, overwhelming bombardment of sound, I found it possible to observe the whole squalid scene in far greater detail.

I noticed how many people in the room had red faces, for instance: some flushed from alcohol, some from the heat, and many more from the exertion of dancing. The only pale ones in the entire room were sitting at my table: Astrid and her friends somehow managed to remain as cool and dry as statues, even with the inferno raging around them.

It was also fascinating to see the expressions on so many of those red faces. While some were smiling and laughing, far more of them—especially those on the dance floor—had a fierce, animal-like intensity. Wide-eyed, hyperaware, and breathing heavily—athletes, perhaps? Then I realized: no, *people having sex*. The thumping, repetitive movements; the sweat, the grunting; the ecstasy. Of course this is what people do here on a Friday night. This is Hamburg. All roads lead to sex.

As my gaze drifted to the band onstage, I realized that they, too, were going through the motions of sexual intercourse. John stood with his legs apart, pulsing up and down with the beat of the music: he was humping the microphone, plain and simple. Paul stood to his right, stomping and humping as well, all the while shooting flirtatious smiles at the audience. I could only imagine that in bed, Paul would be the more charming of the two, while John would be the more forceful. (Yes, I find it a little disturbing that such thoughts would enter my mind at a time like this, but such is the all-consuming power of sex that permeates this place, like an invisible gas.)

Occasionally, Paul would sing a line of harmony, and he'd press his face right next to John's, singing into the same microphone, their lips nearly touching. On certain phrases, they'd both close their eyes and shake their heads in a little ecstatic scream.

I also noticed, for the first time, the strong smells that hung in the air of the windowless basement: a combination of sweat, alcohol, and hormones. If you had to construct the aroma of sex in closed laboratory conditions, you would probably start with sweat, alcohol, and hormones. It's a classic recipe, handed down from one generation to the next.

To be fair, there were nonsexual smells as well: a great deal of tobacco, for one thing, and a strong smell of beer, which made up the vast majority of beverages both consumed and vomited. I also detected the well-defined smell of urine, wafting in from the bathroom from time to time. (I hadn't yet ventured into the men's *toilette,* and I wasn't about to start. I didn't want to imagine the unspeakable crimes against hygiene that went on inside.)

But without question, the overriding smell of the place—and the look, and the sound—was sex. Sex defined the inside of the club every bit as much as it defined the neighborhood of the Grosse Freiheit, and the city of Hamburg. If Paris is the city of passionate love, then Hamburg is the city of meaningless sex. And here, within these walls, in the noise and filth and stink of the Kaiserkeller, beat its very heart.

Astrid tapped my shoulder and shouted something into my ear. She repeated it, with gestures, and I realized what she was saying:

Do you want to dance?

And just like that, I felt the room go silent.

Now before I describe what followed, let me take a moment to explain my policy on dancing. I rarely initiate it myself, as I'm not very good; and I rarely agree to it, because it tends to make me feel lumbering and inept. Some people just have a sense for it—graceful and uninhibited, they seem to float on the dance floor, and inhabit the music. Not so with me. My body, I've been told, moves like a printing press.

However, when I'm good and drunk, my body seems to move in a more fluid manner, and I rarely feel embarrassed. I don't know if I'm actually moving better, or if I just don't care. Whatever the reason, alcohol and dancing are a good combination for me.

The only other thing that will get me to brave the dance floor is a beautiful girl. Like the one who was now leading me by the hand, into the music.

Astrid. How many times had I dreamed of this moment? A dance: the very thing I had craved from her since that first day in her office.

We faced each other and started to move. Not touching at this point, not yet. The other couples nearby were divided pretty evenly between those who were touching and those who weren't. I always take my cues from those around me, and particularly from my partner. Astrid began by doing something that resembled the Twist (a dance I was familiar with). I tried my best to copy her movements, but she was far more graceful and inventive: her arms shot out from her sides in ways I'd never seen; her hips and knees found rhythms within rhythms; her feet glided weightlessly. She was a beautiful, graceful dancer. How could she be anything else? I couldn't help but smile at the sight of her. And she smiled back. I could have watched her all night.

The band was playing a medium-fast honky-tonk type number. (Paul was singing—I couldn't make out the words.) It was a strong, repetitive rhythm, not difficult to keep up with. And explosively loud, of course, even with the earplugs. After a little while, I found it was actually quite easy to dance to: I could simply time my awkward movements to the steady thumping of Pete's drums, and I could make it look like I knew what I was doing. And actually having a good time.

Astrid was now doing some crazy moves—spinning around, juking out her thumbs like a hitchhiker—and making me laugh. I tried some crazy moves in return, none of which looked particularly cool, but at least they were moderately funny, and made her laugh, too. We started to loosen up, and it felt good.

I'd always thought that we had a strong physical connection, and now it was lighting up the room. We read each other's moves and reacted. She made a wild move and I shot one right back. We were reading each other perfectly, and laughing like a pair of schoolchildren.

In between moves, we managed to have the following conversation, entirely without words:

—Do you have something in your ears?

—What? No.

—Yes, you do. I can see them.

—I had to; it's just too loud.

—Oh come on, take them out.

—I can't. I'll go deaf.

—Please?

She reached her hands toward my ears. I caught them in my hands. And we stood dancing for a few moments in this strange pose: her hands on either side of my head, my hands holding hers. This made us both laugh even harder. I didn't want to let go.

Finally I indicated defeat and pulled the *Ohrstöpsel* out of my ears.

The sound hit me like a tidal wave. I was three feet from the stage and my ears were suddenly naked, unprepared for the blitzkrieg.

It was painful for a second, but then . . . the pain receded. And what took its place was a pure, electric energy. It penetrated into my organs, like before—but now it was moving me, physically, like a high-voltage charge through my limbs. I was no longer fighting the music; instead, I was animated by it, like Frankenstein's monster. My hulking, tentative dance steps of only a few moments earlier were now jet-powered and jet-propelled. I was moving with force and conviction, but seemingly without effort. My body was overtaken by the music. "It lives! It lives!"

I took hold of Astrid's hand and led her into some whirling, spinning movements, jitterbug style. (I don't really know how to jitterbug, but I've seen enough movies to know vaguely how it works.) Astrid took the bait, and soon we were twirling, stepping together, stepping apart, moving from embrace, to arms extended, and back again. And it all worked! Somehow, our movements clicked, and our bodies flowed. It was thrilling: we looked like professional dancers, and I felt like one, too! There is something about this woman that makes me better at everything I do.

Astrid cackled and threw her head back, and for the first time since I'd met her, I saw her cool alabaster face turn red—with passion, with exertion, with sex. Was I the person responsible? Was I the one making her so happy and so impassioned? All signs pointed to yes.

We finished a flourish-y move with our faces almost touching, my hands on her waist—and just then the song ended. The crowd applauded and so did we, but our faces didn't budge. It would have been so easy to kiss her. The sexual tension was as loud as the music. But then I saw her cast a quick look up at the bandstand, and I knew she was looking at Stuart. I didn't need to see the expression on his face. I could feel his jealousy. And on Astrid's face I saw a flicker of guilt.

We stepped apart, still applauding, and made our way back to our seats. From the stage Paul said, "*Danke schoen,* everybody. We're takin' a short break. See you soon."

Astrid was breathing hard and glowing with perspiration. "Alan, that was fabulous," she said.

"You were fabulous," I answered, my ears ringing.

Klaus and Jurgen gave us a big round of applause and slapped us on the back. Astrid and I exchanged a look, suddenly shy with everyone watching us. And I knew what was coming. Within seconds, Stuart appeared by her side.

"Hello, everybody," he said. Klaus and Jurgen greeted him like a conquering hero and Astrid immediately threw her arms around him. "My rock and roll hero." (She pronounced it as "hewo.") They kissed. Probably a longer kiss than appropriate for the situation, but I could only assume it was for my benefit.

Stuart sat down with us and ordered a drink from a passing waiter. (The rest of us mortals have to walk to the bar.) "Everybody having a good time?" he asked.

"*Ja,* fantastic!" said Jurgen, and Klaus echoed the same.

Stuart turned to Astrid. "I saw somebody dancing."

"Yes," she said. "Did you like it?"

He smiled a cool smile, behind his sunglasses. Too hip to be jealous, and too well-mannered to be anything but gracious. "Dancing is good," he said. "Dancing is good."

I watched him chat quietly with Astrid, a private conversation not meant for the rest of the table. She jutted her chin up as she spoke to him, in that way women do when they're offering their mouths up to a man, that anytime he wanted to kiss her would be just fine. I tried not to stare at them, but I did. It seemed so odd, and so cruel, that only minutes ago I had her full attention, her full commitment, and now I had neither. I felt myself growing bitter again, watching another young couple fall in love.

Finally, Stuart turned to me. "So, Alan, have you decided you like our music after all?" he said, just friendly enough.

My mind raced with responses. All the things I could say, or should say, as I watched him get closer and closer to Astrid, now affixed at his side.

I couldn't manage any of them. Instead, I grinned stupidly and shrugged. "Rock and roll," I said. This got a big laugh from the table. I'm glad I could amuse them.

We continued our convivial chat, the five of us, talking of this and that. But for the remainder of the evening, Astrid and I never exchanged another look.

October 29
per Luftpost

Dear Artie,

What is wrong with women? I don't mean to say *all* women, I just . . . okay, maybe it *is* all women.

I always make the same mistake: I assume that girls see things and feel things the same way that I do, that maybe they live in the same world as I do. And I am proven wrong, again and again.

So this German girl, Astrid. I saw her tonight—and, like *every* time I see her, we had a great time. We danced for most of the night and she said I was fabulous. We always make each other laugh, we always enjoy each other's company. Don't women always say, *I want someone who can make me laugh*? Done!

Furthermore, there is a strong physical attraction between us. A *chemical attraction*. Something we both feel deep down, on a primal level. And it's not just the attraction of a man and a woman: it's the attraction of the *right* man and the *right* woman. I'm convinced that some couples simply aren't suited for mating. Remember when you got naked for the first time with Maria Gusto and you told me that she smelled like sour milk? That was your DNA announcing that you and she were not a good match, no matter how sexy her legs or enchanting her smile. Your chromosomes didn't match, and I'll bet if the two of you had a child together, he would be a slow learner.

Well, with Astrid and me, everything smells right, everything feels right. Our children would be magnificent.

And yet . . . there's another guy in the picture. Isn't there always another guy in the picture? Some women, apparently, are born with another guy in the picture.

He's one of the musicians from next door, and his band was playing tonight. And the band is *okay*, you know, they're a *bar band*—and this guy, Stu, can barely play his instrument.

And he sits down with a group of us during a break, and he's wearing his sunglasses (yes, indoors) and trying to look like James Dean, and everybody is treating him like he's James Dean. Like he's a star! And he plays in a stupid bar band at a shithole in Hamburg! And everybody's telling him how great he is, and he doesn't really say anything, he just sits there with his arm around Astrid, and drinks it all in. Why should he say anything? All he has to do is sit there in his Ray-Bans and everybody fawns over him like a newborn baby. Is he funny? No. But he wears sunglasses and plays in a band. It's so maddening. I didn't even stick around for the next set of music, as I didn't think I could stand to hear a note of it.

Anyway, sorry to drag you down with my tragic tales of romance. I'm starting to wish I hadn't broken up with Suzy. Do you see much of her these days? She stopped writing back to me, and I can't say I blame her.

Jesus, I'm an idiot sometimes.

Your Pal,
Alan (The Idiot)

October 30

After I finished the letter to Artie, I went to bed and slept fitfully. I kept thinking about me and Astrid dancing, and laughing, and falling in love—had it really happened? Yes it did—and where was she now? Probably in bed with a pale, spotty English boy, possibly on the other side of my bedroom wall.

I fantasized that Stuart and I were standing side by side in front of her, naked (or at least in our underwear), so she could compare us. Who had the nicer face (me), who had the nicer body (me), who had the better sense of humor (me)? She would then ask us a series of questions, whatever she wanted, about all the things that mattered to her, all the things that she felt were important in choosing a sexual partner, no matter how trivial. Stuart and I would take turns answering her questions, respectfully (at least *I* would be respectful), and by the end of it, she'd have all the information she needed to make a smart, informed choice.

Actually, that sounds like the Miss America pageant.

I got very little sleep, but I stayed in bed for a long time, squirming. At about 11 in the morning, I heard a noise from the hallway. Someone—or possibly two people—were leaving the boys' room and walking down the stairs. Was it Astrid? I was dying to know, but I didn't dare open the door and risk seeing them face to face. I waited until they were safely down the stairs, and then I dashed out of my room and up to the roof, which has a clear view to the street.

Shivering in my thin pajamas, I peered over the side. Only one person came out the front door, and it was Stuart. Thank God, I thought. If I'd seen them together just then, I swear I would have jumped.

I went back to my room and tried to warm up, tried to gather my thoughts and emotions. I felt sick to my stomach. Cold. Confused. I'd worked myself into a frenzy imagining they'd spent the night together, and now, apparently, they hadn't. Or had they? Did she love him? Or did she love me?

I had to talk to someone.

I threw on my coat and ventured into the hallway. I knocked on the door.

"Come in," came a voice.

Timidly, I pushed it open. John and Paul looked up. They were sitting on separate beds, facing each other, each holding a guitar. John was wearing a pair of glasses I'd never seen before. He took them off as soon as he saw me.

"Hello, Alan," said Paul. "What's up?"

"Am I interrupting?" I said.

"We're just working out a song," he said.

"I can come back."

"Everything okay?" Paul asked. John just scowled.

"I just . . . it's just, with Astrid, I don't know . . ." I stammered to find the words, not even sure what I wanted to ask. "Do you think . . . is she . . . ?" My words trailed off.

"Oh dear," said Paul. "Does somebody need a hug?"

I may have whimpered a tiny bit. "Yes."

Paul put his guitar down and gave me a big, manly hug.

"Oh, for fuck's sake," muttered John.

"You and Astrid had a nice time last night, didn't you?"

"Yes," I said, wiping my eye.

"We noticed," said Paul.

"Yeah, and Stu noticed," said John, not at all nicely. More like an accusation.

"Did he say something?"

"No."

"Then how—"

"Well how do you think he's going to feel?" said John. "You're trying to steal his girl."

I protested that I wasn't trying to steal anyone's girl, I'd simply met someone I really liked, someone who was sending me nothing but positive signals, and who I felt was maybe falling in love with me, too.

John didn't answer, but started noodling on his guitar instead. I didn't recognize the song, but I got the sense that, whatever the lyrics were, they were probably making fun of me.

"Look," said Paul, "if you had a nice time dancing with her, why don't you come out and dance with her again? There's nothing you can do about them, you can't control that, but you can keep showing her a good time, eh?"

I shook my head. "I don't want to put myself in that situation. If they're in love, fine. If she wants me to leave them alone, fine, but why does she keep showing me all this attention, and all this affection?"

John looked up wearily. "We're working on a song here," he said.

"Sorry," I said, and took a step toward the door. "What's the song?"

"It's called 'Memphis, Tennessee,'" said Paul. He handed me a handwritten lyric sheet. "You know it?" He plucked a little phrase on his guitar.

I shook my head.

"Chuck Berry? You know Chuck Berry, right?"

"No," I said.

"Are you kidding me?" said John. "You're from the States and you don't know Chuck Berry?"

"Oh wait," I said, "didn't he do one about Beethoven?"

"That's right," said Paul. "'Roll Over Beethoven.'" He played a faster guitar lick that I recognized.

"For your information," said John, "Chuck Berry writes the best lyrics of anybody in music."

"*Hurry-home-drops on her cheek,*" said Paul.

"The man's a fucking poet," said John.

"Oh really?" I said, with a certain amount of condescension.

Paul smiled. "Oh that's right. You fancy yourself a poet, don't you? John writes poems, don't you, John?"

I asked John what his poems were about.

"Just stupid bollocks," he said. "What are yours about?"

I told him I was working on a poem cycle about death and deformity.

John stared at me for just a moment, and then he pulled his face into a distorted grimace. He twisted his mouth around his tongue and grunted out some gibberish while he clenched his hands into deformed claws. He was doing his spastic act again. "Unug! Unuggg!" He strained to form the words. Paul laughed.

"Unnnuggg! Unnunnunnnuhhhh!" John fell to the ground, in a series of twitches and convulsions. Paul laughed even harder, which I suppose only encouraged him. John lay there with his body in spasm for a few moments. I wouldn't give him the satisfaction of a laugh.

"So," I said, turning back to Paul. "What's the song about?"

Paul pretended to kick John's crippled body. "Get a job, you bloody gimp!"

"I just meed my mants," croaked John.

Jesus, this could go on all night.

"It is," said Paul, "a tale of unrequited love."

I looked again at the lyric sheet, but couldn't read the

handwriting.

"It's about a fella who's on the phone, trying to track down the love of his life. They broke up because her family didn't approve. And then at the end, you find out the girl is only six years old."

"So he's a child molester?"

"No!" Paul thought about it for a moment. "Well, I don't know. John, do you think it's about a child molester?"

John said, "Unug anguh anguh anguh!" and rolled around on the floor.

October 31

I decided I should stay in Wednesday night. I had a paper due the next day for Wensinger's class: two pages on Hamlet (yawn—I could do it in my sleep). But I also wanted to get some work done on my poem. I've completed barely two pages of it, and I don't even know where it's going, other than a vague thematic direction. I've decided on the title, though. I'll call it, simply, "Hamburg." The portrait of a city at one particular moment in time, like *Dubliners*, or *Winesburg, Ohio.* I suppose Astrid will figure in it somehow, but I haven't figured out that part yet.

As expected, the paper for school took no time at all (Hamlet + his mother = Oedipus). But then I sat down with "Hamburg" and I hit a wall. Literally. Everything I've written so far involves rubble and bombed-out buildings and collapsed walls. What does it mean? What's the point? Sometimes I read the words I've written and I think I'm a complete idiot who has no business writing poems, or anything else for that matter.

> *Hamburg*
> *The sour smell of death*
> *Rising from the charred remains of the children*
> *Burns my eyes.*
> *The cold spinning blade*
> *Cuts through the body of the beast,*
> *Crushing and grinding*
> *Into sausage.*
> *O Hamburg, my Hamburg*
> *Ours is a Dance of Death*

A dark song of Despair
In a flowing, stinking cesspool of blood.

I think I can go even darker.

I'm not going to rush it, though. I'll go out tonight. I'll go to the Kaiserkeller. Because man does not live on death and deformity alone.

I'd been thinking about what Paul said. Yes, it might be completely hopeless to chase after a girl like Astrid. But I'd just had the most wonderful time with her—the best time I'd had with anyone in ages, and why should I walk away from that? You've found her, now go and get her.

She wasn't there. Not in her regular seat, near the stage; none of her buddies were there, either. I did a full walk-around of the bar and the dance floor. No Astrid. I briefly waited outside the ladies' room. No Astrid.

The boys were onstage. They didn't notice me at first, but at some point Stuart saw me. He probably thought I was there just to sniff around for his girlfriend (which, to be fair, was *exactly* what I was doing). He gave me a look. I couldn't tell exactly what kind of look because of the sunglasses, but it appeared to be a small, self-confident smile. Possibly triumphant and gloating, but not necessarily. Could also just be "welcome to the club." Inconclusive.

I had a quick drink at the bar and I was about to leave when I heard from the stage:

"We're doing a new song tonight." It was John. He was looking straight at me. "By the great poet Chuck Berry. Almost as good as Alan over there."

I raised my glass to him.

"Here's 'Memphis Tennessee.' One-two-three-four—"

Long distance information, give me Memphis, Tennessee

Help me find the party trying to get in touch with me . . .

It was interesting to hear the song, fully formed, after seeing them learn it just the night before. It wasn't a great performance, the crowd didn't go wild the way they sometimes do. (And I'm sorry, but Chuck Berry is not a poet. He might have a clever turn of phrase here and there, but a poet? Heavens no.)

What impressed me about the band is how professional they sounded. Competent. To learn a song that quickly and yet sound like they've been doing it for years. They may be apocalyptically loud and jarringly unsophisticated, but they are able musicians, I'll give them that much. They make the songs their own.

And, yes, "hurry-home-drops on her cheek" is a pretty good line.

I was taking a final sip of beer when a young woman tapped my shoulder.

"*Bitte,*" she said. "Are you with ze band?"

She was pretty. Actually, very pretty. She had long blond hair and liquid blue eyes. And she was standing with two of her friends, both of whom had equally blond hair and wore big, red-faced smiles. And all three seemed very interested in me.

"No," I said. "I mean, I'm just—I'm a friend."

"Oh!" said Blonde Number One. "You are from England?"

"No," I said. "America."

"Oh!" All three lit up. Maybe I was the first American they'd ever met. "We love ze Beatles."

"The Piedels!" said Blonde Number Two. They all giggled. "Do you know what this is, what means the word *piedels*?"

"No."

They giggled some more. "*Piedels* means . . ."

Blonde Number Three took over. "It means the penis of a young boy." All three of them erupted in giggles.

I'm trying to remember the last time a girl said the word "penis" to me in a bar.

They introduced themselves. Renate, Helga, and Gitta. And asked me if I wanted to dance.

Well I think you know my policy on dancing, so, with not one but three pretty young ladies doing the asking, I naturally said yes. And we danced. And danced and danced. And I'm not sure why. I think it was the tag-team effect of Renate, Helga, and Gitta: when one of them got tired, the next one took over, and in this way they kept me going for nearly an hour. I was able to use many of the same moves I'd used with Astrid, and I was surprised how relatively competent I now felt. I didn't feel an intimate connection with any of the blondes, like I had with Astrid. But I didn't care. It was fun. And I didn't care if all three of them kept their eyes fixed on the bandstand, where they swooned every time Paul gave a flirty smile and every time John said the word "fuck." As far as they were concerned, I *was* with the band, despite my denials.

And the more I danced, the more I got to thinking. If everybody in Hamburg was having sex, *why wasn't I?* Why had I pinned all my hopes on the one girl who had a steady boyfriend, when there were so many other *frauleins* available, here in the sex capital of Western Europe? *Frauleins* of every shape and size, every taste and smell, every position and fetish. So I continued to drink, and continued to dance.

I kept dancing even after the boys came offstage and the other band took over. Renate, Helga, and Gitta seemed not nearly so fond of this group (Rory Storm and his outfit), which meant they could now pay more attention to me. We got a little more physical, a little more flirty. Gitta in particular did a lot of dance moves with her hands around my waist, drawing our hips together for one teasing moment and then stepping apart. Hips together, hips back, to the beat of the music. God, I'm glad I didn't stay home tonight and write.

At one point I went to the bathroom and found myself pissing next to John.

"I see you've discovered Renate and Helga?"

"And Gitta," I said.

"Ah yes, Gitta." He thrust his hips further into the urinal.

"They're pretty, right?" I said.

"And they will fuck you, ya know."

"How do you know?"

"Just a hunch."

Hmm. The thought had certainly occurred to me. Coupling up with a stranger in a bar isn't my standard mode of conquest—I prefer going on dates and making my moves slowly, over the course of an evening—but it does have a certain ease and efficiency. Bars and casual sex go together for a reason.

John walked over to the sink and pulled a small tin out of his pocket. "You want one of these?" He spilled a couple of pills into his hand.

"What are they?"

"Prellies," he said. He popped them in his mouth and downed it with two cupped hands of water from the sink. "Preludin. Diet pills, right? But they keep you going all night. It's like speed."

"Are they dangerous?" I said.

"Dangerous? They're fucking brilliant."

"I don't know," I said, trying hard not to sound like a sissy.

"Suit yourself." He put the tube back in his pocket and

squinted at himself in the mirror, fluffing up his hair in an attempt, I would imagine, to look more like Elvis Presley. He tried several different looks, and squinted from different angles: I'm pretty sure he's functionally blind without his glasses.

"Okay," I said, "I'll try one." I'm not sure why I said that; it just came out. John looked surprised, but shook two pills into my hand. "They're good with beer," he said. "Keep the beer coming, it'll level you out."

I lowered my mouth to the sink and sucked them down.

"Good lad," said John.

It didn't take long for the drug to kick in. Roughly three songs in, I could feel myself dancing noticeably faster and harder. More like an athlete, dancing in double-time, and squeezing more moves into each routine. Even during the slow songs, I could feel myself moving entirely too much, in a way that was completely inappropriate to the music, to the extent that people were actually staring at me, but I didn't care. This felt good, this felt right.

At approximately ten songs in (the boys were back on the bandstand now, and dammit but their songs really are easier to dance to), I noticed that I was sweating rather profusely, and my shirt was almost completely soaked through, but I didn't care. I kept replenishing myself with beer, which tasted *amazing*, and seemed to do a good job of "leveling me out" as John had put it, as well as keeping me nicely hydrated so I didn't pass out.

Gitta's interest in me seemed to wane as we got into the second and third hour of dancing, but that was okay because Renate now seemed the most eager of the blondes and took an unswerving delight in keeping up with me on the dance floor. It's possible that she was on Prellies as well, but I think she was just drinking more than the others and happens to have a constitution that gets stronger and stronger with every drink until she finally passes out (which I hoped wouldn't happen for a while). At one point—or was it several?—she ran her hands through my hair and pretended to be grossed out by all the sweat dripping from my head, but I think she was turned on by it.

At about midnight, a fight broke out near me, and I found my reaction to it rather curious (by this time I'd gotten two more Prellies from John and had probably drunk into the double-digits in beer, as well as a good sampling of schnapps). It was two Germans fighting this time, the local riffraff I would imagine, battling over God knows what, flailing away with their fists and sometimes with chairs. I didn't get involved with the fight, but I didn't run away from it, either. I found it fascinating, and I actually tried to get closer to the mayhem, even while I never stopped dancing. I was mere inches away when one of them broke a bottle over the other's head (it didn't make a shattering sound like in the movies, but more of a dull thunk, like hitting someone in the head with a baseball bat), and even that didn't cause me to miss a beat.

The fight got broken up by one of the bouncers, a hulking brute named Horst. I only know his name now because, shortly after he beat the shit out of the brawlers and tossed them out the door, Paul summoned him to the stage to sing "Be-Bop-A-Lula" with the band, which I gather was some kind of reward for breaking up fights. I think I was the only person dancing to it—I was unstoppable at this point—but I joined the rest of the crowd chanting *"Horst! Horst! Horst! Horst!"* while the bouncer performed with all the flair of a dancing gorilla.

By about 3 in the morning, things were getting a little

blurry. I don't remember everything, but I do recall a few specific images:

I remember me throwing up in the bathroom.

I remember Renate passing out, not on the floor but at the table, her face pitched forward onto an ashtray (which, fortunately, had nothing burning in it at the time).

I remember hearing a "last call" from the bar and the boys playing their last song.

I remember Gitta going home with Paul.

I remember Helga going home with Pete.

I remember seeing Renate still passed out on the table and thinking I wasn't going to get laid tonight after all.

I remember getting into a conversation with an old and unattractive woman on the street who revealed herself to be a prostitute. She was missing several teeth but told me how handsome I was. She put her hand on my crotch and asked if I wanted to come play with her "squish mitten."

I remember me saying okay.

I remember her walking me down some horrible dirty street to her horrible dirty apartment while she coughed her lungs out from another filthy cigarette and wondering what the hell was I doing—and how the hell I was going to get out of having sex with a filthy prostitute—and I must have said something out loud to that point, possibly something rude, because she slapped me in the face and pushed me into a pile of garbage.

I remember feeling enormously relieved.

When I finally staggered home, I could hear the sound of drunken sex coming from next door. Gitta with Paul, Helga with Pete. Or maybe they switched. Or maybe they were all together. Perhaps there were other girls as well, and all of them were having sex in a small room at the same time, like a Roman orgy, or an X-rated Marx Brothers movie. I didn't particularly want to stay up and listen, but the Prellies were still doing their bidding, and sleep was impossible.

I put in my earplugs and worked on my poem for a while, and then switched over to my diary and started this entry which I thought would actually be a very short entry but I see it has gone on too long and I see now that the sun has come up and I seem to finally be tired so I am

November 1

Oh my God, what did I do last night? Oh dear God.

November 2

I spent all day yesterday in bed. Much of it sleeping, much of it trying to remember other times in my life when I felt this sick, this close to death. There was the time in fourth grade when a nasty head cold turned into pneumonia and my sister convinced me to write out my will on an Archie comic book. Or the time I ate a bag of rancid peanuts during a family trip to Miami Beach and proceeded to vomit in the swimming pool at the Fountainbleu Hotel (causing the shutdown of said pool for two days, and earning me the unbridled hatred of every guest there). Or my first week at Columbia when, inspired by Dylan Thomas, I visited the White Horse Tavern and drank five shots of whiskey, smoked a pack of cigarettes, and rode back to my dorm face-down in a taxi.

But all of that seems like kid stuff compared to how I felt yesterday. The combination of beer, schnapps, Preludin, and four hours of dancing is something my body was completely unprepared for. (How could *anyone* dance for four hours straight? Let alone someone who's terrible at dancing? I shudder to think about what I looked like.) Even turning over on the bed, from my left side to my right, was painful. My head throbbed, my muscles ached. I was dehydrated from the alcohol and exhausted from the speed.

It boggles the mind to think that my neighbors, the rock and roll bad boys, put themselves through punishment like this six nights a week. I've seen them drink beer like it's water, and people are constantly sending them rounds of whiskey or schnapps from the audience. I suppose you could argue that playing a guitar doesn't take as much energy as dancing does, but their marathon performances usually seem to end with sexual conquests, as well—so no, I really don't understand how they do it.

In reading through my diary entry from that night (thank goodness I wrote it all down or else I'd never remember), I'm nonetheless thankful for two things. First, I didn't actually consummate my relationship with the toothless prostitute. That would have been a difficult memory to live with. And second, I'm glad Astrid wasn't there to see me. She would never lose control like I did. She would never make a fool of herself. She's a better person than that. Clearly I am not. I am a weak, sad, out-of-control drunk who fancies himself a poet but really is no better than one of those hobos who sleep outside the Port Authority, filthy and peeing in a tin cup. I picked up the photo she took of me and stared at the handsome, confident man who stared back: young, optimistic, and in love. What a joke.

I am never going back to the Kaiserkeller, I can tell you that.

Or at least, if I do go back, I will not drink.

Then there's the other little matter of school. I slept through my Shakespeare class yesterday, which normally wouldn't be a big deal, except I was supposed to turn in my laughably easy paper on Hamlet, which, of course, I couldn't do. So today I had to make that right.

I walked the whole way to school. My headache was still raging, but the cold November air felt good in my lungs. By the time I got to Wensinger's office, my face was covered in cold sweat, and when I stepped into the heated building, I felt a sudden wave of nausea. Herr Professor was getting ready to leave but waved me in.

I apologized for missing class. I explained that I had been sick.

“Sick?” he said, with a barely raised eyebrow. “With what?”

I couldn’t lie. Not now, not in addition to everything else. “I stayed out late,” I said with a sad smile. “I overslept. I feel terrible.”

“I see.” His eyes, peering out from wire-rim glasses, couldn’t have been colder. “So you were not sick.”

“No, Herr Professor.” It felt good to be honest.

He slowly circled back to behind his desk and sat down. He looked up at me with a bemused expression. He didn’t ask me to sit down, of course, because that would have altered the power dynamic in the room, he leaning back in his chair while I shifted unsteadily on my feet, desperately wanting to lie down. “And what are you doing here?”

“I wanted to turn in the paper.” I held out the paper. He didn’t move. I stood there with my arm extended for what seemed like an eternity. Finally he gave the smallest of smiles.

“No,” he said.

I placed the paper on his desk.

“You will pick that up, please.” Now he sounded angry. But only for a moment, until I picked it up and slid it back into my notebook. His calm smile returned.

“Herr Levy.” He opened a small box on his desk and took out a cigarette. He lit it and took a deep draw, expelling the smoke straight over his head. The smell almost made me retch. “If you were going to give yourself a grade in my class, what would it be?”

I cleared my throat. “I think I’ve done A work for the most part,” I said, “and if you read this paper, I think you’d find—”

“No,” he said. “I will tell you why I will not read your paper. Because you and I had an agreement. You would turn it in on Thursday, and I would read it. But you have not kept up your end of the bargain. Why should I?" He blew another puff of smoke over his head.

"Can I make it up?" I asked.

He looked puzzled. "What does this mean, *make it up*?"

"Could I write another paper, or take a test?"

"Oh, I see! To make it up. To me. To do me a favor! To apologize!" He let out a high-pitched laugh, almost a giggle. "Yes, *this* is how it works in America. You get in trouble with the teacher, you don't do the work, you don't follow the rules, and then and you go in and say, 'Sorry, man, can I make it up to you?' And this gets you an A in America? This is what an A student looks like?"

I returned his stare. "A minus," I said, "on average."

"Yes, because you are *a poet*." He took another drag. "I'll tell you what I'm going to do with you, Herr Levy. I'm going to fail you. You may keep coming to class if you wish, but your grade will be an F."

"You can't fail me!" I said, as if quoting from a rule book that clearly doesn't exist.

"Why not?"

"For missing one class?"

"No," he said. "For your smugness. For your arrogance. For your condescending attitude toward me and my class. For your sheer and utter conviction that you alone are a genius and that no one—not even Shakespeare himself!—is worthy of your precious time."

I felt a lump in my throat, another wave of nausea, but I swallowed it. He wanted to break me. I wouldn't give him the satisfaction.

Wensinger stood up from his chair. "Let me give you some insight, Herr Levy. As you navigate your way through life. The world owes you nothing. You and all your people."

He stubbed out his cigarette. “Now go on, isn’t it time to go somewhere and get drunk?”

I turned and left.

November 3

The walk home from Wensinger's office was miserable. My head was still pounding, and the pool of acid in my stomach seemed to expand with every step. My body, starved for sleep, had been violently awakened by the clanging bell of Herr Professor's emotional abuse, and all I could do was keep marching toward the bed that I knew would take me away from all this.

Whenever I feel rejected, or humiliated, or beaten down (and I think Wensinger did a fine job on all three counts), I content myself with thoughts of revenge. Not physical revenge. More like, "Just you wait, I'm going to be so successful, so highly regarded and universally treasured, that (person who rejected me) will be *really sorry* for (specific rejection) and will regret it for the rest of their life."

I suppose that's why, when I got back to my room and got into bed, I wasn't able to sleep. Even with my eyes closed, all I could think about was how much I wanted to get on with my life and my career, and create the fabulous works of art that would negate my failures and silence my critics. I got out my manuscript for "Hamburg" (still only two pages long), grabbed a pen, and sat up in bed, ready to bring forth a little more genius into the world.

But none came. I couldn't write a single word. I could barely bring myself to read the handful of sentences I'd committed to paper already. It wasn't that I hated what I had written; I simply couldn't concentrate on something as small and specific as writing a poem. Not when my mind was reeling with so many bigger issues: my life, my career, my body of work, the meaning of my existence, Astrid. And what the hell

I was doing in Hamburg studying with a prick like Wensinger.

At some point, there came a knock on my door.

It was Pete. If anyone was capable of cheering me up, it was probably not Pete.

"Hey mate," he said. "You got a minute?"

At least it would get me out of my own head. "Sure," I said. I placed my manuscript back in my notebook, which felt like a relief.

Pete trudged over to the single chair in my room and sank into it. He rubbed his face, as if to wake himself up. "I was about to go out for a meal."

"Sorry, I already ate." I wasn't in the mood to buy him breakfast for some pointless observation about Astrid and Stu.

Pete nodded and looked down at his shoes. I was familiar with this look. He was not going to follow it up with any actual conversation, but would probably remain in that position for a good long time.

"What can I do for you?" I said.

He rubbed his face again, a little bit pained, and took another endless pause. "Look," he finally said. "I know they're me mates. I know they're me band. But sometimes I just . . ."

I would have to pull it out of him. "Just what?"

"I just fucking hate 'em!" he blurted, like a child who'd been keeping a secret, and followed it with a strange laugh that I'd never heard before.

"Well," I said. "Collaborating is hard—"

"They never shut up! You know that. You hear 'em. There's always somethin' going on. Talking, joking, let's do this, let's do that. It's twenty-four hours a day of fuck-all!"

I nodded.

"And it's their bloody attitude! I can't stand stuck-up

people! That bloody John thinks he's the cat's pajamas. And Paul. What a couple of ponces. And do they ever, once, listen to my ideas? About the band? No! I've got ideas, me. I got things to say!"

I reassured him that yes, he was the most talented member of the group.

"And the best-looking!" he added.

I nodded sympathetically. He continued to stare down at his shoes, looking more and more determined. At long last he said, "What would you think if I moved in with you?"

It took me a moment to understand the question. "You mean, here?"

Pete made a clumsy attempt to explain his reasoning, fumbling around with words and half sentences, some of which included "me independence," "birds," and "kippin' in the afternoon," but he didn't make a whole lot of sense.

Finally he offered me ten marks a week in rent, and reassured me that he "wasn't bloody queer."

I told him I'd have to think about it. It didn't seem like a terribly attractive offer (though the extra money wouldn't hurt). Maybe I just couldn't stand the idea of rejecting someone who was already feeling rejected, after I'd spent most of the day feeling rejected myself.

"Cheers, mate." He lumbered back to the door and left, not once looking at me.

I did a little work for my other classes in the afternoon. There was no point studying for Shakespeare, since it appears I'll be failing that. But I have two other classes, and if I wasn't ready to throw myself into poetry just yet, at least I could throw myself into *The Sorrows of Young Werther* for German Lit. I was just getting into it when there was another knock on the door.

This time it was Paul. "Hello Alan," he said. "Have you got a minute?"

Paul bounced into the room, absolutely the opposite of the dour, lethargic Pete. He had a look around and asked all sorts of questions about my clothes, my classes, and the books I was reading. It was small talk, obviously, but he's good at it, and makes you believe that he's actually listening and actually cares. It wasn't until he sat down in my chair—much like Pete had—that he revealed the true purpose of his visit.

"I understand Pete wants to move in with you."

Yes, I said.

"Did you tell him yes?"

"I told him I'd think about it. Why?"

"Well, here's the thing," he said. "I would absolutely love it if Pete moved in here with you."

I laughed. "I thought you guys all got along so well," I said.

"Oh we do. All of us, except for Pete. He's a bit of a drag, you know? He's always off doing his own thing, and the only time we ever see him is onstage, and then once again at night—and I'm the poor sod who has to share a room with him! John's in the room with George, I'm in the room with Pete, and of course Stu . . ." He stopped.

"Where does Stu sleep?" I asked, despite not wanting to know.

Paul looked glum.

"Just say it," I said.

"Most nights, over at Astrid's."

I felt my insides plunge.

Paul looked ready with the obligatory hug, but I changed the subject.

I explained that I really didn't *want* a roommate, that the room was cramped and depressing enough, and I didn't want to get in the middle of some internal band-squabble. "And he's just so dull," I said.

"No he's a good lad," said Paul. "I'm being tough on old Pete. He's a decent guy. He's a good drummer. He's just not as quick as the rest of us, you know? He's runs a little bit slower, that's all."

"Maybe you should get a different drummer," I said.

Paul smiled. "Maybe you should get a roommate."

I told him I'd have to think about it some more.

"You might just like havin' one," he said, standing up to look around the room. "Someone to shoot the breeze with. You ever get any girls up here?"

I shrugged, maybe a little too casually. "Well of course," I said.

"Caw!" said Paul, waving his finger at me. "Mr. Movie Star Looks, the *frauleins*, I know what goes on in here."

"Ah, the *frauleins* . . ." I sighed, like a world-weary Don Juan. "The eternal dance. *L'amour*."

"Mmm," said Paul, nodding in agreement. I could tell he was impressed with my casual use of French.

"*L'amour*," I continued, "*est la poesie des sens*. Love is the poetry of the senses."

"Ooh, I like that," said Paul. "Is that one of yours?"

"No," I said. "Balzac."

"Mm," he said. "I'm gonna use that."

"It always works," I said, with a wink.

We shared a knowing laugh. Paul gave me a slap on the shoulder, one oversexed stud to another, and he was out the door.

Who am I kidding? Two and a half months I've been here, and I still haven't gotten laid.

I did some more work in the afternoon, but I found myself

getting distracted. I started writing a letter to my parents, to try to explain why I'd be failing my Shakespeare class, but I just couldn't do it. I thought about how galling it was, how absurd! It was like getting an F from Shakespeare himself. I looked at the engraving of his face—the famous portrait from the First Folio—that appears on the cover of his Collected Works. He didn't look mad. Just disappointed.

There was another knock at the door.

It was John. He looked mad.

"I hear you're trying to break up me band," he said, right in my face.

"I'm trying to what?" All I'd done all day was sit in my room.

"You told Pete he could live here, didn't you?"

"No," I said. "I told him I'd think about it."

"Well you're not gonna," he said, jabbing a finger into my chest. "Got it?"

Now I was thoroughly confused. I asked him if he wanted to come in and talk about it.

"No, I'm not bloody coming in," he said. "I'm telling you to mind your fucking business when it comes to the band."

"But I thought you guys hated him."

He gave me a cold, hard stare. "The band *stays together*." He practically spit out the words. "If we want to hate each other, we hate each other. If we want to love each other, we will do that. But I'm not gonna have some toff like you stickin' his nose where it shouldn't be."

"Look," I protested, "I don't care—"

"That's right, you don't care." He was breathing hard. I stepped back, fearing he might hit me. But he took a breath instead, and when he spoke again, it was in a lower voice. "I don't have a family, you see? I wasn't one of the lucky ones. I don't have a mum, and I don't have a dad." He had a strange, intense smile on his face, and something like madness in his eyes. "What I've got is a band," he said, his lips stretched tight. "Don't. Fuck with it."

He turned quickly and walked out the door.

November 4

If you had told me that last night, Saturday night, would start with me going to the Kaiserkeller and end in Astrid's bedroom, that would have made me very happy. I would have said, *Yes, that is exactly what I've been hoping and praying for, thank you very much.*

But alas, life disappoints. Or at least it disappointed me, at this particular moment in my life, when fate brought me exactly where I wanted to be, but for all the wrong reasons. It's like one of those old jokes where the genie grants you your wish, but there's just *one little problem*...

I got to the club around 9. I was a little nervous about how I might be received, after all the business about me "trying to destroy the band." (Like I really give a shit about the power dynamics of five guys who sing together.)

When I walked in, Paul was at the piano, doing a song called *Tutti Frutti*. By now, I'd heard them enough that I was starting to recognize the songs, and starting, even, to have favorites of my own. I rather liked the ones that Paul sang from the piano: most of them (Jurgen told me) were written by the American singer Little Richard, whom I'd never heard of, though I knew some of his songs by way of Elvis Presley. When Paul sang them, he flat-out screamed them, like his hair was on fire. Unlike John, who also screamed his songs, Paul's screams were high-pitched, almost feminine, and even more distinctly Negro: like a fire-and-brimstone preacher shouting the word of the Lord. Except this music wasn't about God. It was, you guessed it, about sex.

Wop bop a loo bop a lop bom bom!

Got a girl named Sue, she knows just what to do
Got a gir-ir-irl named Sue, she knows just what to do . . .

When I got close to the stage, Paul gave me a wink and a thumbs-up. Maybe the housing crisis had passed. Or maybe he still thought he'd have the room to himself tonight.

John, without his glasses, didn't notice me at all, which was probably a good thing.

Astrid was at her usual table, flanked by Klaus and Jurgen, as well as a few other friends, all fashionably dressed, French-bohemian in style, pale-skinned and sensitive, smoking Gitanes as if their lives depended on it.

"Alan!" She waved both hands in the air and blew me a kiss. I blew one back.

But not a hug this time.

She introduced me around to the other friends at the table and insisted that I join them. The only vacant seat was three or four bodies away from Astrid, next to the new people, where I wouldn't have much of a chance to talk to her. But I understood this was how she wanted to play it (at least when Stu was around).

As before, it also gave me a chance to concentrate a little more on the show, since I wasn't hanging on her every word and gesture. (Though I did find myself sneaking an occasional look in her direction, and once or twice caught her doing the same.)

I'd worn my earplugs again tonight, but by the third song in, I decided I didn't need them. I casually pulled them from each ear and stuffed them into my pocket. And I ordered a beer. Just one.

The boys were in fine form, stomping their boots, jumping around the stage, doing splits and leg-kicks all the while hammering away on their guitars. (All except for Stuart, who always plays it cool: he'll laugh at the others' jokes, but doesn't join in.) John pulled a comb from his pocket and used it to mimic a Hitler mustache, never missing a chance to call out the Nazis in the audience:

"How many war criminals do we have here tonight, eh? Show of hands?"

The Saturday audience was more raucous than ever, and seemed determined to participate in the show as much as possible. A few of them drunkenly charged the stage looking for a fight, but were quickly repelled by Horst's lightning reflexes and sadistic punching skills. Others merely shouted insults at the stage, and occasionally song requests, which the boys were quite adept at fielding:

"What do you want to hear next?" said John.

A volley of suggestions shouted back. They seemed to know all the names of all the songs.

"What would *die frauleins* like to hear?" said Paul.

And now all the girls screamed.

"AND WHAT ABOUT THE NAZIS?" screamed John. "COME ON, NAZIS!"

At our table, Jurgen and Klaus shouted out their request in tandem: "Cha cha boom! Cha cha boom!" Astrid joined in their chant: "Cha cha boom! Cha cha boom!" Our whole table chanted along.

"All right, the Nazis win. One two three . . ."

Cha Cha Boom!
Besame, besame mucho
Each time I bring you a kiss
I hear music divine

A truly ridiculous Latin number, featuring Paul in full Casanova mode. All he needed was a cape and a rose between his teeth.

And the audience ate it up.

I sat through two more songs, quite enjoying myself, a little bit lost in the noise and the vibrations. One of the nice things about explosively loud music is that it wasn't really made for talking. For a few minutes—or hours—you really don't have to worry about what you're going to say. (I envy people who feel that way all the time, even around girls.)

I felt a tug at my hand. It was Astrid, pulling me up from my seat.

"Let's dance," she said.

She never lets me down.

We picked up where we'd left off that first night. Not quite as wild, not quite as flirty, but we were dancing again.

We danced steadily for the next hour or so, but only one or two songs at a time. There were no Prellies at work tonight, and I think Astrid didn't want to get too caught up with the dancing, or with me. Every time we stopped and went back to our seats, I saw her glance up at Stu, to make sure he wasn't getting resentful. Another new rule, I suppose.

I danced with one of Astrid's friends (Eva) and a couple of other girls in the bar (I didn't catch their names). I limited myself to two beers, even while I noticed how much everybody around me was drinking. Just for a lark, I started counting the number of drinks consumed by the boys onstage. It was staggering. They each had a stein of beer parked nearby, and whenever any of them got empty, Horst quickly topped it up. By midnight, I counted eleven for John alone. (Evidently, free beer represented a sizeable portion of the meager wages Bruno paid them.) In addition, I counted three different times when someone in the audience sent a tray of Schnapps or Champagne up to the stage, and the boys dutifully chugged them down, much to the delight of the red-faced Samaritan who sent it. They also smoked onstage, often for the full duration of a song, so I would guess that each Beatle consumed a full pack of cigarettes in the course of a night. And, of course, the Preludin.

I figured out, by the way, where the magic pills come from. There's a hulking old woman, Rosa, who sits outside the bathrooms and keeps them tidy; and while I was draining the first of my beers, I saw her slip a silver tube into George's hand. I suppose it's good business to keep the entertainment happy. And awake.

I also started to notice how much Astrid was drinking. I'd seen her drink before—Bacardi and Coke was her usual, and she almost never paid for it: there was always *someone* willing to buy Astrid a drink. But she was knocking them back at a faster pace tonight. I could see it in her dancing, as well. She was getting a little sloppy. And "sloppy" is the last word I would ever use to describe Astrid.

I got the sense that something was bothering her, and eventually I realized what it was.

A couple of cute German girls—not Renate, Gitta, or Helga, but two others very much of their ilk—had parked themselves on the dance floor directly in front of Stu. They were paying a great deal of attention to the mysterious bassist, and he was flirting right back. He chatted with them between songs, and they giggled and blushed at every little thing that came out of his mouth. All the times that I thought Astrid was glancing over at Stu, she was really looking at the threesome that was developing, with Stu in the center. Her expression grew darker, her eyes more blurred—and she drank more

Bacardi. Surely this wasn't the first time she'd seen him flirt with the fans, but for whatever reason, it was bugging her tonight.

We were just walking back to our seats—staggering, in her case—when we heard George play the slow guitar intro to the next song. We both immediately recognized it. Astrid grabbed my hand and pulled me back onto the dance floor.

"Ooh," she said, "let's dance to this one."

It was another Elvis tune; you might even call it his signature song. *Love Me Tender.*

It was also the only song in the entire act that Stuart sang.

Stuart's voice was nicer than expected. He wasn't a screamer like the other lads, but he had a nice sense of phrasing and could carry a tune. He sounded like a choirboy.

But here's the other thing. It's a *slow song.* Astrid and I had never danced a slow song together. Slow songs (as everybody who's gone to high school knows) are just makeout sessions minus the swapped spit. You didn't slow-dance with a girl unless . . . well, unless you had intentions. Which I surely had. But she didn't. Did she?

We faced each other, suddenly shy again, and wrapped our arms around each other. We started to sway. If she smelled of alcohol, I wasn't aware of it. I could only smell her. Like freshly washed linen, with a hint of peppermint.

Love me tender, love me sweet
Never let me go
You have made my life complete
And I love you so

It was a wonderful, magical moment, but it didn't feel right. After months of fantasy, I finally had Astrid in my arms—but it didn't feel like the real Astrid. She was drunk and wobbly on her feet. She seemed distracted, joyless, not connecting with the music (the first time I'd ever seen *that*) but lost in her own troubled thoughts.

And, of course, I had to wonder just how much of this dance was being done for Stu's benefit. Stu, who stood not ten feet away, pouring his heart into a love song, watching a girl who he may or may not be in love with, in the arms of another man.

Love me tender, love me, dear
Tell me you are mine
I'll be yours through all the years
Till the end of time

I could feel her sneak a look at him every now and then. I avoided his gaze, but I did notice that the rest of the band was watching us. Paul gave me a smile and a wink, while John only glowered. George and Pete watched with blank expressions, but looked over to John from time to time to gauge how he was reacting.

Astrid leaned her head on my shoulder. Maybe out of exhaustion, maybe out of . . . what? Love? Surrender? As she pressed her body against me, I wished so desperately that I could make everyone else in the room disappear. All the drunks, all the thugs, all the musicians. If I could just close my eyes and they'd all be gone. Everyone and everything, except for me and this beautiful woman.

At long last, the song ended and we walked back to our seats. She was draped over my shoulder, still in a dance-embrace, but also using me for balance. I carefully placed her in a chair.

"Are you all right?" I said.

"No." She swung her head down and then up again. "Darling, will you take me home?"

I had to ask her to repeat the question. Because I had not the slightest idea how I should answer it.

"You can drive, can't you?" she said. She looked like a frightened child.

What else could I do?

Jurgen and Klaus both offered to help, as did some other friends, but Astrid waved them off. "Alan will take me home." I gathered up all her things while Astrid assured them she was fine and would see them tomorrow.

Klaus pulled me aside. "You will be safe with her, yes?"

"Yes," I said, "I will." Trying to sound sober and in control.

Klaus didn't seem completely reassured, and glanced up to the bandstand, where the boys were starting another song.

Astrid and I walked toward the exit, and I felt like everyone in the room was watching us. The boys were well into the song, and couldn't stop, which must have bothered Stuart enormously. I took one last glance back at him, and what I saw wasn't anger, and it wasn't jealousy. He looked scared.

Astrid tossed herself into the passenger seat and closed her eyes.

"Thank you for doing this," she said.

I nodded and turned over the engine.

Her car was still pristine: no coffee cups, no cigarette butts. It wasn't hard to drive, either. A buddy of mine had a Volkswagen in high school and I got a lot of practice with it.

I drove carefully down the cobblestone streets of the Grosse Freiheit and past the Reeperbahn. There were crowds of people everywhere, all chasing God-knows-what. The business of men and women, transacted here all night, every night, like the world depends on it. And it probably does. I saw men walking alone, men walking with prostitutes, men walking with beautiful women. I wondered if maybe, somehow, somewhere in Hamburg tonight, there was a man walking with his wife.

Her eyes still closed, Astrid made a sound. I realized she was crying.

I asked what was wrong.

She stared out the window for a moment and sniffed. "I don't know what I'm doing with him."

I kept my eyes on the road. She would tell me what she wanted to tell me. Another two blocks rolled by.

"Someday I will lose him. He is a musician, of course I will lose him. Not tonight, not tomorrow, but . . ." She stared out the window again.

We drove some more.

"Does he love you?" I asked.

"I don't know," she said. "I don't know."

I hated that she felt so miserable, and I blamed Stuart for it. I hated that the solution to her problem, maybe to *all* her problems, was sitting right next to her, but she couldn't see it. And it wouldn't be right for me to tell her. Not now, not in this state. She probably wouldn't even remember it the next day, so what would be the point? A gentleman doesn't do such things.

We drove out of the downtown area and over the bridge, where the streets became leafy, and the buildings turned into bigger and bigger houses. Suddenly it was very quiet outside, and very dark. It was starting to rain.

Astrid's house was sturdy and handsome, on a street lined with sturdy, handsome houses. As I'd suspected, she came from money.

I stopped the car in front. She grabbed a tissue from her purse and dabbed her eyes. She seemed a little better now, a little more in control. "I'm so sorry about this," she said. "You must think—"

"I think," I interrupted, "that I want you to be happy." I was telling her the truth, but only the half of it she wanted to hear.

She smiled. "Oh Alan." She touched my face.

Dear God, the temptation is so strong. A thousand times I've wanted to kiss this girl, and every time something isn't quite right, something sneaks in and douses the flame. Tonight she was simply too drunk and too upset. It wouldn't mean anything.

"Come inside with me," she said, taking hold of my hand. "I want to show you something."

We stumbled up the front steps, shielding ourselves from the freezing rain. It seemed to wake her up a little, as she had no trouble running up the short flight of stairs, even when drunk.

"You have to be quiet, my mother is asleep!" she whispered.

It was a nice house, comfortable, very much like a standard home on Long Island but without the plastic upholstery covers.

"Do you want something to drink?"

"No," I said.

"Well I'm going to." She tiptoed into the kitchen.

"No, don't—"

"Shhh!" She admonished me.

She poured herself a glass of vodka and chugged it, then coughed a little and laughed. "It's terrible!" she said.

I wish I could understand women.

We tiptoed up two flights of stairs to the attic. She kept a finger to her lips, and motioned for me to keep following. I felt a mounting sense of dread: anything she could possibly show me at this point—or any sexual encounter she might be planning to instigate—was simply too dangerous, and couldn't be trusted. As my mother likes to say, nothing good ever happens after 2 a.m.

She switched on the lights.

And what I saw was a shock. An assault on my senses, like my first time at the Kaiserkeller.

The entire room was filled with oil paintings, all big canvases, fifteen or twenty of them, maybe even more.

"This is Stuart's room," she said. "His studio."

The effect was stunning. It was a fairly large attic, but every wall was covered—dominated—by canvases. Some were representational, and some were abstract. But they were remarkable and beautifully painted. I noticed a self-portrait done in big, loose brushstrokes, yellow and blue, reminiscent of Van Gogh. I saw a half-dozen canvases that looked vaguely Cubist—geometrically abstract, hinting at motion and three dimensions. Each had a level of detail that showed an enormous amount of work.

"They're all his?"

"Mm-hmm," said Astrid, weaving absently around the canvases like a drunk lady at the museum.

It was just so *unlikely*. The mediocre bass player; the pale, sickly English boy with the sunglasses and the James Dean haircut—*he* painted these? I might have considered the whole thing a hoax if not for Astrid's rapturous look as she beheld them.

"When does he have time?" I asked.

"When they finish their shows. He comes over. He works

until the sun comes up, then he sleeps."

"When does he have time for you?"

She let out what sounded like a laugh. I immediately regretted the words; they sounded a little hard.

"Sometimes I sleep in here," she said. "While he works." The thought must have made her sad, because her face now twisted into a painful grimace. Picturing herself, maybe, curled up on the floor while her boyfriend painted all night, lost in himself and his own world. Maybe she was seeing the rest of her life unfolding that way. "It's really not so bad." Now she was crying again.

I went to embrace her, but she stepped away. "The room," she said, "it's spinning, you know?"

I sat her down in a chair. She looked sick, and took a couple of deep breaths. "He's a genius," she murmured. "He should paint. Always. But here . . . is too quiet, maybe? Not as much fun as . . . all that? Here, he has no one screaming for him, no one clapping. No one to make him feel special."

I spotted a photo, pinned at eye level, on a canvas still in progress, something to look at while he worked. It was a photo by Astrid, I could tell. Moody, black and white, the light perfectly composed. Stuart and Astrid, together. She was gazing through a window, with a forlorn expression, the metal filigree of the window framing her face. Stuart was kissing her on the cheek, his eyes closed, his mouth slightly open: powerless, helpless, hopelessly in love.

And here in front of me sat Astrid, in precisely the same condition.

And here I was, in an all-too-familiar position, as well: stalking them, observing them, and feeling that I had no business being in their company.

"I'm going to lose him," she said. Her eyes were closed

now, too. "I know I'm going to lose him."

I sleepwalked her down the stairs, found her room (minimalist and painted black), and laid her on her own bed, fully dressed. I kissed her on the forehead.

"Thank you, Alan," she mumbled, and promptly slipped into unconsciousness.

I looked down at her sleeping face, still frozen in pain but now, mercifully, at peace. It was like I had just watched her die. My poor, dear little thing.

I ran out into the freezing rain to hail a cab back into the city.

November 5

I had every intention of sleeping late this morning. After all the drama last night, I decided I would blow off my cinema class and just lie in bed for the morning, or the whole day, get some much-needed rest, and feel sorry for myself.

I heard the first knock at about 11 in the morning. I ignored it.

The next knock came approximately ten minutes later. And again about thirty seconds after that. I dragged myself out of bed and answered the door. It was George.

"Good morning, Alan," he said brightly. "Are you awake?"

"What do you want?" I said, rubbing my face.

"John!" George yelled. "He's awake!"

I heard footsteps, and presently I found myself face to face with John. He was angry. Again.

"What did you do with her?" he said.

"With who? I said. "Astrid?"

"You went home with her. What did you do with her?"

I was too tired and depressed to discuss my love life with the pompadoured bandleader. I wanted to say something like, *It's none of your goddamn business. Why don't you worry about yourself and stop sticking your pointy nose where it shouldn't be?*

But John looked very mean and ready to fight, and the fact that I was barely awake clearly put me at a disadvantage.

So I said this, instead: "I took her home and I put her in bed. She was drunk."

John studied me, and peered into my room, looking for evidence. "Too drunk to get the job done?" he sneered.

"No!" I said, a little louder than planned. "I didn't think it was the right thing to do. Not to her, and not to your precious little Stu. So why don't you piss off?"

For a moment I thought John would punch me. George thought so, too: he took a step back.

But John just smiled. "Good," he said. "I'm glad to hear it."

George leaned forward. "I told you he wasn't a wanker."

I asked them if I could go back to bed now.

"All right," said John. "But let me ask you just one question, Alan Levy."

"What?"

He squinted at me. "How could you not know who Chuck Berry is?"

I sighed. "I guess I'm just stupid."

"I'm serious," he said. "You like music, you like poetry. You live in America. You've got this amazing thing going on in your country, this revolution in music, and you're not even paying attention."

"Let me tell you something about music, John," I said. "It's a very personal thing. You have your favorites, I have mine."

"Yeah, but yours are all crap."

Some people you just can't argue with.

"What are you doing right now?" he asked.

"Wishing I could be somewhere else?"

"Why don't you come with us to the record store? I'll show you some good stuff."

I protested, and even lied about being busy with schoolwork, but they wouldn't take no for an answer. John can be very persuasive. He can turn on the charm when he wants to, and is actually very funny when he lets down the tough-guy act. Maybe it's because I did the right thing by Astrid, or because I actually stood up to him, but he seems to have decided that I'm all right.

We ended up at Freiheit und Roosen, a small record store on the Kleine Freiheit. Evidently the boys are all regular customers; the clerk, a turtle-faced teenager named Manfred, greeted them warmly. (Manfred, I gather, is also a Beatles fan and frequent visitor to the Kaiserkeller, though I certainly didn't recognize him.)

John and George did a quick orbit of the shop, looking for anything new. Within a few minutes they had a short stack of discs, and we all squeezed into a listening booth to sample the offerings.

The first, which the boys were very keen to hear, was by Elvis Presley. Titled "It's Now Or Never"—John called it "It's Now Or Neville"—and frankly one of the most bizarre records I've ever heard. The melody is a note-for-note copy of the Italian song "O Sole Mio" (my Mom loved the Mario Lanza version, so I heard it a lot), only with a slow calypso beat and featuring Elvis in full Hillbilly Crooner mode. John declared it to be "crap," and typical of the toothless, emasculated Elvis who had emerged from his Army service, a shadow of his former genius. "I still love you, Elvis," he declared, "but I miss your balls."

Next up was "Cathy's Clown," a new song by the Everly Brothers (of whom the boys are also big fans). I thought it was very pretty, with a nice melody and an even nicer harmony. I told John that it reminded me of the harmonies he and Paul did together. "Maybe," he said, "but we're not as good." He explained that the Everlys had something called "blood harmony," where the voices of two family members are so similar—even *genetically* similar—that they blend together seamlessly. Like two singers singing with the same voice.

John and George discussed briefly whether they should learn this new song, but in the end John (who I gather has the final call) declared that they didn't need another harmony song just now, but should remember it for later.

It was interesting to see John in this mode, neither drunk nor belligerent, not wisecracking or screaming in front of an audience. Here he was, showing traces of humility, good leadership skills, and respect for the artistry of others. Who would've thought?

We heard a few more songs—"Corinna, Corinna" by Ray Peterson, "This Magic Moment" by The Drifters, and "Alley Oop" by the Hollywood Argyles—which didn't make much of an impression on me, although John and George seemed to like them.

The final record on the stack was a song called "Dizzy Miss Lizzy" by Larry Williams. And within ten or twenty seconds of starting the record, they sat up and exchanged a meaningful look. "I like this," said John.

"Me too," said George.

I thought it was a pleasant enough song, but it didn't knock my socks off. I asked them, why this one?

"I just like it," said John. "Dizzy Miss Lizzy. It's a great title. It's a classic twelve-bar blues, it's even got a nice little guitar riff for our George."

"I'd be ever so happy to," said George.

They listened to the song three more times from beginning to end. George got out a piece of paper that he'd smuggled in and, with some stopping and starting of the record, was able to transcribe the lyrics.

You make me dizzy Miss Lizzy
The way you rock and roll

You make me dizzy Miss Lizzy
When we do the stroll
Come on, Miss Lizzy
Love me 'fore I grow too old

They sang along quietly, getting a feel for the song. "Just the three chords, right?" asked John.

"Yeah," said George. "Seventh at the end."

"Like candy from a baby," said John.

As we walked home, they sang it a few more times. There was a brief discussion on who should sing the main vocal, with George at one point suggesting it might be a good "Paul song."

"Well he's not here, is he?" replied John. "So tutty bad-bad Paul." (Paul was shopping for a new shirt, his old one having disintegrated from sweat the night before.) It was declared to be a John song, now and forever.

It's nice, sometimes, to be around people who are enthusiastic about what they're doing, even if it's just shopping for a rock and roll song. My hangover, and my long, difficult night with Astrid, seemed a little less gloomy than a few hours earlier. I suppose this is one of the things that music—and musicians—are good for.

I asked how long it would take to work the new number into their act. Almost simultaneously they replied, "Tonight." They'd go over it with Paul later that afternoon (evidently he's a quick study at these things) and then with Pete and Stu just before the show—"or whenever the fuck they showed up."

When we got home, I asked them the question I'd been pondering all day: Why was it necessary to constantly learn new songs, and keep bringing them into the act?

"Well, you've got to keep it fresh, right? The act. You've got to keep feeding it. You fancy yourself a poet, don't you?"

I told him I did.

"So you read new poems, don't you? You keep learning. The brain is a muscle, Alan, and if you don't exercise it, it gets weak."

I felt a small twinge of shame that I hadn't exercised my poetry muscles in far too long. Barely a page, after almost two months in Hamburg.

"You want to see someone who hasn't grown," said John. "Listen to Rory Storm and his lot sometime. They haven't added a new song in five years. It makes me want to kill myself."

I dropped off the lads at the Bambi Kino and headed over to the Kaiserkeller, hoping I could find Bruno and pick up my mail. He emerged from the toilet, waving away the smell with a well-creased copy of *Die Zeit,* Hamburg's trashiest paper.

"What?" he demanded.

I asked if there was any mail for me. He cursed under his breath in German and limped over to his desk, where there was, in fact, a letter from my parents.

"Herr Levy," he said. "I see you at my club sometimes. You are getting friendly with the English boys?"

"Yeah, they seem okay," I said.

"No!" he shouted, slamming the newspaper. "You stay away from them. They are bad boys. Very, very bad."

He reached into his desk and pulled out a small notebook, which he waved in my face.

"I keep a book!" he spouted. "Everything they do onstage—and offstage—which is a violation of their contract. I write it down here." He flipped through the pages, densely filled with manic handwriting. "October 5. Pulled down pants onstage and waved ass at audience." He looked up at me. "How do you call this? Mooning?"

"Yes," I answered.

"Why?"

"Well, the moon is round, you know."

"Yes." He made a face like he still didn't understand.

"Well, and so is . . ."

"A bottom," he offered.

"Yes," I said. "It's . . . funny."

He shook his head. "I do not find this funny." He went back to the notebook. "October 7. The mean one. What is his name?"

"John," I said.

"*Ja*. I caught him getting . . ." He made a motion of something going in and out of his mouth. "How you say it, the *mouth sex*—"

"Yes, yes," I said. I had no desire to explain to Bruno the origins of the term "blow job."

"—from a prostitute in the men's room. Then—then!—he came onstage and performed with a toilet seat around his neck!" He looked up at me. "Do you have any idea how filthy and disgusting are the toilets in that bathroom?"

"Yes, I do."

He shook his head and stared out the window. "I thought I could work with these boys, I thought I could shape them into something. But they are animals. Filthy, filthy animals. And they *must be* . . ." His voice trailed off, and I was left to imagine what the end of his sentence was. *Punished? Destroyed? Eliminated?*

He took a deep breath. "I did not want to be their enemy, but they leave me no choice." He looked at me. "Have you found out their ages yet?"

I told him I hadn't.

"You know the skinny one, the quiet one with the ears?"

"You mean George?"

"*Ja.*" He wrote the name "George" on a piece of paper. "I think he is the youngest one. Find out how old is *George.*" He said the name like it was a disease.

I picked up my letter and left. I have no desire for any further business dealings with Bruno. I know how it works with people like him. You start a business relationship, and at some point, for some reason, you find that you owe him money. And then he's got you. That's when he starts cutting you into little pieces, which they fish out of the River Elbe and stuff into plastic evidence bags. With people like him, you want to keep it simple. Pay the rent on time, keep your nose clean, and stay out of his way. That's how you stay in one piece.

November 4

Hamburg (cont'd)

The severed arm
Throbs with phantom pain.
The shriveled husk of a hand, a leg, a foot,
Drags behind the mutilé de guerre
Like entrails from a slaughtered calf.
A darkness has descended
From the ash of bombs dropped long ago,
A cloud of poison beckons, embraces,
And vanishes in a whisper
To maim and kill once more.

Too depressing? Not depressing enough? I can't even tell anymore.

November 5
per Luftpost

Dear Mom and Dad,

I got your letter today—thank you for sending the money! I like it even better than peanut brittle! I've been very happy these last few months living in my garret like the starving artist I am, but what a pleasure it will be to spend a little something on myself, for once. Maybe I'll just blow it all on liquor and women and loud music. (Ha ha, just kidding.)

My semester here has been trying in many ways, but I feel like I'm learning a lot. Not so much from my classes, which continue to be dull and frustrating. (I remember a time when I actually *liked* Shakespeare.) But more in the realm of my personal life. When I first got to Columbia, I thought how scary it was to be on my own, away from home for the first time. But at college, there's a structure and a purpose and a community all laid out for you—all populated with kids very much like yourself—and all you have to do is step into it and take your place.

Living here, I've had to do a lot more thinking on my own. Who am I, what am I, what's interesting about me, what's interesting about the world? When there's no real structure to your life, you have to create one yourself—and that involves asking a lot of questions and setting a lot of priorities. Do I want to stay out all night and sleep until noon? Is it worth skipping class every now and then if there's something more interesting to be found somewhere else? Yes, and yes—*sometimes*. The world is a very big place, and I fear that I've seen too much of it only through the lens of academics.

Just walking the streets here, and interacting with the oddball characters I've gotten to know in this very strange part of town . . . I see things and hear things (and *learn* things) that I'd never in a million years encounter even at the best schools in the world. The brain, after all, is a muscle. If you don't exercise it, it gets weak.

I've discovered, for instance, that I have an appreciation for popular music. There's a lot happening in that realm right now—you could even call it a revolution—and I must admit I'd never paid much attention to it. It's not exactly ART, but it's art-ish: there's a certain amount of craft and creativity involved, and while it certainly doesn't move the soul in the same way that the poems of Rilke do, it's nevertheless (for lack of a better word) *fun*. And I've met some very interesting people who are involved with that scene here, mostly through that girl I was telling you about, Astrid. (She and I continue to be very good friends, and I guess that's fine, for now.)

Funny, isn't it, that I came all the way to Germany to develop an interest in Elvis Presley?

Even so, I haven't lost sight of the real reason I came here, and what I believe is my true calling in life: to create, to write, to contribute to the world of poetry. I'm making great headway with my poem cycle (I'm calling it, simply, "Hamburg") and I believe, when I finally squeeze it all out of me, it will be the finest thing I've ever written. And, I hope, establish myself as a serious, consequential poet of the twentieth century. (Does that sound pretentious? Well, I guess I am!)

I suppose what I'm trying to say here is that my time in Germany has been well spent. I've grown as a person, and I've grown as an artist. And even if the academic side of things hasn't gone exactly to plan . . . and even if college ends up lasting a little longer and costing a little more than I first expected, it's all for the best.

Love you both,
Alan

November 6

I decided to go back to my Shakespeare class today. The prospect of seeing Herr Wensinger again was not a pleasant one, but I felt I had no choice. If he wants to fail me, fine. But I won't make it easy for him. And I won't give up on Shakespeare.

Wensinger smiled when I walked into class, and I briefly thought he was happy to see me. But that was not the case. As soon as class started, he made it clear he was ignoring me. While he lectured, he never made eye contact. When he passed out a mimeographed outline of *King Lear,* he made it a point not to give me one. And when I raised my hand to answer one of his insipid questions ("What is King Lear's problem?") he didn't acknowledge me, despite the fact that I was the only one to respond. At long last he said, "Someone else, please?"

I found it hard to concentrate on the lecture, or *King Lear,* or the majesty of Shakespeare's words. I felt like I was at the center of the drama, and that all eyes were looking at me. I felt such a seething contempt for the man who was causing all of this, who was putting so much effort into making me feel small and unwanted, all because—why? I was a foreigner? An American? A Jew?

Or was I really such a horrible person that I deserved it?

When the class ended, I stayed at my desk while all the other kids filed out. Wensinger continued to ignore me while he packed his briefcase. I didn't say a word.

Finally he spoke up. "I don't know why you come here, Levy. You have failed the class, you understand this?"

"Yes," I said.

"Then what is the point? You are making yourself look

foolish."

"I want you to read something," I said. I walked to his desk and I laid down two sheets of paper stapled together. "This is a poem I wrote."

"Oh dear," he sighed. "You think you are a poet."

"Yes. And so does Columbia University. They awarded this poem the Philolexian Prize for Poetry last year." I'd given him a copy of "Locations," my favorite of my poems at the moment, and part of the collection that won the prize, given annually by the English Department.

"Well, well!" said Wensinger. "A prize-winning poet! Well then clearly you are better than Herr Shakespeare, because *he* never won a prize."

"He may have won a prize," I said, a little defensively. "We don't know."

"I suppose that's true, he might have won a prize and we just never heard about it. We know very little about the life of Herr Shakespeare—"

"Will you read my poem?" I said, my voice rising.

"Why should I? I have already given you your grade."

"Because I read yours."

He paused to consider this. He scooped up the pages and held them at arm's length, peering down his nose through his beady little lenses, his lip pulled back in disgust. I noticed the dandruff on his shirt.

"I will think about it," he announced. "I will either read your poem, or I will use it to wipe my ass."

I spent the afternoon wandering around Hamburg by myself. Even the kids in my classes have started treating me differently: avoiding me, not inviting me out to lunch and drinks like they once did. Who knows what they've been told about me. Maybe nothing. Maybe they've just seen how

I'm treated by Wensinger, and assumed that something was wrong with me.

How strange it is to think back to my days at Columbia, or even my days in high school, when I was a reasonably popular kid. I had my circle of friends, Suzy and Artie and the gang; but I was friendly, at least, with just about everyone else, too. Even people I barely knew—I spoke kindly to them, and they to me.

Why such a big difference, between that experience and this one? Was it a cultural thing? Or was it just the workings of one evil man?

I found myself on the Alte Konigstrasse and in front of a record store I'd never noticed before. I went in. My natural instinct was to peruse the jazz aisle, and even a little bit of the classical section. But I found myself drawn to the small section of rock and roll records in the back.

Most of the titles, and the artists, meant nothing to me. There was a new record by Paul Anka called "Puppy Love," which I thought was cute (I've always been a sucker for puppies). I thought about suggesting it as a new number for my neighbors, but I fear it's not rock and roll enough and John would mock me in a particularly cruel way. Same with the new Neil Sedaka record (I've always liked him, too) called "Calendar Girl." Won't suggest that one, either.

Then there's this song called "Everybody's Trying to Be My Baby" by Carl Perkins. He sounds a little like a hillbilly, but so does Elvis Presley. It's a catchy tune, and maybe it would be a good song for the boys (since all the girls at the club apparently want to be *their* babies). I thought it would be kind of fun to bring them a song and then hear them perform it the next night. (Actually, I don't know if that really would be fun, or it's just an indication of how bored I've gotten with life in Hamburg.)

I thought I could buy the record and bring it to them, but then I remembered they don't have a record player. So I had a wild idea: What if I bought a record player with the money my parents sent me? Then I could play it for them at my place. I could host listening parties, in fact: I could invite my neighbors, I could invite Astrid, I could invite Renate, Helga, and Gitta . . .

But do I really want a bunch of rowdy, foot-stomping Englishmen hanging out in my room all night? Laughing, screaming, getting drunk, jumping off furniture, pulling down their pants? It could be the last time I ever got any work done. I'm not sure I could create a poem cycle about death and deformity while rock and roll musicians went rampaging like bulls through my apartment.

Perhaps I'll just tell them about the song instead.

I got back to the apartment around nightfall. I could hear loud voices inside the boys' apartment, an argument. I put my ear to the door.

"Maybe if you were *here* sometime—"

"Shut up."

"Don't tell me to shut up!"

I couldn't tell who was who. Maybe one of the voices was Paul?

"When we call a rehearsal . . ."

"Nobody called a bloody rehearsal!"

"I called a rehearsal, but who bloody cares what I say?"

"Oh sod off—"

Just then the door opened. Which would have been awkward enough except that the person now standing two inches from my face was Stuart, surely feeling as uncomfortable as I was. An unwieldy pause followed.

“Oh. Hello,” he said.

“Hey,” I answered.

Stuart didn’t say anything else, but quickly turned and walked away down the stairs. I looked inside the room. The rest of the boys were all there. A band meeting, it would appear. And me. I could feel the tension.

“Hi guys,” I said.

“Hi Alan,” said Paul. The rest of them grunted and turned back into the room.

Paul stepped into the hallway to join me. His face was red. “Everything okay?” I asked.

He pulled the door shut. “It’s bloody Stuart,” he said in a whisper. “He’s got no bloody interest in this band and he’s dragging us all down. How are we supposed to get better if our bass player can’t keep up? He doesn’t even bother to learn the new songs!”

“Well,” I said, “why don’t you play the bass?”

“I’m not playing the bass!” he shot back. “The bass is for losers and fat guys who stand in the back. No thank you.”

I told him it was just a suggestion.

“It’s frustrating,” he said. “The band is *this close* to being really good. It’s just a couple of elements, you know?” He took a moment to regain his composure. “Anyway. Sorry you had to hear all that. I don’t know what to do about Stuart. I can’t even stand to be in the same room with him.”

I had to ask. “It didn’t have anything to do with me, did it?” I said. “I mean, me and Astrid?”

“No, no.” Paul made a quick dismissive motion with his hand. “Not at all.”

I said I was glad to hear it.

“But can I tell you something, mate?” He put his arm around my shoulder. Yet another hug. “And it’s just my opinion, but I don't think you should give up on Astrid."

"No," I said. "She's with him—"

"I see the two of you dancing!" he said. "I see the way she looks at you. I saw you took her home the other night!"

"Yes, but nothing happened," I pointed out.

"Well, maybe it hasn't happened *yet*. I'm just telling you what I see. She's a fabulous girl and she deserves better than bloody Stu—"

Just then the door flung open. It was John.

"Hey! I don't want you telling him that, Paul!"

"I'm not *tellin'* him, John, I—"

"You've got a problem with Stu, you take it up with Stu. Leave his fuckin' girlfriend out of it!"

Paul rolled his eyes. John turned to me.

"And *you*," he said, staring a hole through my forehead. "Find another girl."

I sighed. "Look, I don't—"

John grabbed me by the collar and pulled me close. His eyes were burning. I could already smell the alcohol on his breath. He looked more than capable of violence. "Leave my band alone and *find another girl*."

He pushed me away and went back into the room, slamming the door behind him.

Maybe John doesn't like me after all.

Things only got stranger that night when I went to the Kaiserkeller. I realize I'm becoming a regular at that place, which is something I never intended to do. I also confess that I'm no longer sticking to my one-beer limit, but I have no plans to ever lose control again. And I will *never* take Prellies again, so help me God.

The truth is, I like the Kaiserkeller. I like the madness of it, the joy, the honesty, the adventure. It's everything that the university isn't. Sure, I could stay in at night and continue studying for a class that has no interest in teaching me anything about anything—or I could go out and have fun. Turn off my brain for a while. God knows I'm not the first poet who's ever found inspiration in the life force of a bawdy tavern.

I got there early. The boys had just started playing. They each nodded a friendly hello as I walked in, even John. If he had a problem with me, he wasn't about to chase away the audience. That's what I like about this place. Once the music starts, it's all about the music.

I watched the performance for a while. I didn't dance but sat at my table, tapping a foot or bobbing my head (something I would describe as "sitting-down dancing," a move well known to inhibited white people).

I found myself enjoying their antics more and more. They were funny. They ragged on each other, they ragged on the audience. They jumped on chairs, they did splits, they kicked and charged across the stage—and whenever things got slow, John would simply go into his crippled spastic routine and call the audience Nazis.

At about 10 o'clock, Astrid walked in with Klaus and Jurgen. I exchanged hugs with all three (man-hugging, I think, is a European custom I'm quite sure will never catch on in the States). Astrid's hug was especially long and warm, and she whispered into my ear (shouted, actually, over the music), "Thank you, Alan. For taking me home last night."

I shouted back something to the effect of *no problem.*

We all sat down together and watched a song or two, and then Astrid stood up and took my hand. "Come with me," she said.

She wasn't leading me to the dance floor, but out the door. For a private conversation. My heart sped up, out of reflex.

Another moment alone with Astrid. I've given up on her already, haven't I?

We walked out by way of the bandstand; Astrid shouted up to Stuart, who was in the middle of a song. "Just for one minute, darling. Okay?"

Stuart shot me a wary look and then turned back to Astrid. "Okay," he said.

Paul gave me a sly smile. John looked angry.

We went outside. It was freezing and we started to shiver immediately.

"So," Astrid began. "Last night. I am so embarrassed at how I behaved. I was . . ." She made a motion of drinking.

I told her I'd seen worse, or something stupid like that.

"And you were wonderful." She pulled her coat a little tighter. "I don't want you to think I don't care about you . . . but I am in love with Stuart, you see?"

Of course she was. I'd known it for a while, but this was the first time I'd heard the words spoken out loud.

"I love him very much."

For so long she and I had flirted with each other, daring each other to fall in love, knowing that it couldn't happen, but pretending that maybe it could.

"I understand," I said.

"I think we will get married. I don't know when, but soon."

"That's great," I said. "I'm happy." I wasn't. It felt like Suzy all over again, except that Astrid and I never even got to be a couple.

"Please be happy. For me?"

"Yes," I said. "You deserve to be happy."

She gave me another hug and held on tight. "It's okay to love a friend," she said.

I nodded, though I disagreed. To my mind, there's either

love or there's friendship, but not both. And the only person who will ever tell you different is a beautiful woman while she's breaking your heart.

"And don't feel awkward around Stuart. We are all friends, yes?"

"Of course," I answered, trying to sound sincere, which I wasn't.

I led her back inside by way of the dance floor. "How about one last dance?" I said. She nodded okay. For old times' sake.

Paul stepped up to the mike. "We'd like to carry on now with a love song. A song about giving all the love inside you . . . to someone very special." He was looking right at me and Astrid. "So hold on to someone you love, hold on tight, and see if you can fall in love just a little bit more . . ."

"Why don't you shut up and play the song?" John asked, which got a big laugh from the audience.

They started playing. John on vocals. A slow, pretty song, one that I've always liked.

To know know know her
Is to love love love her
Just to see her smile
Makes my life worthwhile

Astrid and I started to dance, slowly. The problem was, neither of us was expecting a romantic song. It felt like we had fallen into a trap, slow-dancing like a pair of lovers. I could feel everybody staring at us, and everybody on the bandstand hating and resenting me (look, he's *still* trying to make it with Stu's girl)—except for Paul, who continued to beam down rays of romantic sunshine with his backing vocals. John, I could tell, was putting minimal effort into singing the song, and clearly resented having to do so while watching us dance. I couldn't even look at Stuart, but could well imagine what he was going through, and how badly he wanted to kill me.

Astrid and I smiled at each other, but it was awkward. I tried to think of something to say, something funny, maybe, or self-consciously ironic, but nothing came.

Suddenly I heard a commotion from the stage. A loud electric noise and a blur of bodies.

Stuart had dropped his bass and charged into Paul, tackling him to the ground. The two of them were flailing at each other on the floor center stage, raining (but mostly missing) punches while the rest of the band attempted to break it up. They fought like two guys who didn't know how to fight, windmilling fists, twisting and turning on each other.

Two of the bouncer-waiters rushed the stage and—surely out of force of habit—started beating up the brawling musicians. Horst the bouncer shouted at them to stop: "*Das ist die band! Das ist die band!*"

Horst climbed up on the stage and pulled everyone apart. Paul and Stuart separated and immediately tended to their instruments while the rest of the band wondered aloud *what the fuck was going on*? The audience was shouting at the stage, some cheering and whooping, others starting fights of their own for no reason in particular.

It's the most chaos I've ever seen in this place. And that's saying a lot.

Astrid ran to Stuart's side; he reassured her that he was okay. Paul strutted around the stage, playing it for laughs.

John stepped to the mike. "Welcome to the Friday Night Fights," he said. "We're gonna take a break."

Bruno called out from the back of the room. "No! You vill play! You vill play now! You get your break at eleven!"

There was some grumbling from the boys, but Paul and Stuart looked eager to get back to work.

"Come on, Piedels," taunted Bruno. *"Mach schau!"*

John made a spastic face and picked up his guitar. The rest of the band followed suit, even though Paul and Stuart didn't so much as look at each other.

I walked to the front of the stage. I wanted to apologize to Stuart—and to Astrid—and assure them that none of this had been my intention and that I wasn't trying to break them up or get in the way or steal anyone's girlfriend. I made a gesture to that effect, but as I walked toward him, John stood in my way.

"I think you should go home," he said.

"We were just dancing!" I protested.

"Alan," said John. "You're fucking with the band. Go home."

He was right. I didn't want to get mixed up in band politics any more than I already was. And any more meddling between Astrid and Stuart would be pointless. I gathered up my coat and waved goodbye to Astrid. She waved back, a sad smile on her face. I smiled and gave a thumbs-up to Stuart. He nodded.

I walked out the door and was nearly a full block away when I heard the music start again. "Sweet Little Sixteen," as loud and raucous as ever, like nothing had ever happened.

Life at the Kaiserkeller goes on.

November 8

I woke up early this morning and finished reading *The Sorrows of Young Werther* for German Lit. It's a powerful book, and I can see why it was so popular, especially with the grim, humorless Germans. In its day, it was a publishing sensation (it was said to be Napoleon's favorite novel), and it set off a craze for suicide among young people emulating its hero, Werther, who shoots himself because Charlotte is in love with Albert and not him.

Would I kill myself over Astrid? I don't think I would . . .

I tried to concentrate on Werther's story but I kept coming back to my own. I've spent so much time thinking about Astrid over these past few weeks that I'd begun to imagine our future together, living it out in my mind, feeling joy and happiness, basking in its pleasures as if they were happening now—only to discover that none of it ever *will* happen. Not for me, anyway.

But would I kill myself?

I feel like a fog has settled over me, and it's thick and dense, and sometimes it feels blinding. But if I stop and focus, I think I can see through it, just a little, just enough to give me hope. I can see, ever so distantly into my future, where more opportunities, and many more women, must surely await.

But maybe that's how it began for Werther, too: thinking that he could see a way through his depression, but finding, in the days and weeks that followed, that he couldn't, and that life without Charlotte was not worth living. Maybe he felt the same glimmer of hope that I'm feeling now, and convinced himself that everything would be fine, until the fog overtook him and he blew his brains out.

So the best thing for me to do, I decided, is concentrate on the book and not on myself. I would go back to school and try to enjoy that small part of it, since German Lit is the only class I'm taking that's not taught by Herr Wensinger.

But I never got to find out.

Just as I took my seat at the back of the classroom, Herr Teichmann summoned me to the front of the class and asked me to step outside.

"Herr Levy," he said, "you will please go to see the *Dekan für studentische*. He is waiting for you."

The Dean of Students' office was in the next building, and as I walked there, my first thought was that there had been a death in my family. This happened to my friend Dave Slottow in fourth grade. All eyes were on him as he walked to the front of the classroom and out the door, only to have the principal break the horrible news: his father, a massive heart attack, an hour's wait until his grandmother got there to pick him up. (I think that's the most horrible part of the story, having to contemplate the death of his father while sitting in the office of our horrible principal, making pained, awkward conversation.) I braced myself for the news, and I couldn't help weighing which would be worse, my mother being dead or my father.

The dean, Herr Klimek, was indeed waiting for me and told me to have a seat.

"Herr Levy," he began. "There has been a complaint."

I cocked my head.

"About you," he said. "And your conduct."

He went on to explain that one of my teachers had accused me of "behaving in ways unworthy of the institution, and damaging to the student body at large." Among these behaviors (he read from a letter) were contempt for authority, insubordination, and public drunkenness.

I blinked several times, trying to understand. The person he was describing sounded nothing like me. But Klimek's grave expression assured me it was no mistake.

"We take this complaint quite seriously," he said.

"Was it Herr Wensinger?" I asked.

"I am not at liberty to say." He told me there would be a hearing in two weeks before the *Disziplinarkommission,* at which time I could present my side of the case and apply for reinstatement. Until then, I was suspended from school and not allowed on school property.

There was a pause. Maybe he expected me to protest, or offer some form of denial. But I didn't. I couldn't even think of where to start. Finally I muttered, "Does this mean I fail?"

He leaned back in his chair. "If you are denied reinstatement, then you will not receive credit for any of your courses, no." He must have seen the blank look on my face. "So, yes, it would mean that you fail."

I let out a short laugh—a snort—which seemed to clear my head. "I have never failed anything in my life!" I declared. "This is a lie, and an insult, and if I have to hire a lawyer, I will do so—and I will sue Herr Wensinger and this entire university for slander!" It was clearly an empty threat. There was no way that I could hire a lawyer, or pay him, to defend myself in an academic case; but even so, I was glad I said it. I have a tendency to not stand up for myself, to let myself be bullied, and if I can take any pleasure from this wretched set of events, it's that for once I have shown a little spine.

The dean was not so impressed. He showed no sympathy or interest in pursuing the matter. My outraged words hung there for just a moment, and then he calmly rose to his feet.

"Good day, Herr Levy."

I got up and walked to the door.

"Oh yes. This is for you." He handed me an envelope. "You may read it outside."

It was the poem I'd given to Wensinger. It was folded into thirds, with a short note paper-clipped to the front. The note was typed neatly, with generous margins, like a poem, on his personal letterhead.

Dear Mr. Levy,

I have read your poem and I regret to say that I find nothing exceptional about it.

I find your subject matter dull and tedious. I find your use of language to be clumsy and inelegant. I would not even call it a poem: it is prosaic and pedestrian, without soul and without music.

It is my opinion that you do not possess the skills necessary to pursue a career in poetry. It is better to know this now than to spend many years of your life chasing a dream which is unreachable. I hope you will see that, by telling you this, I am doing you a favor.

Good luck with your future endeavors.
Karl Wensinger

November 8
per Luftpost

Dear Mom and Dad,

I wish I was home right now. I wish I'd never come to Germany. I've made some terrible choices.

And not just in Germany. I've been foolish for so much of my life. I've had every opportunity, every advantage: a loving family, financial security, a first-rate education. How can a person be given so much, and turn it into so little of consequence? Let's be honest—I've never been an outstanding student. I don't get straight As like Miriam does. I've always considered my grades to be less important than my abilities as an artist, but again, let's be honest, I haven't exactly set the world of poetry on fire, have I? The only thing I've ever feared in life is mediocrity, and I feel myself descending deeper and deeper into it.

Earlier today, I

November 9

I couldn't finish the letter. I threw it out, then took the garbage can outside and emptied it into a public rubbish bin so I wouldn't be tempted to fish it out and try again.

I'll tell my parents at some point, but there's no reason to drag them into my emotional mess just so they can watch me writhe in self-pity. At least not until I figure out what to do.

I could argue my case before the university, show them that Herr Wensinger is being a malevolent bully and that this whole episode is a personal vendetta. (Had he really hated my poem so much that he was willing to kick me out of school?) Maybe Wensinger has a history of these attacks on his students, and the university would nod in agreement when I told them I was being unfairly persecuted.

More likely, of course, they would side with one of their own, no matter what the facts, and come down hard against me, the spoiled American Jew. Clearly, to them I was still the enemy. Maybe they relished an opportunity to refight the war. Maybe I should, too, since—as in the two previous wars—the American side is so clearly in the right.

But (and this is what's so depressing) what's the point? Why should I fight to stay in a school where I'm not wanted? Where no one will challenge me, or inspire me, or expand my mind? Why stay in a city where I can find neither love, nor sex, nor even a whole lot of companionship? Maybe it's time to cut my losses and go home. What on earth am I doing here?

I picked up my Rilke and read Letter Eight, in which the poet counsels his young protégé Krapus, who is foundering in the depths of melancholy. "You must be patient like a sick man and sanguine like a convalescent," advises the poet, "for perhaps you are both. And more than that: you are also the doctor who has to superintend yourself."

Yes, I thought, that was my first instinct as well. Superintend myself.

Go out and get drunk.

I walked to the Gretel and Alfons and parked myself at a corner table. I got my first Bacardi and Coke. (Yes, Astrid's drink; I'm sure that's just a coincidence.) I thought about how getting kicked out of university would affect my life, and my future, and my chances of getting into the Iowa Writers' Workshop. And I decided to keep drinking.

I was just into my third drink when I saw Pete across the room, also drinking by himself. I was in no mood to plumb the depths of his dullness, but soon he was standing in front of me.

"Hello, mate," he said. "Do you fancy getting a meal?"

I pointed to my glass. "This is my meal."

Pete sat down. "Well maybe you'd be interested in hearing about what happened after you left the club last night. It was quite a little dust-up."

I shook my head.

He leaned forward. "Stuart is out. He's left the band."

I glanced up from my drink.

"Thassright, matey," he said. "Buy me a drink and I'll tell you about it."

"I'm not buying you a drink."

"Oh come on," he said. "You know you want to hear. One flippin' drink."

I bought him a drink.

"Right," he said. "So you were there for the fight, yeah?"

"Yes," I told him.

"So. After you left, we go back to playin'. Nobody says

nuthin' about the fight, we just play the songs. Nobody's even lookin' around. Then, we break at eleven, John says, 'Band meeting. Outside. Now.'"

To summarize the meeting:

Stuart announced he was leaving the band. He said he would finish the work he was contracted to do; i.e., continue playing in Bruno's club for the duration of their contract, which ran until the middle of December. After that, though, he was done. In addition, he wouldn't go to any more rehearsals, wouldn't learn any new songs, and wouldn't play any of their "secret" gigs at the Top Ten Club. (Bruno was right about that much: the band had been sneaking over to the other club during their set breaks and performing as backup for a singer named Tony Sheridan.)

As Pete recounted the story, I began to wonder just how much of this drama had been engineered by cheeky little Paul. He had been wanting Stuart out of the group for months, and now he'd gotten his wish. He'd been jealous of Stuart's friendship with John, and now Stuart was going away. And—here's the real question—how much had Paul been manipulating *me*? All that encouragement to keep chasing after Astrid, all that "you've found her, go and get her" business—how much of that had been a knife in the ribs to Stuart? How much of that had been planned to get Stu *into* Astrid and *out of* the band?

It's funny how people's looks, and even their manner, can be so deceiving. Baby-faced Paul, full of romance and sentimental ballads—and inside beats the heart of a shark.

If nothing else, I could see him being a successful businessman someday.

"What happens with the rest of the band?" I asked.

"Don't know," said Pete. "Might be a gig in Munich or West Berlin, but I think it's just Bruno blowing smoke up our arse. Maybe we'll go home, maybe this is the end. Though if you asked me, I think we sound just as good without a bass as we do with one."

"What about Astrid?" I asked.

"Bloody thrilled about it, she is. Already talking about moving in with him, him going back to being an artist. Bloody artist . . ." He sniffed. "You seen his paintings? Bloody rubbish, in't they?"

I shrugged. I didn't like to think about Stuart's paintings. They depress me. Their sheer number, their variety, their size, their level of detail. How admired they are by teachers and casual observers alike. Everything my poems aren't.

"I say, good for him," said Pete. "She's a fine-looking piece. I can tell you this: every one of us wanted to get a leg over her. Right since day one. And she chose him! The pale, spotty, queer one. No accountin' for taste, eh?"

I wondered. Maybe every single one of them had gone through what I was going through now. What if the whole band—all except Stuart, anyway—had had their heart broken by Astrid?

I refused to believe it.

"Do you suppose," I ventured, "that maybe she still has some unresolved feelings? About me, I mean?"

"Ha!" he snorted. "Not bloody likely! She never liked you, mate. Sorry."

My back stiffened. Pete—dull-as-dishwater Pete, a man without an interesting or insightful bone in his body—was presuming to tell *me* what Astrid thought, or how she felt? I wanted to grab him by his ridiculous leather jacket and throw him up against the wall, but I kept my composure. "And how," I asked, oh-so-calmly, "would you happen to know that?"

He didn't even bother to look up. He had no idea how

much he was infuriating me, but stared instead at his breakfast, which he continued to shovel into his mouth, regular as a metronome. "I think that's just how she is, you know, with everyone," he mumbled. "I seen her with other blokes. She gets around more than you think, mate."

Now I just wanted him to fuck off.

He soon obliged, heading to the Kaiserkeller, where he had another six hours of drinking and pounding on drums to do. But as I watched him go, I was surprised to feel a twinge of envy for this dull, annoying little man. Never mind all the sex he was having. He had a place to go and friends waiting for him. He had an *audience* waiting for him. Not so for me.

I had a few more Bacardis, but all I could taste was the hangover, massing its troops on the border, ready to advance and lay waste to another day of my life.

PART THREE

November 10

At noon I willed myself out of bed, even though I could have stayed there for the rest of the day. I felt the need to get my body moving, just to prove that I could.

It was freezing outside, and my first half-hour of walking was sheer misery. I did a tour of the Harbor piers and into the Portuguese quarter, where you see lots of seafood restaurants with dead fish in the window—a parody, I thought, of the dead-eyed prostitutes who look out from the windows of the Herbertstrasse. A fitting metaphor for me. Where some men find passion and adventure, I find only dead fish.

I wanted to keep moving.

As I turned a corner to head back toward St. Pauli, I heard a car honk.

"Alan!"

It was Astrid, driving her Beetle. She waved me over, smiling broadly. I started to smile back, but then I thought about my conversation with Pete: what if it was true that she never really liked me? I had started to believe it, tossing in bed last night, but now here she was, calling my name and rolling down the window.

"Where are you going?" she asked.

I lied and told her I was on my way to school.

"I will give you a ride." It was a simple statement. Nobody argues with Astrid. Her spirit is a force of nature.

She seemed a little quieter than usual—maybe she was still embarrassed about our dance the other night, or the fight it had caused—or maybe the car just *seemed* quiet compared to the Kaiserkeller. We mostly made small talk, about the weather and some restaurant she had tried last night. I didn't feel like telling her about my problems at school, and I decided to play dumb about Stuart leaving the band. She'd tell me if she wanted to.

She asked me what class I was going to, and if I was enjoying it. I lied, again, and told her Shakespeare, and that things were okay, even though I was bored with the teacher and disappointed in the other students.

"Then maybe you should not go," she said.

"I have responsibilities," I mumbled. She looked at me. She could probably tell something was wrong—she's perceptive that way—but I didn't want to get into it. There was no point trying to get closer to her.

"Okay," she said. We drove on in silence.

She pulled up alongside campus. I reached for the door handle, debating whether I would walk home or take the bus.

"Alan." Astrid took off one of her leather driving gloves (yes, she wears driving gloves). On the third finger of her left hand was a thin gold ring.

"He proposed," she said. "We are getting married."

She said it in a curious, detached tone of voice. Not like the American girls I know, who wave the ring in your face and jump up and down like they've just won the lottery. With Astrid it had a more realistic undertone, as though she acknowledged the difficulties that lay ahead, along with the joy.

I felt nothing. Not anger, not sadness—I'd been through those emotions already. I'd imagine it's like the days following the death of a loved one: you find that nothing has actually changed, but the fact of it becomes more and more real.

"Congratulations," I answered. I didn't think I should kiss her, but it seemed like the appropriate response. So I kissed her on the cheek and gave a perfunctory hug, both of which were awkward.

But this is what's so great about Astrid (and I'm not saying this as someone who's still in love with Astrid, but as someone who understands that *everybody* falls in love with Astrid). She doesn't surrender to awkward moments. She doesn't let a little discomfort ruin the encounter. She acknowledges it and moves on.

"Can you be late for your class?" she asked, and turned off the car engine.

I told her yes, I probably could.

She proceeded to tell me everything about her relationship with Stuart. The first night she saw him in the club, how he looked so different from everybody else in the band. How clear it was that Stuart was never meant to be a musician, and that his genius for painting was obvious to everyone who had ever met him.

I nodded. It was still painful. It would be so much easier to dismiss him as a pretentious fool if I'd never seen his paintings.

She told me that Stuart was planning to stay behind in Hamburg after the rest of the boys go off to Munich or back home to Liverpool. He was looking into enrolling at the Hamburg College of Art, and it was possible that Astrid's mother would pay for it.

She told me he'd been painting almost nonstop since he told the band he was leaving, and how he looks happier than she's seen him in months. And how he's absolutely positive he won't miss the applause and the cheering fans, and all the young girls who fall in love with him, just like Astrid did, when he plays the bass with his back to the audience.

And as she sat there telling me everything, spilling all their secrets, all her plans and fears, I made a mental note: *This is what love looks like. This is how love behaves.* The next time I'm trying to express love, in a poem or in a letter, I will remember this. Love is what Astrid feels for Stu.

"Alan," she said. "Skip your class today. Come to my house. I want you to do something for me. Maybe as an engagement present?"

I asked her what it was. She said it's a surprise.

I'm ashamed to admit that my first thought was, *maybe she finally wants to have sex with me.* Yes I am that shallow. Yes I live in a world of fantasy that revolves completely around myself. What is wrong with me?

We got to her house in a matter of minutes. In the daylight it looked even more quaint and suburban, and thus even more familiar. She introduced me to her mother, an elegant, middle-aged matron who offered me a cup of tea and asked me the standard questions about America.

Astrid took me by the hand and led me up the stairs to her room. I don't think she even remembered that I'd been there before. I started to mention it, but she shushed me. She pointed to the stairs leading to the attic, where I heard someone moving.

"Is Stuart here?" I whispered.

Astrid nodded yes, and pulled me into the bedroom, shutting the door behind her. "He's working. He only stops to eat a sandwich."

"I don't think he'd be happy about finding me in here!" I whispered.

"Don't be silly," she said. "He is working now, he will not stop."

"Then what?"

"Okay," she said. "Please sit."

I sat on the edge of her bed. Which felt like an even worse idea.

"You told me once you were brave and willing to try something exciting, yes?"

My heart pounded.

She opened up a dresser drawer and pulled out a pair of scissors. "I want to cut your hair," she said.

Say what you will about Astrid, she does manage to surprise you.

She explained that she'd been wanting to cut Stuart's hair for weeks now, only he wasn't having it. She wanted to give him what she called a "French Cut," the style favored by the bohemian kids in Paris. She showed me a photo in a French magazine: some French model with his hair looking like . . . I don't know, Julius Caesar? All of a uniform length, and combed forward, spilling over the forehead and right down to the eyebrows. It looked like someone had put a bowl on his head and cut around it. I couldn't imagine why a man would want to make such a spectacle of his hair.

Sensing my unease, Astrid went into sales-pitch mode. It's how the handsome boys are wearing it, she said, *trés chic, trés mode,* and I had the perfect face for it. She knew my face, she insisted. Hadn't she proven it by taking that magnificent photo? She promised I would look even more like a movie star than I already did, and *die frauleins* would be drawn to me like kittens to milk.

I looked at the magazine again. I suggested that the hairstyle was the same one she wore on her own head. A pageboy haircut, you'd call it.

"No, no," she assured me. "It is much different for men."

Well, that's a complete lie—they are identical—but she must have figured I was too insecure with my own masculinity to agree to a girl's haircut. And she's quite right. Only a fool would agree to such a thing.

Why, then, did I agree to it?

Because it was Astrid. She's a girl you simply can't say no to. Because everything she says and everything she does has a sense of excitement. You follow her because you know she'll always take you somewhere new and fun and different, and she's never disappointed you once.

My parents used to say, when I was young and easily influenced, "Well if so-and-so told you to jump off the Brooklyn Bridge, would you do it?"

And I realize that yes, if Astrid ever made that request, I would soon end up bobbing like a cork in the East River.

It took her about twenty minutes to finish the job. And I'd be lying if I said I didn't enjoy it. Twenty minutes of Astrid hovering in front of me, her head inches from mine. All the attention, the physical contact, her fingers gliding over my scalp and through my hair. It was maybe the most intimate thing we'd ever done together. And yet, there was Stuart, the man she loved, setting down his footsteps, back and forth, just above our head. I felt myself being pulled back to a familiar place, even though I knew it was too late.

"Do you use anything on your hair?" she asked. "Any oils or lotions?"

"In America," I told her, "we call it greasy kid stuff."

She was fascinated with the expression, and repeated it back to me: *greasy kid schtuff*.

I assured her that I never use anything on my hair.

"Good," she said. "I wish the English boys felt the same way. Can I tell you something? There is nothing sexy about greasy hair."

I told her about my own experience with Suzy, about the cans and cans of hairspray she went through, how the air would fill with a toxic cloud of glue. I realized I had never mentioned Suzy to her before. (I hadn't talked to anyone here about Suzy, come to think of it.) It felt safe to broach the subject with Astrid now that she was wearing a ring. Safe—yet once again, more intimate than ever.

When she handed me the mirror, I was shocked. There was no other way to say it: I looked like a girl. Very much, in fact, like the girl who was standing in front of me now, trying to gauge my reaction. "Huh," I said.

"You look fantastic!" Astrid bounced in circles around me, running her hands through my hair. "Alan, I'm not kidding you, this is a very handsome look for you. And very manly."

She wasn't convincing me.

"Promise me," she said, "you will give it a chance. Let it settle into place. Give it two days before you start combing it back the old way."

"And what's in it for me?" I asked.

"Well, you will attract all the girls. There is no question."

"Yeah," I muttered, "if they're lesbians . . ."

"All right, how about I will take your picture again? But only if you keep it. And, you must come to the club tonight, and show it off to Stuart. I want him to be jealous. And you are very good at that."

I wanted so much to ask her: *Did I ever have a chance with you? Was there ever a moment when you considered choosing me over Stuart?*

I didn't, of course. I simply agreed to her terms and left.

I avoided eye contact with anyone for the rest of the afternoon. I walked around the city, but it felt strange having the wind toss my hair about like a horse's mane. I went home and read for a while, but I started to get depressed. An hour ago I'd been a complete failure; now I was a complete failure with a funny haircut.

I got to the Kaiserkeller a little after 10. Rory Storm and his group were playing when I walked in, and I knew what that meant. They'd all be sitting at the same table: Astrid, Stuart, the rest of the boys, and all their friends. There'd be no hiding. I took a deep breath and approached their table.

George was the first to notice me, and he burst out laughing. He nudged Pete, who started laughing, too. Soon the whole table was in hysterics.

Astrid jumped up and put her arm around me. "I think he looks wonderful!" she said, running her fingers through my ridiculous hair. Sure, they were all laughing at me, but who among them wouldn't be happy to have a girl like Astrid mussing up their hair instead of mine?

"You did this to him?" Stuart asked, grinning widely.

"Yes!" she said. "Because Alan is not a great chicken like you are."

I turned to Stuart. "She is a very persuasive girl," I said.

"Oh, I know," he said. We exchanged a sympathetic look—two guys who'd fallen in love with the same person. We had that in common, at least.

"Congratulations," I told him. "I'm happy for both of you."

"Thanks, Alan," he said, and we shook hands.

It turned out to be a fun night, which was just what I needed. I didn't mind being the comic relief. I didn't tell anyone about my issues at school, and it felt good knowing nobody would care.

Despite all the fireworks of the past couple of days, everyone was in a good mood, and the evening came to feel like a celebration. Stuart and Astrid were engaged now, and everybody was happy for them. And happy that all their friendships had survived. There'd been fights, there'd been jealousy, there'd been tears; but now here they all were, sitting around a table, laughing, drinking, and being friends.

And the boys, I think, were happy knowing that their band had survived. They would find a new bass player, I suppose, but there was no doubt that they would keep on playing, and keep on getting better. Paul, I think, was the happiest of all at this prospect, and he was a one-man dynamo onstage. More jokey than ever, more flirty than ever, screaming out his songs with a whole new passion.

I'd never really considered how hard it must be to perform the same show for six or eight hours every night, and make it all seem fresh and exciting (imagine if actors on Broadway had to work this hard). Tonight they were putting their all into it, and the audience was loving them. The whole band sounded better than ever.

John sang most of his songs that night with silly nonsense lyrics, which never failed to crack up the rest of the band.

Well give me putty
(that's what I want)
A lot of putty
(that's what I want)
I wanna eat beef!
(that's what I want)
Oh-oh, out of rye bread

Astrid and I danced to three or four songs. She couldn't stop running her hands through my hair and telling me how handsome I looked.

Stuart didn't say much, but I caught him studying my head quite a few times over the course of the evening. Judging by that, and by the way he and Astrid clung to each other and kissed between sets, I wouldn't be surprised if I see a new hairstyle on him sometime soon. Maybe on all of them.

November 10

per Luftpost

Dear Artie,

I trust that you will enjoy the enclosed photo of me, and hope that, within a couple of days, you will stop laughing.

Seriously, though, what do you think?

It's called a French Cut, and some of the really interesting, really cool kids here are wearing it like this. I got talked into it by that gorgeous photographer girl I was telling you about. (She didn't take the picture, but she's promised to take another one of me soon.) I've officially given up on her, by the way: she's engaged and . . . bah Hamburg, I don't want to talk about it.

I'm getting more and more friendly with those musicians who live next door, and I find I'm growing weirdly fascinated with music in general. I know you've done more of that stuff than I have. The only music I've ever performed, really, is a couple of plays in high school and of course that horrible production of *The Music Man*. I just find it so much more interesting than my stupid, boring classes. I spend hardly any time at school anymore.

I really can't wait to get back to Columbia. I look forward to seeing all of you guys again. I may be coming home slightly ahead of schedule. Or maybe I'll just stay here and turn into the next Elvis Presley.

And by the way, I think it's totally fine if you want to go out with Suzy. I don't think she's really your type, but hey, why not give it a try? She's a swell girl, and I hope the two of you end up with a bunch of hairy Jewish children.

Your hairy Jewish friend,
Alan

P.S. I told you Kennedy would win! But I worry that he might be dangerous. He's so good-looking, I feel like he could get away with anything, lead us anywhere, and America would just follow because he's so goddamn handsome.

November 11

I slept late again today and didn't get out of bed until 11. What a foul and degenerate bum I've become. And what a night owl! It's shifted my perspective on things, now that I'm seeing more of the nocturnal world (which I associate with manmade and sensory pleasures, like dancing and music and alcohol) and less of the early morning world (which I associate with God and nature and sweetly chirping birds).

And of course I don't have homework to worry about, now that I've been kicked out of school.

I find I'm sleeping better than I have in ages. Part of that, I suppose, is that I now keep more or less the same schedule as my next-door neighbors, so their noise and horseplay no longer keep me awake. I also suspect they're not partying at home as much as they used to: for them, like me, the novelty of living in Hamburg has worn off a bit, and the physical exhaustion of their performance schedule has surely taken a toll.

I thought I'd knock on their door and see if they wanted to have breakfast, but I didn't hear any sound coming from inside, apart from a low buzzing noise that could have been a snore, so I thought it best not to disturb them.

I went to the Café Moller for my strudel and coffee, and entertained myself with this morning's *Herald-Tribune* (I've discovered a nearby luggage store that sells the paper, thus saving myself a long, frigid walk to the newsagent's every day). I'd nearly finished the crossword puzzle when I looked up to see Paul, John, and George walking past the window.

I hurried to catch up with them. "Hey guys," I said, "where ya going?"

They didn't break stride. "This lucky bastard," said Paul, indicating John, "is buying a new guitar."

"That's exciting," I said.

"Johnny's moving up in the world," said George.

John snorted a little and continued walking.

"What are you getting?" I asked, like I knew anything about guitars.

"A Rickenbacker."

"Ah!" I said. "German?"

"American." John cast me a cold look. "Like you."

I nodded. "So America makes good guitars, then?"

John didn't answer. He was walking quickly, like he was afraid the guitar wouldn't be there by the time he got to the store.

I'd wanted to tell them about the Carl Perkins song I'd heard at the record shop, and maybe get them to listen to it with me, but I could tell this wasn't the right time.

"Mind if I come along?" I asked.

Paul looked surprised and glanced at John, who shrugged. "Sure," said Paul.

We trudged for nearly fifteen minutes in near silence, crossing the street single file: John leading the way, his hands thrust in his pockets; Paul with a cigarette dangling from his hand, and George bringing up the rear.

"What do you think about Stuart leaving the band?" I finally asked John.

"I think he's a grown-up and he can do whatever he wants," he replied.

"But won't it change the whole chemistry of the band? And if you don't have a bass player—"

"Alan," he said sharply. "I'm buying a fucking guitar. I don't want to talk about it."

We grew silent again.

The Steinway Musikhaus was located on the far end of the Reeperbahn, and John heaved a sigh of relief when he saw the guitar was still in the window. I followed them inside.

It was funny, and a little endearing, to see John's eyes light up when the salesman handed him the instrument. "Whoa!" he exclaimed, cradling it in his arms like a newborn baby. "She's a beauty, in't she lads?"

They oohed and aahed like a couple of grandparents.

George filled me in on the details: it was a 1958 Rickenbacker 325, three-quarter size, natural honey finish, solid top, alder body and neck, with three pickups and an open top roller bridge. Each of the details he described in the same hushed, loving tone I'd heard my father use to describe the options that came on his new Buick LeSabre.

John noodled a bit on the guitar, a look of sheer wonder on his face. He handed it briefly to Paul, who did some noodling of his own (he seemed nearly as good playing a right-handed guitar as he was with his own lefty version) and then passed it over to George. "Smooth as silk," he pronounced. John quickly grabbed the guitar back and wrapped his arms around it like a jealous lover. "Gerroff!" he said. "She's mine!"

He paid full price for the instrument—you don't haggle with Germans—but managed to get it *ratenzahlung*, or on the installment plan: he slapped down some cash, signed a few papers, and walked out the door, the proud owner of the most wonderful guitar in the whole world.

He literally danced in the street with it, twirling it around in its canvas carrier like Fred Astaire with Ginger Rogers (if Ginger had been made of wood and wired for electricity), in and out of traffic, horns honking and people yelling, none of which could rouse the smitten young man from his reverie.

George suggested they find a hotel room. Paul pronounced them man and wife.

I asked John what he was going to do with his old guitar.

"I hadn't really thought about it," he said. "Paul, you want the Club Footy?"

"Sure I suppose," he said, "I'll give it a try."

John was a lot more talkative on the way home, singing (literally) the praises of the new instrument, crowing about how much better the band was going to sound and how he couldn't wait to play such-and-such on it, or go out and find it new songs.

"Hey, speaking of new songs," I said.

We were only two blocks away from the record store and, owing, perhaps, to John's euphoric mood, they agreed to come in and check out "Everybody's Trying to Be My Baby."

We attempted to squeeze into a listening booth, but with four of us and a guitar, it just wasn't going to happen.

"Alan," said John. "Wait outside, and keep hold of the Rickenbacker. I swear to God, if you let anything happen to it, I'll kill you."

I sat down on a chair, the new guitar across my lap, while the boys piled back into the booth.

I watched them as they listened to the record, but I couldn't tell if they liked it. Strange, I thought, that I would actually care, one way or another. It was just a dumb rock and roll song that I'd stumbled upon, but I felt like it was some kind of a test, like my audition—not for the band, but for "with the band."

They bobbed their heads a little bit to the beat, but I didn't see any smiles or enthusiastic glances. I could see them look out at me from time to time, almost suspiciously, reconciling the thought of me, an American square with a funny haircut, with music they were listening to.

They played the record again. Absently, I looked down at the guitar on my lap. I started to unzip the carrier so I could take a closer look, when I heard a loud thumping on the glass.

John opened the booth door and stuck his head out: "Take your fucking hands off it!" he yelled. "I will kill you!"

I zipped the bag shut again. So much for being "with the band."

They played the record for a third time and afterward had a long and very businesslike discussion. I tried to make out what they were saying. It was mostly between John and Paul, with an occasional interjection from George. It was like a team of doctors discussing a patient, debating a diagnosis, conferring over the best course of treatment—while I, the next of kin, looked on helplessly, desperate for a scrap of good news.

They played the record again, and this time I noticed George copying the lyrics on a piece of paper (which appeared to be the receipt for John's guitar). That had to be a good sign.

At long last they emerged.

"Well?" I asked.

"It's a decent song," said John. "Not a great song."

"Oh." I tried not to sound disappointed.

John continued. "I don't think it's a good song for me. And Paul didn't love it for himself either. But George here liked it, didn't he?"

"And you know," mock-whispered George. "It's so rare these egomaniacs let me sing anything at all."

"You're going to do that song?" I asked. "My song?"

"Yup," he said. "Thanks for finding it, Alan." And he shook my hand.

I was absolutely elated.

That night I got to hear the world premiere of "Everybody's Trying to Be My Baby," sung by George. I was actually nervous when he announced it, and feared for how it would go over with the audience.

Well they took some honey
(twang twang)
From a tree
(twang twang)
Dressed it up and they called it me

Lo and behold, twerpy little George did a great job. It didn't have as much hillbilly flavor as the Carl Perkins version, but it had an innocent charm. And the girls in the audience went wild. I'd never thought of George as being particularly handsome, but when he started singing about all the girls falling in love with him ("Fifty women knocking at my door"), the ladies in the audience clearly *believed* him. When he finished the song, he was greeted with wolf whistles and catcalls. He took a long bow, reveling in all the lusty attention.

Klaus, standing next to me, leaned in and shouted over the noise. "You see? Even a baby like him gets girls when he sings in a band." George, he told me, was younger than the others—he'd recently turned 17—and, unlike his oversexed bandmates, was most likely still a virgin.

Judging by the reaction to this new song, he won't have that problem for long. *You're welcome, George.*

And speaking of which—guess what else happened tonight? In the sexiest city on earth, on the smuttiest street in the raciest club with the horniest women in the whole universe, in the year of our Lord 1960, Alan Levy of Scarsdale,

New York, finally got some action.

Praise Jesus.

Astrid wasn't there, but I was having a nice time with Klaus—talking about girls, mostly, but also music and film and literature. Klaus has become a real friend over the past couple of months. If only the kids at my school were half as interesting.

Onstage, the boys were sounding better than ever, thanks in part to John's new guitar, which had a great sound. Even I could hear the difference. And you could just see how excited he was to be playing it, and how the rest of the band drew from that energy.

I couldn't help but notice—and Klaus and I spoke of it often—how much they'd improved, even in the couple of months that I'd been listening (and even with Stu on his way out). They've gotten tighter, and more confident, and more nuanced as musicians. (I know, it's hard to imagine rock and roll music being nuanced, but if you hear it enough times, it actually is.)

Paul announced that they had a special guest vocalist for the next song, and a burly German man waddled up to the stage. He grabbed the microphone and sang:

For Goodness sake,
I've got zie hippy hippy shake

"Who is he?" I asked.

"He's a gangster," said Klaus. "A real gangster. They say he kills people."

"And they let him sing with the band?"

"Wouldn't you?" Klaus asked.

We watched him sing for a few moments, drunk and

completely off-key, stumbling around the stage, his shirt stained with sweat.

"And now," said Klaus, "he will probably get all the girls, too."

"Jesus, we've got to form a band," I said.

Just then, I felt a tap on my shoulder. "Hey American, you want to dance?"

She looked familiar, but I couldn't place her. She was beautiful, though, with long, dark hair. She wore a short skirt and fishnet stockings. I said yes.

As we made our way onto the floor, I asked how she knew I was American.

"Everybody here knows you," she said. "You're friends with the Beatles, aren't you?"

"Yes," I said. "Actually, I am."

Sometimes it's good to be with the band.

We danced for three straight songs. She was a fabulous dancer, and even a little more polished in her movements than Astrid. Not quite as playful, but more in control, and more elegant. And the way she looked at me! Very intense and straight in the eye, though always with a coy little smile. It wasn't like we were laughing together and playing and having fun—it was more like a magnetic attraction.

She told me her name was Bettina.

After the third dance I bought her a drink. She was a model, she told me, but also studying fashion design at the *Meisterschule,* which is where Astrid studied. It turned out the two girls were old friends. She was surprised, however, to hear that Astrid was now engaged to Stuart. "Marrying a musician," she said. "That's not something good girls do."

"I thought all girls had a thing for musicians."

She smiled and took a sip of her drink. "I like your hair,"

she said. She reached out to touch it. "May I?"

I don't know why, but I found that wildly erotic, the fact that she asked.

"Please do," I said.

She ran her hand through my French Cut. In a manner I could only describe as *casually sensual*. "Mm, that's very nice," she said. "May I do it again?"

I gulped down the rest of my beer and we hit the dance floor for a slow song. We held each other close and moved our hands over each other's bodies with an ease that felt both natural and unexpectedly quick. The stroking of my hair, perhaps, had broken the ice, and now we both felt quite free to explore—at least with our hands, and at least confining ourselves to backs, shoulders, torsos, and, of course, our respective haircuts. Hers was soft and delightful; she seemed to feel the same way about mine.

We had a few more drinks and danced a few more fast songs. I felt myself getting hotter and hotter. I'm quite sure that my face was turning red, and was now just another in a sea of red faces, churning and overheating in the sexual cauldron of the Kaiserkeller.

When the next slow song came on (Stuart's version of "Love Me Tender"), Bettina and I wasted no time. Our tight bear hug of a dance turned immediately into a kiss—not a long and lingering kiss, but a short kiss followed by another short kiss, as if to confirm the first one. We finished the dance in silence, feeling the full effect of what we had just started, hardly even moving at all, our foreheads pressed against each other.

"Do you want to go somewhere else?" she whispered. Her English was very good.

Yes, I did.

I grabbed my coat and said goodbye to Klaus, who shot me a wink. I asked Bettina to just give me one quick moment—I was dying to pee. I gave her a kiss on the lips for insurance.

I sprinted—yes, sprinted—into the bathroom, desperate to empty my bladder as fast as I possibly could, but it took a maddeningly long time for my erection to subside.

As I stood there, John sidled up next to me.

"I see you've met Bettina," he drawled.

"Yes," I said. "Oh my God is she beautiful."

"Mmm," he said. "And you know she's a prostitute."

I immediately stopped peeing. And stared straight ahead.

John must have seen the broken look on my face. "Don't worry about it," he said. "She's clean. She's approved."

I shook my head, not understanding.

"All the whores here get inspected by the city. They get a certificate saying they're clean. A ticket to ride. So cheer up. At least you won't get the clap." He patted me on the back and left.

I stood for a moment, staring forward, penis in hand, trying to make sense of this latest absurdity. Trying to understand how one of the great nights of my life had suddenly come crashing down around me in a big, ugly, sleazy mess. (Not just a whore, mind you, but a city-certified, tested-and-approved whore.)

I briefly considered running away. Just making a break for the door and never looking back. Writing off the whole thing as a simple, albeit tragic, mistake that I would one day laugh about.

But then I thought about the new Alan, and all the brave, adventurous things he was now capable of. Maybe this was possible, too. Maybe going to Hamburg and having sex with a prostitute was like going to Paris and eating snails: mildly distasteful at first, but ultimately an acquired taste. I remembered Suzy telling me (how ironic that it would be Suzy) about the first time she ate snails in Paris: how she resisted at first, and felt a small twinge of revulsion, but then settled in and enjoyed them thoroughly. And even ordered a second helping.

I splashed some cold water in my face and looked in the mirror. I discovered a long time ago that, when you have a tough decision to make, it helps to look at yourself in a mirror, and state it, out loud, in the form of a question. When you're looking deep into your own eyes, it's hard to tell a lie. "Is this something I want to do?" I asked. The answer came quickly: *Yes*.

Bettina is a beautiful girl. She just happens to charge money for an activity that I'd always assumed was free. (For me, anyway, because, you know, I'm sensitive.) Besides, prostitution is perfectly legal in Hamburg. And thanks to my parents' generosity, I have a little extra cash hanging around "to buy myself something special." How proud they would be.

And let's face it, I'm not such a good little boy anymore, am I? I got kicked out of school. For "public drunkenness." If I'm going to be a juvenile delinquent, I might as well enjoy some of the perks.

I marched out of the bathroom. Bettina grabbed my arm and we walked out the door, Jurgen and the entire band leering.

"Shall we go to your place?" she said.

"Sure," I said, although all I could think was the word *prostitute*.

It was only three blocks to the Kino, and we passed it making small talk about the weather and other pointless things. At the club, we could barely keep our hands off of each other. Now we weren't touching at all, not even holding hands, just trudging through the cold, side by side. When we got to the front door, she stopped me.

"Are you all right?" she asked.

"Of course." I forced a smile. And wondered when would be the right time to ask *how much?*

"Are you sure?"

"Yes," I said. "Absolutely." There was a brief pause that hung in the air just long enough to make it crystal clear that I wasn't so sure about this at all.

She seem puzzled, and even a little bit hurt.

"Look," I said. "I've never done this before."

"You've never been with a girl?" she asked in an *isn't-that-adorable* sort of way.

"No," I said. "With a . . ."

"With a what?"

"With . . . paying for it."

She looked at me, still confused, and then burst out laughing. "You think I am a prostitute?"

"Aren't you?" I said.

"Why would you think I'm a prostitute? Do I look like a prostitute?"

"No!" I said. "Somebody told me."

"Who?"

"John. You know, from the band."

"John. The funny one? The one who is always making jokes?"

The world was spinning again. "So . . ." She smiled and wrapped her arms around me. "Alan," she said, "I came home with you because I think you're cute. And I think you're a nice guy. And I *really* like your hair." She ran her hand over it again, this time grabbing a fistful and pulling my head right toward her open mouth. We kissed again. Long and lingering this time.

"No charge," she whispered.

I thanked her.

"If you're a good little boy," she purred, "I might even buy you breakfast."

November 12
per Luftpost

Dear Artie,

Have you ever been with a girl who was into biting?

And not just a nibble on the ear, or a playful tug at the bottom of your lip. I mean something that's intended to cause pain or maybe even to draw blood?

Here's the reason I ask.

So last night, I finally got to taste a little sample of Hamburg's most famous delicacy: cheap and easy sex. It's been a long time coming. For almost three months, I've been surrounded—seeing it, hearing it, smelling it. The whole city feels like an orgy, and it's been very frustrating to stand on the sidelines for so long, full of resentment and disdain for all the revelers at the party getting their rocks off on a regular basis. (And then having to chase after this photographer girl for months and get nothing out of it except a couple of warm-and-caring hugs.)

Well, all that ended last night. As we used to say on the softball team, I finally busted out of my slump. Her name is Bettina, and she's beautiful. We met at the club and, after a night of hot and sexy dancing, we went back to my place to close the deal.

And it was fantastic. I mean, really exciting and dramatic—which is maybe just how Europeans do it, since they're not burdened by our nagging American puritanism (which, in my limited experience, usually announces itself in awkwardness, begging, and bungled apologies afterward).

There were no apologies, no uncertainty, and no caution:

just four sheets to the wind. It was fast, and loud, and absolutely amazing. I don't know if I'm the sort of person who can open myself completely to casual sex with someone I barely know—I'm a little old-fashioned that way in that I prefer at least the illusion of falling in love—but this was definitely a step in the right direction. I honestly felt I was on the brink of enjoying sex just for the sake of sex, the way sailors and sluts and Italians do. A purely sensual experience, cut off from all the guilt and shame that I normally feel, and which, I would have to assume, was put there by my mother. I was, for maybe the first time in my life, basking in the glow of pure pleasure.

Until I felt the first bite. It was on my neck, like a vampire. It jolted me a little, but I didn't say anything. We fooled around some more, and then I felt another bite on my chest. I must have made a little noise, like a yelp, because Bettina started to laugh, and bit me again. And the more I yelped, the more she kept biting—my lip, my thigh, my nipple. Eventually I told her to stop, and she did. She even apologized. But I get the sense that if I want to continue having sex with this girl, I'm going to need a box of Band-Aids. A big box.

Is this something I should be worried about? Is this casual, European-style sex play? Or the sign of a deeply demented individual? Since I probably won't have time to wait for your reply, please tell the authorities—if they find me butchered to death, or half-eaten in my depressing Hamburg apartment—that at least I died happy.

Yours Truly,
The Delicious Alan

November 13

Bettina didn't stay the whole night. She doesn't strike me as a let's-stay-in-bed-and-cuddle-all-morning kind of girl. She was there for the sex, and, once finished, she was done with me and on to the next. A little businesslike, perhaps; but not *as* businesslike as I'd been led to believe.

I think she likes me, though. She gave me a big kiss on her way out and left me her phone number. The nice thing about my situation, though, is that if I want to see her again, all I have to do is show up at the Kaiserkeller with my new haircut. It's a pretty good bet that I can lather, rinse, and repeat. That's how it seems to work here in Hamburg.

As I lay in bed, stretching like a cat, basking in afterglow and the musky scent of my bed linens, I started feeling better about my life. Yes, my academic career seems uncertain. Yes, I'll probably get kicked out of the Hamburg program for good—and at some point I'll have to tell Columbia about it, and hope that they take me back.

But there are also some positives . . .

I'm young. I'm unencumbered. And I'm living down the street from an establishment, open to the public, that I've come to believe is one of the finest sex laboratories in the world.

I will study the ways of sexual technique—and God knows it's a wide-ranging field, with as many methodologies are there are people on earth. Hamburg is a port city, so I imagine the community is rich in the cross-currents of erotica; a sexual melting pot, if you will, with skills and perversions gathered from the four corners of the earth. And I will learn as many of these as I possibly can. This will become my field of study.

For if sex is a science—quantifiable and empirically tested—it's also an art. I hope that, as I continue to have sex with a wide variety of partners, they will help me to see the human spirit more clearly, in all its variation. I hope that, by getting to know more and more women in the carnal sense, I will come to know better how they think, how they feel, and how they love.

Jesus, I'm going to fuck my brains out.

I lazed around in bed for most of the morning, high on endorphins and thinking about my future. Eventually, I got up and wrote a letter to Artie. (Somebody has to be witness to my glorious night.) When I finished that, I picked up Rilke again, intending to read the fourth and fifth letters (my favorites) but I was just too wired up, too intoxicated with thoughts of sex, past and future. I wanted to talk about it. My mind was spinning.

When I heard some movement coming from my neighbors' room, I threw on some pants and knocked on their door.

Pete answered, looking ragged and hung over.

"Good morning," I said. "May I speak to John, please?"

Pete looked like he didn't understand the question.

"It's a personal matter," I added.

Pete continued to appear confused. I wondered just how long he would stand there, but then John appeared at his side, even more filthy and bedraggled.

"Hello, neighbor," he drawled.

"Bettina," I said, with the indignation of someone who'd just had the best sex of his life, "is not a prostitute."

"Yeah, I know," he said.

"Then why did you tell me she was?"

"Just fucking with you, mate. No hard feelings."

"It just so happens," I continued, "that she and I had a wonderful night together. Passionate and amazing."

John nodded. "Did she bite you?"

"Not . . . that I remember," I sputtered.

He put on his glasses and had a closer look at my neck. Like a beaten wife, I instinctively covered the mark. "Maybe just a little," I said.

"Do you fancy it?" he said. "The biting, I mean."

"Well," I cleared my throat. "It's different, I suppose."

"Mm." John studied my face.

"But everything else about it was really, really normal."

"Mm," he nodded. "You like it normal, do you?"

"I don't mean *normal,*" I said. "I mean amazing. Mind-blowing!"

He nodded again. "Good for you, mate." He turned into the room. "You hear that, lads? Alan here had it off with Bettina, and she blew his mind."

I heard low murmurs of approval: "jolly good," "very impressive," "top hole."

"She's a lovely girl," said George. "We call her The Piranha."

"By the way," John said, "your hair looks ridiculous."

He slouched back into the room.

"Hey John," I said, and got to the real purpose of my visit. "Have you sold your guitar yet?"

"No," he said. "Why?"

"Because I'd like to buy it."

He thought I was joking at first, or maybe he wrote it off to my sexual hangover and feelings of empowerment (which may have been valid). But when I offered to pay him two hundred marks on the spot—thanks, Mom and Dad—I got his attention.

"Meet me in the café," he said, "and we'll talk about it."

When he showed up at the Moller fifteen minutes later, Paul was with him. It was a business discussion, I suppose, and they had a dead-serious attitude. I felt like I was asking for their daughter's hand in marriage.

"Why do you want to buy a guitar?" John asked, looking suspicious.

"I want to learn how to play," I said. "It looks like fun."

They exchanged a skeptical look.

"Have you ever played one before?" asked Paul.

I told them about my Uncle Ernie, who played in the swing band and showed me a few guitar chords when I was younger.

"What's the point of it?" asked John. "You want to join a band?"

"Maybe," I said.

The truth is, I'd been thinking about it a lot. I'd had a few conversations with Klaus on the subject, and I found my mind returning to the idea often, now that I have more free time on my hands. "And anyway," I said, "it sounds like your band is about to have a vacancy."

They both laughed. "I told you that's what this was about," said Paul.

"Is that so crazy?" I asked. Impulsive, maybe, but when you're an artist you have to trust your impulses. "You said the group was missing a couple of elements. What if one of them was me?"

"You don't even know how to play." Paul was still laughing.

"I can learn," I said. "Stuart learned. And not all that well, from what I can hear."

I saw a flash of anger cross John's face, but only for a moment. "Stuart," he said, dead-calm, "is a bloody genius. I like having geniuses in my band."

"Are you a genius, Alan?" asked Paul, raising his loopy eyebrow.

"I don't know," I said, with Ivy League confidence. "Who is to say?"

John smiled and leaned back in his chair. "Do they think you're a genius at that fancy German school of yours?"

"That fancy German school," I said, "is full of fucking idiots."

This amused them. I told them about how Wensinger had me expelled from the program (a fact I haven't mentioned yet to my parents). My rebel-outlaw status seemed to amuse them even more, and I found myself spilling the whole sordid tale, which was a relief. I explained about the academic hearing, where I can ask to get reinstated.

"Why would you go begging to those Nazi fucks?" said John. "What's the point of doing something if you hate it?"

I told them I hadn't decided yet.

"Then I'm deciding for you," said John. "I've decided you should grow some balls."

"The point is," I said, "I've got some free time, and I'd like to take up the guitar."

"Mmm," said John, unconvinced. "And you may be a genius."

Which brought me to Crazy Thought Number Two.

"Well, you know I'm a poet, right?" I said. "Maybe I could write something for you."

This made them laugh again. "Now you're gonna write bloody songs, too?" said John. "Like Chuck Berry?"

"Why not?" I said. "Have you guys ever thought about writing your own material?"

"No," said John.

"Yes," said Paul. "We've written dozens. Lennon-McCartney originals."

"But they're all bloody crap," said John.

"Oh, the boy's too modest," said Paul. "Some of them aren't bad at all."

"Nobody wants to hear original stuff," said John. "They want to hear the hits. They want to dance. Nobody's gonna dance to our stuff, and they sure as shit won't dance to yours."

"Okay," I said. "I'm just offering. And I'm willing to pay cash for the guitar."

John folded his arms. "Tell you what," he said. "Show me one of your poems. If I like it, I'll sell you the guitar."

We all left the café together.

It's not often that people ask to read your poems. (Maybe if you're T. S. Eliot, but even then, I doubt it.) I'm always flattered when people do, because reading should be a pleasure, not an obligation.

But my experience with Wensinger left a sour taste in my mouth. I don't for a minute believe any of the things he said about my poem or my ability as a poet, because the opinion of Columbia University must surely rate higher than that of some third-rate poet in the provinces of Germany. But his comments stung. And there have been times in the past few days when I've questioned nearly everything about myself and my talent—or lack thereof.

Ultimately, I decided there was no harm showing my writing to John, because he's just a musician. (Though, in fairness, he does seem to have an interest in words, and chooses his own words carefully, if sometimes a little aggressively.) I had another copy of "Locations" in one of my notebooks. I still believe it's my best poem to date, and everybody who's read it—except for Wensinger—has been impressed.

John answered when I knocked. I handed him the two sheets of paper. He already had his glasses on, and studied the title.

"'Lotions,'" he drawled.

"'Locations,'" I said, already annoyed.

He scowled. "I'm not gonna read it with you standing right in front of me."

I slipped back into my room and padded around, tidying things up and folding some of my clothes. I put my ear to the wall at one point, just to make sure there was no laughing. There wasn't.

Five minutes later, John knocked.

He held out the poem. "It's crap," he said.

I grabbed the paper. "Well, I think you're wrong."

John squinted, looking almost apologetic. "I can't help it," he said. "I'm not gonna lie. It just doesn't do anything for me."

"Well, it was good enough for the awards committee at Columbia University," I sniffed.

"Well," said John, "it's possible they're a bunch of fucking idiots, too, don't you think?"

I tried to contain myself. There was no reason to think that this yob would appreciate good poetry, not when his favorite poet was Chuck Berry. I put on my haughtiest, most New York Literati voice. "May I ask, my dear boy, what you didn't like about the poem?"

He shrugged. "It's the language. It's just too much." He took the poem and read the first stanza:

There are many locations
Which shall remain with me
For the duration of my existence.
And yet some have transfigured . . .

"You don't like that?" I asked, attempting to sound condescending.

"Why do you use such big words?" he said. "Why don't you just say, like, *There are places I'll remember*?"

"Well, I hardly think—"

"*—all my life. Though some have*—what does 'transfigured' mean?"

"Changed."

"*Though some have changed.* What's wrong with that?"

"That's ridiculous." I would never rewrite someone's poem, not right to their face. Even if I don't *like* a person's work, I still respect it, and I respect the artist who created it. That's what a gentleman does.

"Why don't you say what you mean?" John didn't sound insulting or even critical, just curious. "Why do you dress it up in all that pretentious shit?"

I sniffed again. "Words, my dear boy, are a form of music in and of themselves."

John immediately went into his retarded cripple act. "Oh is they? Gaaaahhhh!"

"I'm sorry you didn't like it," I said, summoning all the well-bred smugness I could muster. "To each his own, I suppose."

I tried to shut the door but he stopped me. "Alan," he said. "I like the fact that you write poems. It takes guts to even try it, you know? A lot of people go their whole lives and never try anything."

"Perhaps," I said.

"You can have the guitar."

I paused. "Well I'm not sure I still want it."

"I'll tell you what," said John. "You can have the guitar, if I can have this." He held up the poem.

"You want my crap poem?"

"Yeah," he said. "And two hundred marks. In cash. Let's not forget about that."

November 14

I took delivery of John's guitar right after our conversation. He didn't include a carrying case, which is fine, since I'm not ready to play it in public. I don't have an amplifier, either, which is potentially a bigger problem. I've learned that without an amp, an electric guitar just sounds thin and twangy. But at least it sounds like music, and the boys assured me that an amp is completely unnecessary when learning to play. (I wonder if they're concerned about the prospect of loud music coming from next door. I suppose I can't blame them for that.)

It's a handsome instrument. And heavier than I would have thought. Here are the specs (as provided by George, who seems to be the guitar nut of the group): a Hofner Club 40 (hence the nickname "Club Footy"), single-cutaway hollowbody with a spruce top, maple back and sides, adjustable floating bridge, and trapeze tailpiece, with a solitary pickup and rosewood fingerboard. I have no idea what any of that means.

On the inside of the hollowed-out body is a sticker that reads, *Guaranteed not to split*.

Maybe not as fancy as I thought.

I'll admit that I had a little buyer's remorse at first. Two hundred marks for a guitar that I don't even know how to play. Probably not the wisest investment I've ever made, but that's exactly what I like about it.

I like holding the guitar. I like the way it feels. It seems a little dangerous, like a rifle or an axe. I like swatting at the strings, and running my fingers up and down on the frets.

And I like the idea of a writer being proficient with

a musical instrument. Isn't poetry all about rhythm and phrasing, the rising and falling of sound and expectation? I've always had a vision of Thomas Jefferson taking a break from his latest draft, noodling around on his violin while he worked out some bit of phrasing in his head: "inalienable rights? . . . *Un*alienable rights?"

I found a book of guitar chords and some basic technique at the library. I don't actually have a Hamburg library card, so let's just say I borrowed it on my own. (Jesus, what a rebel I've become!) I sat down to fiddle around with my new toy and learn a few chords, maybe a song or two, and by the time I looked up, it was nearly 6 o'clock and my fingertips were practically bleeding. (Woody Guthrie famously had a sign on his guitar that read, "This machine kills fascists." I think mine will read, "This machine kills time.")

I got to the club early, as I was in the mood to hear some music. The boys had just started and they didn't have a ton of energy, but for my purposes, that was perfect. It was easier for me to watch their fingers and figure out what they were doing. I didn't recognize a whole lot. A couple of chords here and there (and also what I perceived to be bar chords, which I have yet to master) but for the most part, they might as well be playing a different instrument. Very nimble and fluid, not clunky and hesitant like me. I wonder how much time it will take for me to get good. Is it possible that I'm a musical prodigy and I've just never known it?

Astrid came in with her group at around 10, and I was glad to see her. She seemed very happy, with that sparkle of joy and optimism that so often comes with a brand-new engagement ring.

She also pointed out that Stuart now had the same haircut as I did.

He no longer looked like James Dean, but with his high cheekbones and his steely eyes now partly eclipsed by his new bangs, he looked even more mysterious and artsy.

And almost as girly as me.

"John has been teasing him about it all day," said Astrid. "You would not believe the names! But I think he is jealous. All the girls like Stuart even more now."

You've got to hand it to Astrid. She gets things done. I wonder how many other men in this town will end up jumping off the Brooklyn Bridge just because Astrid told them to.

She told me Stuart had now officially moved into her house: even though he's been living there more or less constantly for the past few months, now it's official and fully sanctioned by her mother, who has come to *adore* her future son-in-law. Stuart's family, on the other hand, does not approve of their boy marrying a German, and she sees some potential hard times ahead in dealing with "the bloody English."

As I watched Astrid setting forth the rest of her life to me, shouting it over the loud music, big and expressive with her hand gestures, elegant and yet adorably awkward, I realized I'm not over her yet, and I probably never will be. I know I've lost her. She's in love with another guy, and those things happen. You move on. Or maybe you never do.

The love of Rilke's life, Lou Andreas-Salomé, was a married woman, and yet they remained close (and not in a *just-friends* kind of way) for the rest of his life. Is such a thing possible with me and Mrs. Stuart Sutcliffe? At some point I will be going back to America, and I hardly see Stuart or Astrid living anywhere except Hamburg or Liverpool. But life has a way of unfolding in strange and unexpected ways, especially in matters of the heart. Never say never, I suppose.

I had a nice conversation with Klaus. When I told him about buying John's guitar he told me that he had recently bought a secondhand bass.

"The bass?" I said. "Isn't that the instrument nobody wants to play?"

"I think it is easier than the guitar," he said. "I think it will take me less time to get good at it." We talked some more about forming our own band, and what it would take, and how much time we'd have to put into it; all of which sounded like great fun. Even just *talking* about forming a band felt fun, and a little dangerous, even though I'd been playing the guitar for exactly two days.

We were joined at our table by another musician, who I recognized as being part of Rory Storm's band.

"Alan," said Klaus, "this is Ringo."

Ringo wore a bright red suit, like the rest of Rory's group, with a matching tie and handkerchief. Onstage, they looked like a bunch of magicians at a seaside resort. The Hurricanes struck me as more professional than the Beatles, but not necessarily in a good way. They performed little dance steps with their songs, and Rory had some choreographed moves to go with his slick and shameless mugging, all of which seemed a little cheesy. (And judging by the reaction of the Kaiserkeller crowds, they weren't as popular as my vulgar, freewheeling neighbors.)

Ringo seemed nice enough, though.

Klaus and I told him about our band, and shared some of the names we were considering: Rommel and the Panzer Division, Anne Frank and the Hideaways, All Quiet and the Western Front . . .

"What I hear," said Ringo, "is both you lads want to join the Beatles."

Klaus and I looked at each other. "Who told you that?" I asked.

"Paul," Ringo answered, in that same peculiar accent as the rest of them.

"That's ridiculous," I answered. "I can barely play."

"*Ja,* me too," said Klaus. "Paul really thinks that?"

Ringo shrugged. "He said as soon as you both found out about Stu leaving the band, you suddenly got interested in playing instruments."

"That's just not true," I said. I was lying, of course; I'd been thinking about that possibility for a while now, and every time I played my guitar.

"Okay." Ringo shrugged and turned away to listen to the music.

"I mean, if they *asked* me to join the band," I said, "that would be one thing . . ."

"Alan," said Klaus. "I don't think they will ask you."

"Well, I don't think they'd ask you, either," I said, pointedly.

"I understand that." Klaus looked irritated.

"Ringo," I said. "How does somebody get asked to join somebody else's band? I mean, what would it take?"

Ringo took a sip of his beer. "You have to be good," he said. "You have to be really good. And of course you have to get along with everyone. That's very important. A band spends a lot of time with each other. If you don't enjoy being with the other fellas, it's a bloody slog. Rehearsing is a drag, playing is a drag. You'll never get better, and you'll never make any money, if you don't enjoy bein' in the band."

Klaus and I nodded.

"Is that how it happened with you and Rory?" asked Klaus.

"I'll tell you a secret, lads," said Ringo. "You want to know why they hired me?" He shot a stealthy look down at his hands and wiggled all ten of his fingers. *"It's because of me rings."*

Everybody's got a gimmick.

Onstage, the boys were ripping into one of Paul's biggest piano shout-songs: "Long Tall Sally."

I'm gonna tell Aunt Mary 'bout Uncle John
He said he had the misery but he got a lot of fun
Now baby, yeah-eah baby

This, I'd come to learn, was the traditional last song of their set, so Rory and Ringo would be taking over soon. Astrid tapped me on the shoulder.

"During the break," she said, "we're all going over to the Star Club. You want to come with?"

It still amazed me that, in addition to their six-hour marathons at the Kaiserkeller, the boys spent a good portion of their break time performing at another nightclub. The Star Club, I understand, is a fancier venue that pays its performers better.

Klaus agreed to go, but I declined. I'm still a little uneasy around Stuart, and I was getting comfortable at the grimy little Kaiserkeller. I didn't want to miss any of the action.

Sure enough, just as the boys and their inner circle walked out the door, I saw three familiar faces: Renate, Helga, and Gitta—my little blond triplets.

I played it cool. I watched Rory do his shtick, and before long, I felt a hand on my back.

"*Hallo* Alan!" It was Renate. She was looking far better than when I saw her passed out with her face in the ashtray. "What have you done with your hair?"

"Do you like it?" I shouted.

"*Ja,* it's fantastic!" She ran her hand through it. What is it about this haircut? Women can't keep their hands off it.

We danced to Rory and the Hurricanes for a while, and I bought her a couple of beers. I knew that with beer it would take her that much longer get drunk and pass out, which I felt was in her best interest as well as mine.

At 11:30 on the dot, the boys came back from the Star Club, followed by Astrid and her friends. As Renate and I danced, John put his hand on my shoulder. "He's a good lad, this one," he said to Renate. She beamed, and I shrugged modestly.

George patted me on the shoulder as well. "In America, he's the King of Sex." Renate giggled. I blushed.

"You must be very good friends," she said.

"Yeah, we give each other crap all the time," I said.

I could tell she didn't understand the expression meant.

"Did you notice that Stuart and I have the same haircut?"

Renate's mouth dropped open, and she smiled widely. "Wow!" she said. "Stuart is my favorite!"

We continued to dance and she continued to smile, but I got the distinct impression she was thinking about Stuart.

I guess I'm okay with that.

During our first slow song together, our hands started to wander, and before the song was over we decided to go back to my place. (It's finally beginning to dawn on me: if you come right out and *ask* a girl if she wants to have sex, very often the answer will be yes. Why has nobody told me this before?)

I gathered our coats and Renate asked if I would get her a schnapps for the road. I obliged reluctantly and made sure to take a large sip before handing it over. If anybody's going to black out tonight, it'll be me.

When we got outside, Renate stopped and gave me a

serious look.

"Everything okay?" I said.

"Alan," she said. "I am a little bit embarrassed to ask this."

My mind reeled. Yes I'm getting more comfortable with casual sex, but it's still pretty mysterious and terrifying.

"And I hope you don't think it's strange of me . . ."

Dear God, what?

She came so close that our noses were practically touching. "Could my friends come with us?"

November 14
per Luftpost

Dear Artie,

Have you ever heard of something called a "four-way"?

I'm not sure there is such a thing, maybe I'm making it up; maybe I'm a pioneer in this particular field. I only know that, in the words of Lou Gehrig, I consider myself the luckiest man on the face of the earth.

I won't even tell you the details, Artie. That would be boastful and vain and completely disrespectful of the women involved. I'm better than that.

And whatever I may have said about the Germans, I will say this. They are a generous people. They can be very welcoming, in the right circumstances, especially when several are being convivial at the same time.

Or maybe it's just the women. There has to be some weird psychology going on with a generation of German girls who watched their fathers declare war on the world and march humanity into the gas chambers. Maybe they all got so angry and disillusioned that they're subconsciously driven to do everything they can to piss off their fathers. Maybe everything I'm seeing here in Hamburg—and enjoying, to the point of exhaustion—is just one big *Mein Papa* Issue.

Here's hoping I can help them work things out.

Your pal,
The King of Sex

November 14

Hamburg (cont'd)

Dead bodies stacked like firewood
Remain untouched, unwanted even by flame.
Now they begin to rot,
The slow decay of flesh, the creeping tide
Of death upon death upon more death

Oh, fuck this.

November 19

I've taken a few days off from writing. And for that I apologize. Writing is all about discipline, and I've been delinquent—in more ways than one. It feels good to get pen back to paper, even if it's only to write about myself. The idea of working on my poem cycle, on the other hand, seems completely futile. I'm just not in the mood.

Frankly, I've just been too exhausted. My nights at the club are fun, no question, but they are long and wearying affairs. I'm not used to drinking this much, and I'm not used to dancing this much. I'm also not used to—well, all the rest.

It's almost not a challenge anymore. The night before last, my old friend Bettina wandered into the bar and was happy to see me. Suffice it to say that we picked up pretty much where we left off—and, yes, there was more biting.

(We have a lot of fun together, but I suspect she's an angry person on some level. What else would drive you to bite someone during an act of physical intimacy? Sado-masochism? A tooth fetish? Was she bitten as a child? I'd like to understand where it comes from, but the scars are unsightly and I have only so many layers of skin.)

I also made the mistake of getting reacquainted with Preludin. It's been very helpful as far as staying up late, and I think it probably helps my sexual performance—as well as my ability to satisfy more than one partner simultaneously. It's also become readily available, as I get more and more friendly with the support staff at the Kaiserkeller. Rosa, the woman who tends the restroom, is happy to supply me—as long as I'm willing to pay a minimal price and ogle at the pictures of her Rottweiler, Wolfie, who is the great love of her life. She supplies the members of both bands as well, dispensing motherly advice along with drugs and condoms, like the kind of den mother you wish you'd had in the Boy Scouts.

But the Preludin boost certainly comes at a cost. My hangovers are wretched affairs. I feel it in my head, and in my guts. My stomach is full of acid and I frequently get the taste of bile—or something worse—at the back of my throat. It's pretty unpleasant, but at least it doesn't last the whole day. By late afternoon I start to feel awake, and I'm ready to go out and start the whole parade all over again.

I hope I'm not becoming an alcoholic. And/or a drug addict. I realize that I'm showing some of the classic signs, and my behavior would probably set off any number of alarms at a sanitarium. But I have faith in myself. I don't see my life playing out in that manner, as a self-destructive artist who drinks himself to death in his filthy garret—or the filthy storage room of a low-end German cinema (even though that does have a nice ring to it and would probably help to sell books).

I don't know if I have the discipline to be an alcoholic. Maybe discipline isn't the right word: maybe *torment*? On some level, I think, you've got to be profoundly unhappy, and at least a little suicidal. Thankfully, I've had no more thoughts about suicide (and I've stopped reading that depressing Goethe book). What I'm having right now, I think, is merely a short fling with moral depravity.

If there's any positive that has come out of all this, it's my guitar-playing. It turns out that lying in bed while noodling on a guitar is a perfect activity when you're hung over. It takes concentration, but not much exertion. And it's soothing. It actually makes my headaches feel better. The vibration of the strings gently nudges my brain cells into reflection, meditation, introspection. I've spent countless hours over the past few days watching shadows on the wall while I practice chords and chord progressions. My playing gets better all the time.

One of my guitar books has the chords for a bunch of Broadway songs, and I've learned how to play "Old Man River," which I've always thought was beautiful. I don't actually sing along with it, because that would be a travesty: it sounds a lot prettier when I just hum the melody, or whistle. I'm also attempting to learn "Till There Was You" from *The Music Man*, which I know from our production at Columbia, but the chords are difficult. Maybe I'll suggest that one to my neighbors, too.

And what am I thinking about during these long hours of musical reflection? My future, I suppose. It doesn't seem quite as clear as it once did. I don't know if I want to be a college student anymore. I'm not even sure if I want to be a poet.

My dad once told me, when you're choosing a career, stop and consider what second place looks like. At the time, I thought it was horrible advice. What a depressing way to live your life—thinking about your future only in terms of failure? And letting the fear of failure make your decisions for you? Why not think about winning instead, and let that be your motivation?

But I have to confess that now, when I look at Herr Wensinger, I begin to see what second place looks like for a poet: teaching at a backwater college, growing old and bitter, fucking with the lives of young people just to alleviate the boredom. God help me if I end up like that.

So what am I interested in? At the moment, all I can think about is music and sex. Both of them perfectly pleasant. But as a future? As a job? Something I want to pour all my passion and energy and years of life into? I just don't know.

I finally dragged myself out of bed and down to the Moller for breakfast. I was surprised to see John there by himself. He always seems to have a crowd around him, whether it's his bandmates or a gaggle of fans: he's one of those people who can always find an audience.

"Mind if I sit down?" I asked.

He squinted up at me and grunted. I took that as a yes. He was reading the English newspaper and slurping corn flakes from a giant bowl of milk.

"I'm enjoying the guitar," I offered.

"Good," he said.

"Are you happy with yours? The new one?"

"Yes," he murmured, with mock solemnity, and took another slurp of his milk, a raspy stream of bubbles straight from the bowl.

"You know where I can really hear the difference?" I said. "On 'Sweet Little Sixteen.' It sounds so much fuller and richer with the Rickenbacker, don't you think?"

He put his spoon down. "You know, I don't understand you, Alan," he said. "Why you're so interested in music all of a sudden when you have so little respect for it."

"That's not true," I said. "I like music very much."

"But you don't respect it. Not the way you respect poetry."

"Poetry," I said, "is an art form."

"And music isn't?"

We discussed the relative merits of poetry versus music, which led in turn to the merits of Mozart versus Elvis Presley.

"My dear boy," I said, graciously. "Do you honestly think that Elvis Presley is comparable in any way to Mozart or Beethoven?"

"Alan," he said, "this is where I think you're very limited. I think you've got this notion that some things are big and important because people at your fancy school tell you they're big and important. And you learn about these great artists, only they're all dead. You've got to open up your mind. It doesn't matter if music is big or little, if it's a hundred instruments or three. It's how it makes you feel. Right? That's what matters. When we play the Elvis songs, 'Love Me Tender,' they cry their fucking eyes out. And they don't even understand the words! How do you explain that? Something in the music touches you."

"I'm sorry," I said. "Art—great art—stands the test of time. I don't see Elvis holding up for hundreds of years the way Mozart has."

"Well, you're wrong. Someday they'll teach Elvis at that wanking school of yours."

"Huh!" I snorted. "Maybe they'll teach the Beatles, too." I immediately felt bad that I said that. It wasn't my intention to make fun of his band, merely to make a point.

John didn't seem to take it personally. "Stuart used to be like you," he said. "Very fancy. Artist with a capital A, all that. But Stuart lives with his eyes open. He learns from everything and everybody, and that's why he keeps growing as an artist. He's always adding something to the canvas, you know? He may not be the best musician ever, but he never stops bringing in new ideas."

"Yeah," I said. "And now he's leaving the band."

"Yeah, maybe," John said. "That's his choice." He stared out the window, his eyes heavy. I hadn't considered how difficult it must be for the leader of a band to lose a member of the band, especially one he admires so much. It must be like losing a member of the family. No question, this was John's family.

"I think he'll stay involved," he said. "One way or another.

I do rely on that pretentious . . ." He searched for the right word. "Fuck." His eyes darted down the street. "Stuart likes to say that a good painting is one where you can look at any piece of it, any square inch of it, and it's beautiful, just on its own. Right? That's what a song should be like. Every piece of it should be interesting, you know, beautiful. I didn't get that until I met Stuart." He squinted into the distance. "That pretentious little fuck."

"Here's a thought," I said. (There's no time like the present to pitch an idea.) "What if I sat in with you guys some night, with my guitar?"

"No," said John, and went back to his cereal.

"You let people come up and sing with you all the time," I said. "Horst, and that gangster guy—"

"Yes, mate, so they don't kill us."

"I'm getting pretty good," I said. "You might just be surprised."

He took another big slurp. "What's happening with your school? Are you begging them to take you back?"

I hadn't thought about school much. My hearing is scheduled for tomorrow. I guess my plan was to see how I felt about it tomorrow, and decide then if I would even bother going in.

But the answer suddenly came clear.

"No," I said. "I'm done with school."

"Good," he said. "I'm glad to hear it."

It's funny how saying the words made me feel like a weight had been lifted. For the first time in weeks, I felt no obligation to my teachers, my parents, or anyone else who would judge me and make me feel small. I felt free. I didn't have the slightest idea what I would do tomorrow, or the day after, or how I would make a living in Hamburg, or how I would get home, but I would figure it out. For the first time in my life it felt like I had options.

I must have had a rapturous glow on my face because John then asked a very strange question. "Alan," he said. "Do you believe in God?"

I sputtered a little. "I'm a theist," I said, my standard answer. "But as far as believing in a specific God—"

"Last night," John interrupted, "I think I may have pissed on a nun." He looked at me with wide-eyed innocence. "Do you think I'm going to hell?"

I wasn't sure if he was joking or not. "I don't know the answer to that," I said.

John nodded. "I worry sometimes about going to hell," he said.

John is a bit of a mystery. He has so many defensive layers—sarcasm, anger, aggression—and then he'll surprise you with these moments of vulnerability. He shows an awful lot of himself.

"Why," I finally asked, "did you piss on a nun?"

"I was drunk and I didn't feel like walking to the bathroom. So I leaned out the window, and there she was. She walked right into the stream."

It seemed like a perfectly reasonable explanation.

"Maybe there is a God and maybe there isn't," said John. "But if there is one, I think I just got him wet."

I left him a few minutes later, wrestling with his eternal soul and another bottle of milk.

November 19
per Luftpost

Dear Mom and Dad,

I hope you are well. I was thinking the other day that this is the longest I've ever gone in my life without seeing the two of you. Kids grow up, and kids move away—farther away, even, than the Upper West Side—but I know it's never an easy thing for parents to accept, or to be happy about. I want you to know that I do miss you both very much.

Don't worry, there's nothing wrong with me. I think there's an awful lot right with me, as a matter of fact, and I hope that you'll share in my happiness when I tell you this:

I've decided that I'm dropping out of school.

I'm simply not enjoying it, and I'm not getting anything out of it. I've tried—all semester long I've tried—to understand how they do things here, and to fit into their system. I've tried to adjust my own expectations, and compromise, even, on some of the things that *I* think are important in pursuing an education, with the things that *they* think are important. I've tried to learn from my teachers, and follow their instructions, and be a good soldier, and do what I was told.

But at a certain point, one has a higher moral duty than simply following orders. (I think the Germans in particular might want to give this a try.) I choose to think for myself.

And I don't mean to imply that I bear any ill will toward the Germans. I think they are a decent people, very welcoming for the most part, even though some of them have a propensity for causing pain, both psychological and physical. I'm not sure what that's about.

If I'm not able to get class credit for any of the courses I started here (and I think it's unlikely), I will simply stay on for an extra semester at Columbia, even if I have to pay for it myself. I'm going to try to get a job here, and get in the habit of making money. I've come to like Hamburg very much, and I think I'm going to enjoy it even more once I'm living here as a real Hamburger (ha ha), and not just a visiting student. I think that's the more honest way to experience a city, and probably a better education.

I've learned so much here already, more than I can say (and none of it from the university). I've stumbled onto a situation here, through my German friends and through my living arrangement, where the opportunities for learning are boundless. Things that I never dreamed I would learn, from people I never thought I would know.

I might even want to stay here beyond the end of the semester. (That's just speculation at this point, but I'm sure I could talk Columbia into giving me a deferment. I think they will understand that sometimes the best education is no education at all.) I will continue to read the great works of literature and learn from them on my own, without the interference of mediocre minds.

And I will try to figure out what I want to do with the rest of my life. Maybe it's poetry, maybe it's something else. But it's time I started looking.

Love,
Alan

November 20

Another late night at the club, another quick and meaningless sexual encounter, and then . . .

I'd been thinking, for the past few days, about my money situation. I probably have just enough to get by till the end of the semester. I couldn't possibly ask my parents for more. But I'm leading a rather Falstaffian existence at the moment, and that doesn't come cheap. The beer at the Kaiserkeller is inexpensive, but it adds up. I enjoy buying a round for the table every now and then, and Jurgen and Klaus do the same for me. And, of course, there's the women. I've learned that, even in Germany, you cannot buy a woman a beer if you want her to have sex with you. It has to be a cocktail, you see, because that's classy. And no woman will give herself to you without the belief, or at least the pretense, that she is classy.

But then I had an idea. I got dressed quickly and set out for the one place where I could surely find a solution to my problem.

The Kaiserkeller.

It's been a while since I've seen the place in daylight. (It's been a while since I've seen *anything* in daylight.) Without the blaring music and the frantic sexual energy, the building looked like a dead body laid out in the street.

I was glad to find Bruno seated at his desk. He said he had some mail for me. I got right to the point. "Herr Bruno, do you think I could get a job working at the club?"

He looked puzzled. "I thought you were in school."

I explained.

"I have no jobs," Bruno said. "What I need now is new musicians. Do you play?"

"A little," I said. He looked hopeful. "But I'm not very good."

Bruno pulled a small bottle of medicine from his desk. It appeared to be some kind of oil, which he carefully measured out in a teaspoon. "I am very disappointed with the English boys," he said, and swallowed the oil in one gulp. His mouth made a grimace. "I work with many young musicians. Some of them I become very fond of." He poured out another spoonful. "Some of them," he said, "have been like sons to me." His eyes turned dark. "But not these boys. These boys have no . . . *affection* for me whatsoever." He sucked down another spoonful of the oil and made a dry-retching sound that turned into a raspy cough.

He saw the horrified look on my face and showed me the bottle. "*Lebertran*," he said. "Cod liver oil. Have you tried it?"

"No," I said.

"You really should, it's very good for your health." He slid the bottle toward me on his desk.

I leaned forward to get a look at the label, but I didn't dare touch it.

"I think the English boys are simply too young for this kind of work," said Bruno. "I think they are under twenty, at least."

"George is only seventeen," I said, peering at the bottle.

I could hear Bruno stop and turn toward me. "How do you know this?" he asked in a soft voice.

"A friend told me," I said.

I immediately regretted saying it. I tried to backpedal a bit, making it clear that I'd only heard it second-hand, and I had no actual proof of anyone's age; but I could tell from the satisfied smile on Bruno's face that he'd gotten just what he wanted.

"What are you going to do to them?" I asked.

"A good question," Bruno replied, his eyes turning all dreamy with thoughts of . . . revenge? Murder? He quickly snapped himself out of it. "Come with me," he said. "I want to show you what they have done."

He led me downstairs to the stage. "Look at it!" he shouted. "You see how they have destroyed my stage?"

I had never noticed, but the stage was badly chewed up, with big chunks of wood missing from the floorboards.

"They do it with the stomping! Always with the stomping! It is a game for them, to destroy my stage!"

I had certainly seen the boys stomp their feet. At first I had written it off as showmanship, although later I came to suspect it was a way to keep Pete's drumming on the beat when his energy flagged. But maybe it was just a plot to stick it to Bruno.

"What would you do? To people like this?" he asked, his face pushing in on me. "People who treat you in this manner? Who destroy your property?" I could feel his breath on my face. "*What would you do?*"

I tried to defuse his anger, which seemed on the verge of explosion. "I think . . . I would talk to them about it," I offered.

I thought the explosion would surely happen right there, but it didn't. Bruno took a breath and his face relaxed. "All right," he said, in his most reasonable tone. He smiled. "I will talk to them." He put his hand on my shoulder. It felt cold and damp, like a fish. "And you will arrange it for me."

He instructed me to bring the whole band to his office tonight, during their first break. I was to say that Bruno had requested a meeting, and I was to tell no one else. (This last part struck me as particularly sinister.)

"And you'll all have a *talk*," I said, trying to keep the mood light.

Bruno chuckled. "Yes," he said, his eyes brightening. "I will show them how we *talk* in Hamburg."

I had no intention of leading the boys into what sounded like an ambush. I immediately went back to the Kino to warn them, but they weren't home. I made a quick tour of the neighborhood—Moller's, Gretel and Alfons, the record store. No luck. I was about to get on a bus for Astrid's house (I knew at least Stuart would be there) when it occurred to me where I would find them.

The Star Club stood right on the Reeperbahn, in a building formerly known as the Hippodrom. I had never been inside, but I could see why the boys liked it. It actually looked like a theater. Big and modern, with microphones and spotlights that were brand-new, and not German Army Surplus.

Sure enough, the boys were there (except Stuart), seated at a big table with two men I didn't recognize.

I apologized for interrupting. "Something is up with Bruno."

The two strangers seemed to know exactly who I was talking about. Paul introduced them to me as Tony Sheridan, a singer who worked at the Top Ten, and Peter, the owner.

They invited me to sit down and I told them all about my encounter with Bruno. They listened politely but appeared unconcerned.

"I think you may be in danger," I said.

John turned to Tony. "Bruno wouldn't kill us, would he?"

"No," Tony answered. "Bruno doesn't kill musicians. He just tries to scare them."

"Well there you go, Alan," said John. "Have you got anything else?"

"No, I—"

"Then would you please get the fuck out. We're talking business."

I excused myself and left. It's strange how I wobble in and out of the boys' orbit. One day I feel close to them and part of their inner circle, and the next day I don't belong at all. I suppose that's how it is with bands: they become tight with each other, united against the world. It must be nice to have an artistic relationship like that—I've never felt that way as a poet, or even as an actor. Maybe joining a band is exactly what I need.

I got to the Kaiserkeller that night a little after 9. Rory and the Hurricanes were onstage and I sat at a table next to Paul. I reminded him about the appointment with Bruno at 11.

"Maybe you should have a policeman stand outside the door," I said.

Paul laughed. "You're nervous about this, aren't you?"

"I don't trust Bruno," I said. "He seems unstable."

"It's just the business," he said. "People say all sorts of daft things. Have a drink."

The boys did their set. I didn't feel much like dancing and, oddly, I knew no one there. No Astrid, no Klaus and Jurgen, none of my previous sex partners. I started feeling very alone, and very paranoid. Where were my friends? Had Bruno gotten rid of them, the way he was planning to get rid of the boys? I gazed at the red-faced swarm of dancers, all consumed with fighting and fucking, and I started to feel unsafe.

The boys rang out the last notes of "Long Tall Sally" at exactly 11 o'clock. I gathered them up.

"Is there anything you want to tell me before we go in to see Bruno?" I asked.

"Yes," George said, "I don't like your shirt."

We pushed through the crowded bar area, and I was

struck, once again, at how the five of them couldn't even walk through a room without a bunch of girls grabbing them, flirting with them, blowing them kisses.

Bruno stood, formally, when we entered his office. I was glad to find him alone: I'd imagined henchmen by his side, their pockets bulging with weapons.

"Well, my little *Piedels*. How good of you to come."

"Hello, Leggy," said John.

"Ello Bruno!" said Paul. "How's our lad?" Paul looked like he was moving in for a hug, but stopped himself. If there's a less huggable man in the world than Bruno, I have yet to see him.

There were two chairs set up in front of his desk. John and Paul took those, while the other three leaned against a wall.

Bruno turned to me. "Thank you, Levy. You may go now."

"Hold on," said John. "We'd like him to stay."

Bruno looked confused.

"He's with us," said John.

All eyes were on me. I backed up against the wall, next to Pete.

"Is this true, Levy? You are *with them*?" Bruno asked.

Funny, isn't it, how you can be lured into doing things so horribly unsafe and so clearly not in your best interest, just by an act of fellowship and good will. By some primordial desire to *belong*. "He's with us." All day long I'd been dreading this moment; now I didn't want to miss it.

This, I realized, *is exactly why people join bands*. Or street gangs.

"Yes," I said. "I'm with them."

Bruno gave me a dirty look, then turned back to the others. "I know you have been playing the Top Ten," he said.

"Let's don't play games and pretend I don't know this."

Everyone looked at John, who merely shrugged.

"I am willing to forgive this betrayal," said Bruno. "But with one condition. You will sign this."

He handed some papers to John.

"It says you will not play at the Top Ten, or any club other than mine, or else you will be subject to prosecution."

"Well, aren't you the cheeky one," said John.

"Yes," said Bruno, his hands folded on the desk. "I am."

John considered. "Why on earth *wouldn't* we play the Top Ten? They pay us better than you do. It's a nicer club than yours."

"Because," said Bruno, with an almost comical degree of menace, "this is how we do business in Hamburg. We have our own rules. And our own way of *enforcing those rules*."

I made a mental note of the two doors that led from the office, and traced my path of escape.

The boys looked at John again. He glanced at the paper, although I realized that without his glasses he couldn't read a word.

"In that case," he said, "you can take your contract and shove it up your ass." He dropped the paper on the desk and leaned back in his chair, folding his hands like Bruno's. "You crippled Nazi."

The rage in Bruno's eyes could have heated ten furnaces. I could see his head shaking, ever so slightly, as he struggled to contain the violence. With a supreme amount of effort, he announced, "You impudent little shit."

The two of them stared at each other, horns locked, as if daring one another to escalate this thing into the fistfight it so badly wanted to be. This is precisely why John keeps the tough-guy act so fresh: Paul's in charge of the hugs; John's in charge of the fists. They make a good team.

Bruno finally spoke. "Get out!" he snarled.

The boys shuffled toward the door, keeping up a casual, even jovial, façade. Whether they were faking it or not, I don't know. But it was impressive. They clearly have more experience with people like Bruno than I have. I followed behind them, avoiding eye contact.

As they exited, George turned to Paul. "Did we just get fired?"

"No!" Bruno roared. "You will finish the jobs I have paid you for!"

"You still love us, don't you?" John asked.

Not a trace of a smile from Bruno. "I am not finished with you," he said. "*Any* of you."

I took that to include me.

There was some talk about skipping out on the gig entirely, but they agreed that would be unprofessional. Better to finish the night here, and then move things over to the Top Ten tomorrow. "My dad used to tell me," said Paul, "never skip out on your wife, and never skip out on a gig."

They played a solid set, although it was clear their minds were elsewhere. For Stuart, maybe a life of domestic tranquility, minus the loud noise and adoring crowds (would he even be in the group the next time they played?). For the rest of them, a bigger club, a nicer stage, more money. That's how you get ahead in show business: you do a little better next time. From the Indra to the Kaiserkeller to the Star Club. And maybe someplace even bigger after that. "To the toppermost," as they like to say.

I also noticed a remarkable amount of stomping during the set.

They stomped their way through "What'd I Say," "Money,"

"Tutti Frutti," and all the others. Their boots beat down on the stage like sledgehammers and made the walls shake. I could see chunks of wood flying up from the floorboards. Bruno was right: they really were trying to destroy the place. It was war.

I didn't stay for the last set. I wasn't in the mood to dance or chase down another *fraulein* for another night of drunken sex. All the joy and abandon I've come to associate with the Kaiserkeller seemed entirely absent that night. Sitting there by myself, without Astrid and her friends, I could see the place now as nothing more than a dirty, dangerous gallery of vice, full of desperate men and women. I ran up the stairs. It felt good to get outside.

I have a small lock on my bedroom door, and I double-checked that it was secure. I also barricaded the doorjamb with my flimsy desk and chair in case anyone tried to break in during the night. If Bruno was planning to mete out punishment, I didn't want it to land on me. And, unlike my neighbors, I didn't have anywhere else to go.

November 20
per Luftpost

Dear Artie,

I got your letter today and enjoyed it very much. I needed some cheering up. Things have gotten a little weird around here (trouble with the landlord, etc.) but my apartment is quiet tonight—"a little *too* quiet," as they say in the cowboy movies—and I was happy to be in your company.

First of all, congratulations on you and Suzy. I never thought I'd see you head-over-heels in love (I don't think I've ever heard you *mention* the word love). And God knows I never thought it would be Suzy.

I'm happy for you both. I know how great a girl she is.

If I'm honest, I have to admit I'm a little jealous. I have some friends here who just got engaged, too, and they're sooooo madly in love, just like you. There was a time when I would have mocked them—and you—and insisted that we're all too young to be making commitments, and we should be playing the field and sowing our wild oats, etc., etc.

But I have to tell you, I've played the field plenty since I've been here. And it's fun. And I'm not saying I regret it, or that I'll never do it again. But it must be nice to come home to somebody at night. Nice to have a girl who'll talk to you and spend the night without hours and hours of small talk and schnapps. I had that once, with Suzy, and I didn't appreciate it. I hope you don't make the same mistake.

On a happier note (for me), I'm also pleased to hear that you're getting more and more interested in music. I've always thought you were a very talented actor, but you're an awfully good singer as well, and you have a beautiful voice. I'd always figured you for a Broadway-type star, but hey, if you like straight-on singing better, that's a pretty good job, too.

Music has become a real passion for me as well, and I spend whole days playing my guitar, learning songs, figuring out other songs, trying some of my own stuff. I wish they had a good radio station here, but if you want to hear any good music you have to seek it out at the music store. (I'm definitely getting a record player when I get back to New York.)

I find music to be satisfying in much the same way that acting is, only more so. It's all about putting on a show and engaging an audience, but it's so much more vital and energetic. It's like art stripped bare, absorbed immediately in the soul, the way sugar is absorbed immediately in the blood. In the words of Chuck Berry, "My heart's beating rhythm and my soul keeps singing the blues."

So yes, I've become a bit of a rock and roll guy. Although I agree that there's a lot of interesting stuff being done in folk music as well, like Pete Seeger. Folk music may turn out to be a good fit for you. And maybe even for me. It's really all about the lyrics, isn't it? And the guitar playing that's required is pretty basic (I'll bet I could play a lot of it even now).

Maybe when I get back we can play some stuff together? Form a group, even, or write some songs. Though it sounds like you've found someone to partner up with already. He sounds like a good guy, and very talented. I hope it works out. Partnerships are hard. Gee, look at all the coupling I miss out on when I go away for one lousy semester!

In answer to your question, yes I think you should consider changing your name, if you're serious about being a performer. Garfunkel is lovely, and a proud reminder of your (our) heritage, but it doesn't strike me as being all that "show biz." I don't know if America is ready for a Jewish folk singer. Maybe you should call yourselves Tom and Jerry instead.

That's just my opinion, anyway. Funny how I came here to learn all about Rilke and Goethe, and I turn into an expert on show business.

Ain't life strange?

Your pal,
Alan

November 21

I honestly don't think Bruno would kill me. That would just be foolish. However corrupt the local government might be, you can't just kill an American citizen without some kind of serious consequences.

But I've seen people get beaten up in Hamburg. Inside the club, and outside on the street. In the club, it's usually a rowdy customer, or people who start fights. Out on the street, I've always assumed it was some financial dispute. But the conflict I've been dragged into is ultimately financial. Bruno thinks the band is cheating him, stealing money out of his pocket, and trying to destroy his property. (I think they're just trying to get a better deal somewhere else, but it doesn't matter what I think.) And now I've made it known that I'm on their side. "He's with us." I hope I don't get beaten in the face.

I was lying in bed this morning, musing over where I'd *prefer* to be beaten, when there was a loud knock on my door. I tensed my body under the covers, and didn't make a sound. The knock came again, even more urgent. I lay silent for a few more moments, but after the third flurry of knocks, I relented. Killers, I reasoned, wouldn't knock.

When I opened the door, I found myself facing my worst fear: a gang of aggressive, beefy-faced German thugs. Wearing uniforms.

"*Polizei,*" they announced.

I attempted words, but none came. I immediately thought about Anne Frank, and all the other Jews (including my own distant relatives, who my parents speak of only in hushed tones) who answered the door just like this and soon found their lives obliterated.

"You are the English?" said the beefiest one.

"No," I said, "they're—" I stopped. I felt that sense of *belonging* again. "Why do you ask?"

But just then I heard another *polizei*, from the hallway: *"Sie sind hier."*

They had found the boys, and were flashing their badges and talking in the serious tone that you hear only from police officers and high school principals.

"Which one of you is Gay-org Harrison, please?"

George volunteered that it was he.

"Your papers, please."

(Just like in the movies.)

The *polizei* had a quick look over George's passport. "You were born in 1943. This makes you how old?"

"Seventeen," said George.

"Yes," he said. "You must be eighteen to work here."

"Yes," said George. "I've heard rumors to that effect."

By now, I was standing directly outside their apartment, next to the other cop, who turned to me and said, "You will excuse us."

They stepped inside the room and closed the door behind them.

I listened through the door and heard more serious talking, interrupted occasionally by a snarled protest, which was immediately cut short. Germans are not coy about letting you know who's in charge. The discussion went on for a good fifteen minutes.

Finally the door opened. The policemen emerged, and descended the stairs without a word.

I joined the boys in their room. All four of them (again, no Stuart) looked like they'd had the life sucked out of them.

George was being deported. He had twenty-four hours

to leave the country, or else be "subject to prosecution." (The same words Bruno had used.) The police would be back tomorrow, and if George was still here, he'd be arrested.

They fumed and sputtered, cursing Bruno, cursing the Germans, cursing the fate that had struck just when they were on the verge of taking a step forward.

I felt particularly bad for George. He'd annoyed me at first, with Astrid, but he seemed like a good lad, always with a wisecrack, trying to keep up with the others. Now, it appeared, they were about to leave him behind completely.

"I wonder how Bruno found out," he said.

I felt the blood rush to my face, but no one seemed to notice.

Pete was dispatched to get Stu and Astrid. Stu, John announced, would have to be part of any discussion regarding the future of the band, and they all seemed to be counting on Astrid to figure a way out of this mess. The others would get everything packed up and moved over to the Top Ten. Along with their new gig, they'd also been offered a dormitory-type room at the rear of the club. They'd been planning to move in at the end of the week, but decided it was better done now.

I asked if they needed any help.

"No, thanks," said Paul. "Probably best for you to avoid Bruno, eh?"

I asked Pete if I could walk with him over to Astrid's house.

"No," he said. "I'll do it meself." And that was that. Now that I'm no longer employing Pete as my personal spy, we don't have much to talk about.

John said, "Off ya go."

Once again, I wasn't *with them* after all.

I went on another long walk. This time I started down by

the harbor and then up through the *Planten un Blomen*, which always reminds me of Central Park. It was freezing, and the wind whipped even colder off the river. The cold didn't bother me. I was walking with urgency, burning calories and rubbing my hands to keep warm.

I felt horrible about George. I'd gotten him deported, this kid who was probably making money for the first time in his life, this poor guy who now had to go home and tell his parents he'd failed as a musician.

And would the band even survive? Had I also destroyed that? This enterprise they'd started? They have fans in Hamburg, people who look forward to seeing their shows every night. Now, because of me, they wouldn't have that anymore. I'd broken up the Beatles.

As I walked along the river, I saw someone up ahead, walking by himself, and I realized it was Ringo, from Rory Storm's outfit. He was wearing a trench coat and a big sailor's cap, taking photos and skipping stones into the water. I ran to catch up.

"Hello Ringo," I said.

"Oh hello," he replied, and looked back into the camera.

I could tell he didn't remember my name. "You're a photographer?" I asked.

"No," he said. "I just like taking pictures. I fancy the quiet."

I told him about George getting deported, and the boys moving over to the Star Club, and Bruno vowing revenge on us all.

"What the bloody hell?" said Ringo.

"It's a real shame," I said.

"Bloody right it's a shame. I thought we did a good show, them and us. Why would Bruno want to go and ruin that? And who knows what they'll send over to replace them. I hope it's not another band from Leeds. You ever hear a band from Leeds?"

I told him I hadn't.

"Don't," he said. He picked up a stone and scraped the dirt off. "Anyway, they can't replace little Georgie," he said.

"Do you think they will?"

"I can't imagine who with." He threw the stone into the river and turned to me. "Maybe you?"

I hadn't really stopped to think about it.

"I thought you were all gung-ho about joining a band," said Ringo. "Maybe this is your chance."

"I don't think I'm good enough. *Maybe* I'm good enough . . ."

"If you're any good at all, it's worth a shot. They're a tight little band. I think they're going places. You could do a lot worse than to join the Beatles."

It was a fascinating idea, and I started processing it immediately. It was such a brilliant and obvious idea that I soon had trouble concentrating on anything else that Ringo said. We made a bit more small talk but then I left him to his picture-taking and walked back into town. And with every step I took, my mind lit up with one single word:

Opportunity.

The band was about to lose its lead guitarist. (Yes, I was partially responsible, but let's be clear: George was violating the law, he did it knowingly, and he probably would have been discovered eventually.) I am a guitar player. Yes, I'm just a beginner, but I'm a very fast learner (in plays, I'm always the first person off-book). And I know their repertoire. I've heard their songs dozens of times. I don't know the chords for them—yet—but I know how the songs go, how they sound, where the voices come in, the rhythm.

Could I be the new guitarist?

Why not? I'd come to Germany looking to find myself as an artist, and looking for something to feel passionate about. Maybe this wasn't my moment to be a poet. Maybe poetry and drama were merely detours that led me to music. Things like that happen all the time. Apparently, it was happening to Artie.

Do I want to be a professional musician? I don't know. Is this what I want to do for the rest of my life? I don't know that either. But at this moment in my life, it feels right. It feels like fun. Maybe it's just a fling, but what an exciting way to spend my time in Hamburg.

And if I did join the Beatles, maybe I could get college credit for it.

It was dark by the time I got home to the Bambi. I walked around the block a couple of times to make sure no one was lying in wait for me. There was a movie playing downstairs in the Kino, a French melodrama; on a Wednesday night it would be poorly attended. Upstairs, I didn't see any lights on in either room. I went in.

It was strangely quiet. I could hear the low murmur of French melodrama downstairs, but nothing else.

The door to my neighbors' room was locked. I wondered where they were. They had probably moved into the Top Ten by now, but I thought their plan was to spend one more night here. Could they be doing a show at the Keller? I couldn't imagine it, after all the drama with Bruno. I was tempted to go and check, but I thought it was better to avoid that place for a while.

I picked up my guitar and played. It felt good to have the Club Footy back in my arms.

I've been working on it for the past few days, and I think I've figured out the chords to one of their songs. "Rock and Roll Music," the Chuck Berry tune. I'm not positive, but it sounds right when I play

ADGD

ADAD

I ran through the song a couple of times, from beginning to end, and it didn't sound bad. I can even play it standing up, and I think I look good doing it. I have a good feel for the music, and I move well to it, like when I dance with Astrid. I think I look downright professional.

Finally, around 9, I heard the familiar sound of footsteps clamoring up the stairs. My tormentors. My sleep-deprivers. And I was never more happy to hear them.

I flung the door open. They were all there (minus Stuart), bouncing into their room, looking like kids on vacation.

"Hello Alan!" said Paul.

"Hello, guys!" I asked him what was happening.

"Flippin' hell, where to begin?" said Paul. "Why don't you come on in and have a drink?"

I sat on the floor and somebody handed me a beer. John was in a good mood, making jokes and talking in funny voices. Paul and Pete seemed upbeat as well. Only George was quiet. He looked sad. I avoided eye contact.

They told me they had cut all their ties to Bruno. They were officially out of their contract, and now free to commence their engagement at the Top Ten, albeit without George. They would move into the new club tomorrow.

Stuart was done. He had fulfilled his contract to play at the Keller; he was now a former Beatle, an artist and a house-husband, and madly in love. He told them he would fill his time watching shadows on the wall and learning to bake bread. And, of course, painting.

Stuart had handed his bass over to Paul, who would play it on a temporary basis. Paul now sat on the bed, plucking away on the new instrument. If he was upset about being the "fat bass player," he didn't show it. He looked like he was playing with a new toy. (This is a trait, I've noticed, that they all share: put any sort of musical instrument in front of them, and they'll play with it for hours, like kittens with a ball of yarn.)

George was leaving in the morning, getting a train back to Liverpool. He'd spent most of the day teaching John his guitar parts.

John now sat on the other bed, directly across from Paul—the position I'd come to recognize as work mode, facing each other, one lefty one righty, their instruments extended in a mirror image of each other. He was practicing the new guitar parts, even while he talked and joked around with the others. "Look at old Johnny Rhythm now," he said, plucking out a difficult solo.

"Go, Johnny, go," said George.

The important thing, they all agreed, was that the band would continue. This wasn't the end of it, but merely, as John said, "a growing pain named Bruno." They would figure out a way to bring George back, or else they would simply reconvene in England, once their luck in Hamburg ran out.

This I was especially pleased to hear. Maybe I hadn't destroyed the act after all, and maybe I could stop beating myself up for it. Maybe they would start looking for a new guitarist, or a new bass player. (Do I want to learn how to play the bass? No, I don't think so. Nobody likes playing bass. Let Paul do it.)

The evening began to take on a farewell-party atmosphere. One bottle of beer was replaced by another (donated by Horst and the Kaiserkeller staff, sad to see them go), and the boys told me how the night before, Rory had finally succeeded in stomping a hole through the floorboards of the Keller stage, and Ringo's drums had fallen into the crater. Bruno was furious and threatened to break all their fingers.

We laughed and drank, and we all did imitations of the irate Bruno. "You haff broken my shtage!" "I vill grind up your pinkies und make sausage!"

If nothing else, it was the band's first night off in more than three months, and they seemed to be enjoying it.

I was enjoying it, too. If you'd asked me, when I first got to Hamburg, what kind of social life I was hoping for during my time here, I would have said exactly this: a bunch of guys on the floor of somebody's dorm (it seemed like a dorm), drinking beer and laughing our heads off. Guys having fun with other guys, unconcerned, for the moment, at the prospect of chasing girls—because *getting* girls just wasn't much of a problem.

"Here's to the next gig!" said John, raising his bottle of beer.

"To the toppermost!" echoed the others.

Paul put his arm around George. A classic Paul hug. "We're going to miss you, my lad."

George nodded and smiled. He seemed to have accepted his fate, and appeared almost fatalistic about it. I'd noticed it before: George, despite his baby face and jokey manner, had an unusual amount of maturity for someone his age, and the eyes of an old philosopher. "I suppose I'll find something to do," he said, his head down but his eyes darting up. "Get a proper job. Makes me shudder just thinkin' about it."

"Our little George," said John in one of his deep, funny voices—Northern English, perhaps? "Cleanin' out men's toilets like his father and his father's father before 'im. He's got the brushwork of a Harrison, by God!"

Paul stood up. "Hey," he said. "What do you say we bang out a couple of songs, while we're all together—one last time?"

"No!" said George.

"Yes!" said Paul. "Little farewell concert, just for *us*."

"Yeah, come on, guys," said John, now sounding like a dumb American movie. "Let's fix up the old barn and put on a show!"

"Look!" said Paul, grabbing Pete and shaking him. "Even Pete wants to do it. What say, Pete lad?"

Pete shrugged, unenthused, barely cracking a smile. "I suppose," he said.

"Ya see?" Paul screamed. "Even Pete's excited!"

"No!" protested George, as they pulled him up to his feet. "Not in here!" Paul and John marched him over to his guitar.

"Hey," I said. "Why don't you go up on the roof and play there?"

They looked at me like I was crazy.

But soon Paul got on board with the idea. "That's it!" he said. "A farewell concert on the roof!" It would be great practice, he said, for him on the bass, and for John with his new guitar leads. And, of course, it would be "a good laugh."

The rest of the boys soon agreed, and they started hauling their guitars and drums (but no amps) up the narrow staircase that led to the roof.

"Alan," John said. "Go get your guitar. You can sit in with us."

"Really?" I asked.

"Hurry up before I change my mind," he ordered.

I sprinted down the hallway and grabbed my guitar (I also thought to pick up a pen and paper). I sprinted back as fast as I could. I didn't think my opportunity would come this quickly, but fate works in strange and wonderful ways.

On the roof it was dark and freezing, but we were all nicely lubricated. I was nervous. I shoved the pen and paper toward Paul and said, "Give me the chords to 'Long Tall Sally!'"

Paul didn't even have to put down his bass. He scribbled:

G G

G G7

C G D7 C7 G D7

Thank God, I can play all of those.

I slung the guitar over my shoulder and took my place, discreetly, behind Paul and George. I felt a sudden pang of stage fright; I'd never played a guitar in front of anyone, let alone in a band. I put the sheet of paper on the ground and stuck a beer bottle on top of it so it wouldn't blow away. We faced the street.

And then we started to play.

I'm gonna tell Aunt Mary 'bout Uncle John
He said he had the misery but he got a lot of fun
Oh baby, yeah now baby, woo baby
Some fun tonight

I've never heard Paul sing it so loud. His voice rang out like a siren across the dark rooftops of Saint Pauli. I could imagine it traveling for blocks, if not miles, and our neighbors looking at each other, in their living rooms and kitchens, and saying, "*Was ist das?*"

Everyone must have had the same thought, because the louder Paul sang, the more everybody laughed, and the louder they played their instruments. Pete was pounding his drums like he wanted to break them, and the guitars, even without their amps, beat out a noise that cut through the night air like a whip. John and George slapped at the strings so hard I thought they would explode, and even Paul, playing bass for the first time, attacked it like a boxer on a punching bag.

And me? I was playing, too.

It took me a couple of verses to lock into the chord progression, and get a feel for the rhythm. I still had to refer to the piece of paper at my feet, but at a certain point, it clicked into place. I was strumming with passion, with conviction! I wasn't just noodling to myself while I lay on my bed—I was playing music!

It was ecstatic. It was like tumbling, end over end, in the crest of a giant wave. I had to concentrate hard to get the chords right, but I couldn't stop grinning and trading looks with the rest of the guys. They looked as happy as I did. But then they always look like they're having a good time onstage. Now I understand why.

Music is intoxicating. I can see why people devote their lives to it, even if they'll never make a dime at it—even when they're drunk and stoned and strung out on heroin—even when they're trudging through a blizzard carrying their instruments to the next godforsaken dump of a hotel. It was everything that I'd seen and felt at the Kaiserkeller—all that energy and pulsing sexuality—but now it was *inside of me*. Stirring my soul in a way that I've never felt.

Was it the devil? Or was it rock and roll?

I thought about my parents. How they'd feel if they could see me—the nice Jewish boy, the Ivy Leaguer—on a roof in Hamburg, drunk, waking up the neighbors, pounding out a beat with the rest of my street gang/bar band. I started to laugh.

I thought about Suzy. What would she think if she could

see me pouring my soul into a Little Richard song, manfully clutching my electric guitar, hips pumping up and down to the beat? She'd be like putty in my hands. Would she leave Artie for me? It didn't matter. Even if she spent the rest of her life with him, I'd always be the mysterious one: the musician who got away.

When we finished "Long Tall Sally," John announced the next song: "'Money!'"

"Wait!" I said. "I need the chords!"

"Hold on." Paul used my back like a writing desk and jotted the new chords on the other side of the paper:

E A

E A

E B A

E A E B

It was a tricky rhythm, but I'd heard the boys sing it so many times that I quickly caught on. I even tried singing backup vocals along with them (*that's . . . what I want*) but I could tell by the looks I was getting from Paul that I wasn't even close to the right pitch. I laid off the singing. That could always come later. John belted out the words, his voice even louder than Paul's, utterly committed to waking up the neighborhood. Nobody was going to sleep through this.

People on the street started to notice us. Quite a few stopped and pointed up to the roof—*that's where it's coming from*—while several others shouted, "*Halt dein Mund!*" (shut up) and "*Schnauze!*" (shut the fuck up).

This only delighted us all the more, and made John scream the lyrics even louder, substituting the words "fucking" and "Nazis" at every opportunity. A bunch of kids on the street threw rocks at us, which felt more funny than dangerous, even though it presented an extra challenge to try to get the chords right while projectiles sailed past my head.

Then the coolest thing of all. A bunch of girls on the street pointed up at us and yelled, *"Das ist Die Beatles!"*

I waved down to them. Hello, *frauleins!*

"Yay, Beatles!" they cheered.

By the end of the song, two other groups of girls had joined, and they all stood there in the cold, waving and cheering us on. John was now singing "Rock and Roll Music" (I know the chords to this one by heart); he sang it right to the adoring fans, even though he couldn't see five feet in front of his face. When you play rock and roll, you always know where the fans are.

And oh, the way they looked at us! So excited, so turned on, so in love! I'm sure I've never had a woman look at me like that before, and I never really thought it possible. Movie stars get that look. Or Frank Sinatra. Or Elvis Presley. But not a skinny Jewish kid from Scarsdale.

We were playing for the whole city of Hamburg, and as far as I could tell, we were the greatest thing they'd ever seen. The wind slapped our faces, the lights of the city sparkled in our eyes. Hamburg and everything it contained—the excitement, the energy, the sex—belonged to us now, laid out at our feet like an offering to the gods. It was easy to think we could conquer the whole world like this, standing on a rooftop and shouting about love.

We did nine songs in all and stopped only when the *polizei* arrived and escorted us off the roof. They had no idea what we were up to; they were just dealing with a bunch of noisy drunks, which is probably what they did all night, every night. They yelled and pushed us around a little, but finally just told us to go home, which wasn't a problem since we were there already.

My fingers were numb and my head was spinning as we ducked into the warmth of the Kino.

"Did you fancy that?" asked John.

"Yes I did!" I gushed. I could only imagine how I looked: a big apple-pie grin on my face, cheeks red from the cold, my nose dripping snot. John laughed. "Look at him," he said to Paul. "Rock and roll claims another victim."

"Oh, dear me, yes." Paul examined my face like a doctor. "Snatched his mortal soul, I'm afraid."

"ROCK AND ROLL!" I yelled, loud enough to rattle the walls.

"For God's sake," said Paul, "it's three in the morning. You'll wake somebody up."

I was buzzing with adrenaline and could have stayed up all night, but the boys were anxious to sleep. Paul gave me a thumbs-up and ducked into his room. John turned back to me.

"Alan," he said. "Next time you write one of your fuckin' poems, remember how this feels."

I promised him I would.

"I'm serious. Enough with whispering and snapping your fingers. If you've got something to say, step up and say it. Disturb the peace. Make some noise. It's good for your soul."

I slung the guitar over my shoulder. Maybe I'd stay up late tonight and practice some more. Figure out some of the other numbers. Maybe come up with something of my own. Or maybe start working on my poem again. The possibilities seemed endless.

"And you," I said, "should start singing your own songs and not someone else's."

"Fuck that," he said, but I could tell he didn't mean it. This was an idea, I suspected, that weighed heavily on him, and one that Paul probably nagged him about incessantly. But he wasn't in the mood for it now. Even John gets tired sometimes. He rubbed his eyes and turned to his room. "Thanks for sittin' in with us."

"Thank you," I said, and then added, only half-joking, "and I hope I passed the audition."

November 22

via Western Union Telegram

DEAR MOM AND DAD, I HAVE HAD TO LEAVE
HAMBURG SUDDENLY.
WILL ARRIVE AT IDLEWILD TOMORROW NIGHT,
T.W.A. FLIGHT 107
I AM SAFE
ALAN

November 23

I am writing this on the plane. I'm going home. I didn't even have time to gather all my things. Or say goodbye.

Free will is a joke. We think we're in control of our lives, that we choose our own destinies, but we don't. The universe tosses us around like dust and doesn't give a shit where we come down.

I haven't been able to make much sense of what happened. Perhaps writing it down like this will help. The last day and a half has passed in a blur. I'm upset, I'm confused, I'm disappointed, and I can't even fathom how this whole thing turned so ugly so fast.

But I will try.

So. The morning after our concert on the roof, I slept late. I'd been so wired up when we finished that I tossed and turned all night, thinking about life as a rock and roll musician. Playing in a band. Playing with the boys, touring England, maybe touring Europe, who knows what else? It was crazy. I kept reminding myself that I could barely play the guitar, and I couldn't be trusted to sing vocals—what could I possibly bring to the band? Strumming a guitar with the strings muted isn't really that big a contribution.

But I kept thinking about what Ringo had told me, that it was all about the relationships, all about spending time with people you like, and people who like you.

I think the guys like me. Since I got to Hamburg, I've spent more time with them than anyone else. Sure, they're a little odd, and painfully unsophisticated, but I like them, and they were fun to be around. We were practically roommates. Maybe I was just indulging myself, but I felt pretty good about my chances of being asked to join the band.

I was dreaming of such things, sound asleep at last, and I guess I didn't hear them in the morning when they moved the last of their stuff out. I might have slept all day, if not for a strange odor that woke me up around noon. It seemed to be coming from the hallway.

I dragged myself out of bed. Their room was empty. How strange, I thought, that they didn't even knock on my door to say goodbye. Surely they liked me enough that they would have said *something*. (Perhaps they did, and I just didn't hear it.)

But the smell was coming from somewhere else. I went down the hall to investigate, and encountered a very peculiar sight. On the wall was a nail, and hanging from the nail was a smoldering piece of rubber, which, when I looked more closely, turned out to be a half-melted *Willie Boy* condom. There was a small burn mark on the wall just above it, which seemed to indicate that it had been burning there a short time before. I rubbed my eyes and tried to make sense of it all: why was there a burning condom in my hallway?

I heard a sound on the stairs. I turned and saw: it was Bruno. I may have jumped, or let out a small yelp, or both. He glared at me, and spied the burned rubber.

"Did you do this?" he demanded.

"No," I said, "I just woke up." I suddenly felt uneasy being alone in the building with Bruno. The cinema was empty, my neighbors were gone. It was just him and me.

"The English, they are gone?"

"I think so," I said.

He flung open their door and saw the empty room. He marched back to where the condom still hung. "So they are trying to burn down my theater?"

"No," I said. "I'm sure it wasn't that."

Bruno thrust his bright red face in front of mine. "Then how do you explain this?"

My first instinct was to take a step back and protect myself, but I resisted. And in that moment, a calming thought entered my mind: *he's trying to scare me*. That's all it was. If I refused to *be* scared, then he had nothing at all on me—just a sad, angry man. "They wouldn't light a building on fire," I said, calm and rational, "if they knew I was sleeping inside."

He lifted his head. "Well isn't that sweet? You are all so fond of each other, aren't you? I think you suck each other's cocks. Is that what you do?"

"No," I said, looking him straight in the face.

He took a step closer. "Why don't you go back to America, Jew boy? There you can suck all the cocks you want."

I've never wanted so much to hit another man. All the insults I'd endured from the Germans, everything my people had suffered, six million of us dead because of sadistic little creeps like this one. It would have felt so good to knock him to the ground.

But I didn't. I smiled, and I very calmly said, "Why don't you go back to the freak show, Bruno?"

It was a good line, I thought. But, as I've learned from playing tennis, if you stop to admire your shot, you leave yourself unprepared for anything that might come back across the net. I didn't even see the blow from Bruno, it was just a blur—a sudden kick from his bad leg, lashing out like a whip, and the heavy club of his foot cracked into my shin.

I screamed. For a moment I thought he had broken my leg. The kick was delivered so swiftly and so expertly that I realized why Bruno never carried a truncheon. His preferred weapon was right there at the end of his leg.

I struggled to stay on my feet, and lurched toward him. That's when he pulled out his knife. Not to attack me, but to stop me in my tracks. It worked.

"You will be very, very sorry about this," he hissed. "All of you." And marched off down the stairs.

My leg was bruised and bleeding, but not broken. Even though it hurt like hell, I walked over to the Top Ten—I had to warn the guys—but there was nobody there and the door was locked. I did a quick tour of the neighborhood, limping my way from one watering hole to the next, but still nothing.

I walked all the way to Astrid's house, my leg on fire with pain. She and Stuart had just come back from taking George to the train station, but hadn't seen the others. We sat down at the kitchen table and I told them about my run-in with Bruno and showed them my shin.

"Oh my God!" she exclaimed. "Oh, you poor thing."

She got bandages and ice and tended to my injury while Stuart made a pot of tea. It felt warm and comforting to be in their home and I was thankful for it. Astrid has been my guardian angel since the day I arrived in Hamburg; she has never once let me down.

I told them about the burning condom; they didn't have a clue what it meant. "They're a bunch of silly bastards," said Stuart. "John would punch you in the face, but he wouldn't burn down your house. Not his style at all." He finished his cup of tea and excused himself, and went back upstairs to lie down.

"He has been getting headaches," Astrid said. "Playing in the club all night and painting all day, it was just too much. Thank goodness now he has time to rest."

Astrid seemed like a different person. Cradling a cup of tea in her hands and wearing a sweatshirt and jeans, she no longer looked like the club-hopping, avant-garde photographer I had fallen in love with. She was beginning to look, maybe just a little bit, like a housewife. A beautiful and stylish housewife, to be sure, but calm and domestic, not wild and challenging. At peace.

Is this what love does to a person? Is it what happiness looks like? How strange that the very thing we all crave and search for is the very thing that forever dulls us to the world. It must be pretty nice, falling in love, considering how much we give up for it in return.

I thought of telling Astrid about my plans—or my fantasies—about joining the band and becoming their new guitarist, but I suspected she wouldn't be interested. We talked about Stuart and his painting, and her job at the gallery, and her plans to get back into photography full time. I reminded her that she'd promised to take more pictures of me.

"Yes," she said. "I would like that." She took a deep breath and squeezed my hand. "Alan, I feel badly, how I behaved. I want to apologize."

"It's not necessary," I said, quietly. Her hand felt warm, like it always did.

"I was in love with Stuart, but . . ." She struggled to find the words. "But I had to prove it. To myself, you know? I had to see if . . . someone else . . . could make me feel different. Do you understand?"

I nodded.

"It was not fair to you. It was not honest." Her words trailed off and she shook her head.

I understood what she meant. I could have felt angry, I suppose, or felt that I had been used like some pharmaceutical test, where Stuart was the drug and I was the placebo. But what is there to feel angry about? If she'd told me the truth back then—if she'd *known* the truth—what would that have gotten me? Maybe I would have finished my semester at school, and ticked off another box on my education checklist, like I've done every other year of my life. But I would have missed out on everything else.

I squeezed her hand back. "I'm glad I could help," I said.

She blinked her eyes, as if to fight back tears, and was about to say something when the phone rang.

Astrid picked it up and listened, then yelled for Stuart. He came down and we watched her finish the call and hang up. "They've arrested Paul and Pete," she said. "They're in jail."

Bruno had reported all of us to the police, who had picked up Paul and Pete walking on the street. They had admitted to lighting the condom, but denied they were trying to burn anything down. They said it was just a joke (a rather juvenile form of vandalism, I thought, or, as Stuart put it, more of a "fuck you" to Bruno). It wasn't clear if they were being charged with arson or if this was just a scare tactic. I was scared. I have no desire to end up as the pretty Jewish boy in a German prison.

We talked about what to do. Astrid said she could probably get some money together and get them out of jail. I couldn't tell if she meant posting their bail, or paying some sort of bribe, or some combination of the two. Who knows how these things work in Germany?

There was a knock at the door. The police.

Astrid told us to go upstairs and hide. Stuart refused, since he wasn't even there when the so-called arson occurred. But I didn't have the same alibi. I tiptoed to the attic and hid behind one of Stuart's large canvases.

I strained to hear the conversation. The police barked a

little in German, which I didn't understand, and then Astrid talked for a long time. Stuart chimed in a little here and there, but for the most part it was Astrid. She may be turning into a housewife, but she is still a highly persuasive woman.

At one point I heard a policeman say, very distinctly, "Alan Levy."

Astrid answered immediately. "*Nein.*"

The police said something in response.

"*Nein,*" she repeated.

My God, I thought, holding my breath and cowering in a corner of the attic. It's *The Diary of Anne Frank* all over again. And I'm Anne Frank. A Jew, hiding from the storm-troopers downstairs, in danger of losing everything if I made so much as a squeak.

Much to my relief, the police left. I waited ten minutes for their car to drive away, and then I went downstairs again. We talked for a while and considered the options. I didn't see too many good ones.

"Shall we take you to the train station?" said Stuart.

I shook my head. "How about the airport?"

November 24

I'm still on the plane. We're an hour from New York, and I haven't slept at all. I bought a book at the airport but I'm in no mood to read it. I've been staring out the window for most of the flight, thinking about the past few days. And the past few months. A number of regrets linger in my mind.

I regret that I never got to see John again. I wish I could have asked him: If none of this had happened, would you have let me join your band? The answer, probably, would have been no. The truth is, they're all pretty good musicians and I'm not. I think I'm loaded with potential, but really, very few people are good at recognizing potential. We see what's right in front of us, we're good at recognizing the obvious, but seeing into the future is a magic trick, the exclusive domain of prophets and hucksters. True potential, I think, is a secret locked away in all of us, released only by time and opportunity, unseen but eventually discovered. Most people in this world wouldn't recognize genius if it was standing right in front of them.

I regret that I never finished my poem cycle. It would have been nice to step off the plane in New York with a manuscript under my arm, one that perfectly captured the flavor and spirit of Hamburg—one that generations of writers could refer to, and draw inspiration from, the way I've drawn from Rilke and all the others. But I'd been wrong about Hamburg. I'd pegged it, only a few months ago, as a city of Deformity, Death, and Decay, a godforsaken casualty of war. Instead, it was, as Astrid had promised, a city where people came to live. Full of life, *"with the energy."* Vild.

The poem I would write today would be different. It would be a poem of discovery, about a young man—maybe with a young woman by his side—who goes off in search of death, and finds life instead. He discovers that the will to live is unstoppable, and, even though death can overpower and obliterate, it's life that wins in the end.

Maybe it wouldn't be a poem at all; maybe it would be a song. I like the idea of raising my voice a little more often, of shouting out loud and making myself heard. I think of all the poetry readings I've been to—all the hushed, whispered voices, the raised eyebrows, the meaningful nods, the sips of sherry, the earnest discussions, the little cubes of cheese. It's not exactly the Kaiserkeller, is it? Some poems, I believe, are meant to be shouted. Some poems should be danced to, and fucked to, and vomited to. How wonderful it must be to have your words pulse like electricity through the body of an audience, to make their faces turn red, and throw beer bottles at each other. To inspire true, unconstrained passion in your audience—isn't that what every artist is ultimately looking for? (Isn't that what Chuck Berry already has?)

There's no question that I will continue with my writing. It's true that I haven't been as prolific as I would have liked, but I think my poetry has taken on a new richness since I've been in Hamburg, informed by a melting pot of influences and unlikely friends. I'm confident that it will continue to deepen, and intensify, and lead me in new and exciting directions.

I hope I'll continue my music as well. I didn't have time to ship my guitar home, or to sell it, so I've hidden it in a very special place, and someday I will come back for it.

I regret that I never got to experience love, or sex, with the beautiful Astrid. I'm not sure if I believe in the notion of the One Special Person that each of us is destined to meet. I think, over the course of a lifetime, there may be a handful, maybe five or six people who, if the timing was right and the situation was right, could possibly turn into The One. Astrid and I had neither timing nor good fortune on our side, and it simply wasn't to be. Once again, it's the cruel hand of potential—that which has every reason to happen, but doesn't.

The only relationship whose future I can be absolutely certain of is Astrid and Stuart's. They are two people who found each other at the perfect time and for the perfect reasons. I predict a long and loving marriage for them and I hope that someday I can meet their children, of which there are bound to be many.

I've come to admire Stuart a great deal, despite the fact (or perhaps because of the fact) that I barely got to know him at all. Yes, he's quiet and mysterious and wears sunglasses indoors. But he's a serious young man and a serious artist; he may even be a great artist. Like me, he came to rock and roll from another place, from another artistic discipline, and I think that doing so was enormously helpful. His music enriched his painting, and his painting enriched his music. This, I think, is the true journey of the artist: explore everything, try everything, taste everything—but never stop working at your art. (I also suspect that he's had a positive effect on the rest of the band, and will continue to make their music more artistic, if such a thing is possible, if only through his own example.)

My plane is approaching New York City. I can see the Statue of Liberty in the distance. I'll give the old girl credit: she still knows how to make you feel welcome.

I wonder if the band will stay together. I can't believe that they'll rot away in a Hamburg jail for very long. They're just too clever for that. I think of all the noise and excitement they made in that sweaty little basement, how they got people out of their seats and onto the dance floor, cheering, jumping, screaming. And that audience wasn't just anybody. They were Germans! Have you ever thought how hard that would be, to make German people *happy*? Getting those grim Teutonic faces to smile? To entertain people who have *no sense of humor*?

I think the boys are talented. They're bright and fun. Those are good ingredients for success. Maybe they'll all have French haircuts someday, and smoke cigarettes, and maybe they'll even make a record, and get their picture in the newspaper.

More likely, they will discover that the world is a cruel place for our dreams, and whatever their ambitions as a band might be, they will probably fall short of them. Maybe John will go into advertising. Maybe Paul will teach music. Maybe George will live on a mountaintop. Maybe Pete will bear a grudge against his bandmates for the rest of his life. There are a million ways our lives can take us.

I remember a conversation I once had with John. I'd come into his room looking for Pete, but John was the only one there. He was sitting up in bed, his legs folded, guitar spread out across his chest. He was working on a particular phrase, a guitar lick that he played over and over. I asked him what it was.

"I don't know what it is," he said. "But I like it." He hummed a melody that went along with the lick, and repeated them over and over, sometimes with a slight variation. It sounded to me like he was writing a song, but he denied it. "Just something for later," he said. "For when I need it."

We got to talking about the future and where we thought our lives would go. He did more listening than talking—I think his mind was fixed on the simple but appealing melody that had begun to emerge from his guitar.

"What about the band?" I asked. "Do you think you guys can make it? You know, to the toppermost?"

He played the phrase on his guitar again and then looked up. "Yes," he said, very simply. "I do."

I asked him what it would take. How does a band succeed? How does a writer succeed? Or an actor, or a singer? Is it luck? Hard work? Being in the right place at the right time?

"Yes, all of those," he said. He played the phrase on his guitar once more. It was perfect, I could tell. It was just the way he wanted it. "But more than anything," he said, "it's being able to picture it in your own head. Anything you can imagine, you can make come true."

I hope I'll see those guys again.

Left to right: Stuart Sutcliffe, John Lennon, Alan Levy, George Harrison, Paul McCartney, and Pete Best. Photographer unknown.

AFTERWORD

One very special thing about being a diehard Beatles fan is the remarkable amount of information that exists about the band. Yes, we love the songs and the recordings, but so many of us strive to be "Beatles Geniuses" who know all the facts, all the stories, all the trivia. (There are many bands I love, but for the vast majority of them, I couldn't tell you who played what instrument, or where a song was written, or what the producer said when they recorded their first hit.) The mythology of the Beatles is an enormous subject.

When I read Mark Lewisohn's superb Beatles biography *Tune In,* I was astounded by how much is known about the band's first trip to Hamburg in 1960. It's not quite a day-to-day record (like the one that exists for the Beatles' entire recording career), but it's pretty close. There's an abundance of characters and incidents and fascinating details onto which, I thought, it would be fun to hang a story.

I'd been wanting to write something about the Beatles, some kind of witness-to-history thing, and Hamburg seemed like the perfect place to do it. There were enough details there to plot out a story, but few enough that I could make up the rest. My goal was to build an alternate history of the band's visit—or really, of the band's entire *career*—that somehow related back to the tiny fictional character of Alan Levy. (An earlier draft of the novel was presented as a "found diary" that actually claimed to be real. I dreamed of it becoming a publishing sensation, like Howard Hughes' diary—but my conscience, and my lawyer, finally got the better of me.)

And in the end... I had a wonderful time hanging out with

the boys. They are good company. I miss them, as so many of us do. But I've learned that one should never say goodbye to the Beatles. They've shown a remarkable ability, over so many years and so many generations, to show up again: a knock on the door, to deliver yet another surprise.

—DAN GREENBERGER

ACKNOWLEDGMENTS

Thanks to Sarah Rutledge, for great editing and even better ideas; to Amy Inouye and Kate Murray, for putting the pieces together. For help and encouragement along the way: Shelly Goldstein, Hilary Galanoy, Genevieve Dutil, Allison Burnett, Nina Sankovitch, and Shane Eichacher. Special thanks to Vladislav Ginsburg and Ginzburg Fine Arts; and to Astrid Kirchherr, to whose memory this book is dedicated.

ABOUT THE AUTHOR

DAN GREENBERGER is a Los Angeles-based writer for television and film. He is a three-time Writers Guild of America Award winner for his TV work, and his short films have played at festivals across the country. *The Boys Next Door* is his first novel.

His favorite Beatles song is "She Said She Said."

Made in the USA
Columbia, SC
25 March 2022

58136463R00176